PLANETS IN PERIL

By LeMonk

Become
Shakespeare
.com

WORDIT ART FUND

This book has been fully funded by the Wordit Art Fund. Wordit Art Fund
helps deserving authors publish their work by providing monetary
support. To apply for funding, please visit us at
www.BecomeShakespeare.com

First published in 2017 by

Becomeshakespeare.com
Wordit Content Design & Editing Services Pvt Ltd
Unit - 26, Building A-1, Nr Wadala RTO, Wadala (East),
Mumbai 400037, India
T:+91 8080226699

Book Editors: Krupali Uchil & Yashashree Uchil

Cover Designer: Sachin Uchil

©
ISBN – 978-93-86487-25-4

DISCLAIMER

This is a work of fiction. Names, characters, places, events and incidents are
either the products of the author's imagination or used in a fictitious
manner. Any resemblance to actual persons, living or dead, or actual events
is purely coincidental.

DEDICATION

To
My wife Krupali, daughters Yashashree & Varshika and
doggie daughter Cuddly.

You rock!

FROM THE AUTHOR

Are we all alone in the Universe? Do aliens exist? Have aliens been visiting us for millennia? Did an advanced civilization exist on our planet many millennia ago? Did the planet witness an event long ago that almost wiped out life from it?

Such thoughts have given me sleepless nights for many years and if I am not mistaken, many of you out there, must've experienced similar emotions. Answers to the above questions are yet a mystery and the truth may never be revealed, but why not let our imaginations run wild?

However looking at the bright side of things, these very thoughts that drove me crazy also inspired me to write this science fiction novel.

Many characters in this book have been adopted from my previous book **"Batatawadai Puram Adventures and More..."*** published by Leadstart Publishing and to some extent this book is related to my previous book.

Enter the world of Batatawadai Puram with me.......

Warm Regards

LeMonk

Other Book by the author:

Batatawadai Puram Adventures and More...

Batatawadai Puram is a small, isolated (imaginary) village located in the famous Sahyadri Mountains. Outwardly, though it appears to be an ordinary village, it can boast of all the facilities enjoyed by the residents of the biggest and best cities in India.

Join the adventures of Guru, Sri, Nath and Tina, four teens living in Batatawadai Puram, who seem to attract trouble wherever they go. Accompanied by their various friends, elders and teachers, they boldly face daunting obstacles like great environmental disasters, terrorists, and even aliens. They are unwillingly transported to Mars and have to survive the harsh conditions there. However, their intelligence, wit and a bit of luck help them overcome all the obstacles in their path.

ABOUT THE AUTHOR

Sachin Uchil writes under the pen name 'LeMonk'. He lives in Mumbai with his wife and daughters. His previous book "Batatawadai Puram Adventures and More..." co-authored with his daughter Yashashree was loved by children and elders alike.

He is an environmentalist and believes in simplicity and minimalism.

Contact the Author:
Email: authorlemonk@gmail.com
Facebook: fb.me/authorlemonk

*Some terms used in this book:

Vada pav, sometimes spelled *wada pav* or *vada paav* or *vada pao* or *wada pao*, is a vegetarian fast food dish native to the Indian state of Maharashtra. The dish is a simple creation involving a deep fried potato patty with some coriander and spices, served in a bread roll (*pav*) with condiments. It originated as cheap street food in Mumbai, but is now offered in stalls and restaurants throughout India.

Vaman means dwarf.

Vanara meaning humans with monkey like tails.

Asuras are mythological lord beings in Indian texts who, compete for power with the more benevolent devas. Asuras are described in Indian texts as powerful superhuman demigods or demons with good or bad qualities.

Deva means "heavenly, divine, anything of excellence", and is also one of the terms for a deity in Hinduism.

Pishachas, are flesh-eating demons in Hindu mythology. Their origin is obscure, although some believe that they were created by Brahma. Another legend describes them as the sons of either Krodha (figuratively "Anger") or as Dakṣa's daughter *Piśāca*. They have been described to have a dark complexion with bulging veins and protruding, red eyes. They are believed to have their own languages, known as Paiśāci.

Rakshasas were most often depicted as ugly, fierce-looking and enormous creatures, with two fangs protruding from the top of the mouth and having sharp, claw-like fingernails. They are shown as being mean, growling like beasts, and as insatiable cannibals that could smell the scent of human flesh. Some of the more ferocious ones were shown with flaming red eyes and hair, drinking blood with their palms or from a human skull (similar to representations of vampires in later Western mythology). Generally they could fly, vanish, and had *Maya* (magical powers of illusion), which enabled them to change size at will and assume the form of any creature. The female equivalent of rakshasa is rakshasi.

Damru is a small two-headed drum, used in Hinduism and Tibetan Buddhism. In Hinduism, the damru is known as the instrument of the deity Shiva, and is said to be created by Shiva to produce spiritual sounds by which the whole universe has been created and regulated. In Tibetan Buddhism, the damaru is used as an instrument in tantric practices.

Source - Wikipedia

by LeMonk

Prologue
Many, Many Millennia Ago...

The land was dark, desolate and devastated. Frequent flashes of lightning lit up the sky, revealing the true extent of the devastation. It rained fire and gold – literally. Violent winds tore into the clouds, dispersing them hither and thither.

However the flashes also revealed something strange. A single cloud, with two beings atop, gently glided, unaffected by the reigning chaos. The being in front was tall and sinew, his hair neatly tied in a bun, with a few loose strands swaying in the violent winds. He held a huge bow in his right hand while a quiver full of arrows hung loosely by his side.

The other being, huge, muscular with a body resembling cast iron, stood a few paces behind his Lord and Master. Though he knew the extent of the Lord's abilities, that particular feat of the Lord never failed to awe him.

He was well aware of the strong and lovely flying beings and even the flying contraptions of the Asuras. Whereas the flying beings had powerful wings, the contraptions had devices to power them.

But the Lord did not need wings nor did he need contraptions. He could levitate huge objects merely by the power of his mind and could even change the structure and properties of matter, reciting powerful hymns. It was no wonder that despite their immense weight, they stood on a fragile cloud, gliding along, being propelled by the Lord's energy.

"O noble one," said his servant softly, "truth has triumphed."

"But at what cost?"

"The planet is totally devastated, my Lord. Our great continent will be engulfed by the ocean in seven days. There will be no trace left of it."

"Have the Devas banished the evil Asuras, Rakshasas and Pishachas through the portal in space?"

"Most of them were rounded up and banished, my Lord," he spoke in a low tone, "but a few have given us the slip amidst the chaos. After deporting the evil ones, the Devas too left the planet through the very same portal. Perhaps they were ashamed of the utter devastation caused by the war."

"Now our planet will be ruled by the Manavs, that is, the human race."

"But my Lord," he said with some concern, "they have no special powers like the Devas, the Asuras or the Rakshasas. Moreover they can easily be influenced by either good or evil. They have both qualities in them. The few evil ones, who have slipped away and reside amongst them in disguise, may bring out the evil in the Manavs."

"Then we will have to ensure that the good in them is never overpowered by the evil. The few of us, who are left behind, will have to stay amongst the Manavs and ensure that the good in them is kept alive."

"Shouldn't you close the portal my Lord? What if the banished ones decide to return through the portal?"

"The portal is the only way into this part of the galaxy. Closing the portal will forever shut the doors of this planet to the Devas, if they ever chose to return."

"If the banished evil ones return, who will protect the Manavs?" said the concerned devotee.

"I have thought about that and created these three Astras," said the Lord, as he showed three relics radiating such energy that the devotee could barely lay eyes upon them. "They are so full of energy that they will form a protective shield around the planet and keep it hidden from prying eyes."

"But what if these Astras fall in the wrong hands?"

"Only the one with the quality of a true Deva can touch it," he said calmly, "any other being who tries to touch it will perish. You are mistaken to believe that I am the Almighty one. The Almighty energy merely resides in me. When evil prevails in the future, the energy will enter some other form to destroy evil."

"I seek your permission to go away to the Himalayas," said the devotee, with his head bowed low. "I wish to spend the rest of my days in penance. The few of my tribe, who survive, will join me. We have also taken an oath never to speak, or show ourselves to the Manavs, unless the planet is in peril."

"You are my greatest friends and I will not deny you your wish, but there is one last task I wish you to perform before you leave. Take these Astras and do as I say."

"Your wish is my command, your highness," he said humbly.

Present day
October 10th, dawn...

Tina paced up and down the verandah restlessly, time and again glancing nervously over the hedges, onto the road, expecting to see her father's car approach. It was four in the morning and her mother was fast asleep, unaware that she had slipped out a couple of hours ago. However her dog *Coffee*, sat on the verandah with his head on the ground, frown on his brow, wagging his tail gently whenever she passed by.

Tina lived in Batatawadai Puram, a small village nestled high up in the Sahyadri Mountains in western India. Outwardly, it looked like any ordinary village, but it was not so. The village could boast of one of the best schools in the country, a college with a modern research centre and a green and clean environment. All the people in the village were well to do, thanks to the philanthropic efforts of Ishwar, who had become a zillionaire selling Batata Wadas* to the entire world. Ishwar never forgot his humble beginnings nor did he forget his poor village. Though he did not live in the village anymore, he brought about great changes in it. To honour Ishwar and his efforts, the villagers had re-christened their village and named it "Batatawadai Puram".

Tina loved her brother Guru and his best friends Sri and Nath more than anything else. The four of them were the best of pals and had shared a number of adventures together*. She loved to hang around with the boys since they always treated her as one of the gang. Though tiny for her age, she was tough – really tough. And there was a surprise in store for people who thought they could bully her because of her size, for she could climb trees as well as any boy could and had been involved in fistfights along with her pals on more than one occasion.

However that day, things were about to change. She would finally meet Varshika, a girl her age, a friend and new companion. Varshika, the daughter of Sri's aunt, Monika, was born and brought up in Africa. Aunt Monika, who was a doctor, was busy combating a new disease in Africa that had threatened to turn into a pandemic. Being unavailable most of the time, she had decided to send Varshika to her sister's house in India. Varshika would join school in Batatawadai Puram.

Though Tina had never met Varshika, they had become the best of friends on the internet, once they came to know that she would be coming to India. They had learnt everything about each other– likes, dislikes, passions, secrets but had decided not to share pictures and would see each other only when Varshika came to India.

Guru and Sri along with Guru's father had gone to the big city to pick up Varshika. The long wait was turning excruciating for Tina. She had meticulously calculated how long Varshika would take to reach the village. Her flight was supposed to land at noon, two hours for customs clearance and another twelve hour drive from the big city. She should've reached by 2 am. Tina was perplexed by the fact that the clock showed 4 am, yet Varshika had not reached.

Suddenly Coffee was all alert. He first whimpered, got up, dashed to the hedge and to Tina's surprise, sprang clean over the hedge and was on the road in a jiffy. Even as she yelled, she saw the headlights of an approaching car along the narrow, brightly lit lane. Coffee dashed towards the car and came running along with it barking excitedly.

The pandemonium was enough to wake up the neighbours – Sri's household to the right and Nath's household to the left. Fortunately there were no other houses in their

14

near surroundings. As the car reached their gate, lights came on and doors opened. Tina's mother reached the verandah sleepily and was surprised to see her there. Presently Sri's parents, Nath and his mother reached the gate of her house. Everyone approached the car excitedly as Guru got down from the car and opened the huge gate into their compound.

Tina was surprised to find a fair girl (who did not resemble Sri one bit), get out of the car. Unlike Sri, who was lean and tall, Varshika was short with the structure of a dancer – lean and sinew. A sweet smile enriched her face. She could have passed for Tina's sister except for the fact that her gorgeous, emerald green eyes sparkled mischievously.   The unique colour of her eyes, were the highlight of her lovely face.

"Hi Tina!" said Varshika, as both embraced. "I was so eager to meet you that I asked them to bring me directly to you rather than to aunt".

By now Coffee was barking excitedly and scratching the car. Guru yelled at him to be still, lest he peeled off some paint.

"What took you guys so long?" asked Tina. "Was the flight delayed?"

"No," said Varshika, "we took time to get 'Cuddly' out of customs."

Saying so, she opened the trunk of the car to reveal a beautiful golden brown *cocker spaniel*.

"Folks, meet Cuddly, my doggie sister."

Cuddly jumped out of the car and took a few unsteady steps, feebly wagging the stub that she had for a tail.

"She's a bit groggy, both from the sedatives they pumped into her and the gruesome journey".

Coffee ran towards Cuddly, his tail wagging end to end.

Both sat on the verandah, side by side. Cuddly seemed really tired, but enthused.

"Now, young lady" said a stern voice. "Don't you think your aunt deserves a hug?"

Varshika turned to her aunt and flew into her arms.

"Oh aunt, I was so eager to meet Tina that I almost forgot you," said Varshika with a giggle.

"Yeah!" said another voice. "Who's forgotten her baker uncle?"

"O Uncle Keshava! I love you," said Varshika, giving him a big hug.

Sri's parents were the best bakers in Batatawadai Puram and owned a bakery in the village square, a short distance from their cottage.

"Why don't you folks join us for a cup of tea and freshly baked bread?" said Sri's father.

"Any way it's already a half past four," added Sri's mother, "and we can't thank you enough for getting Varshika from the airport."

"Please don't mention it," said Guru's father, rather embarrassed. "What are friends for? And yes, I would definitely love to eat the freshly baked bread along with a cup of steaming hot tea. The aroma is so tempting, that I'm drooling as I speak."

"Why don't you guys unload the stuff from the car and join us?" asked Sri's mother.

"Why us?" groaned Sri. "We're tired."

Sri's mother glared at them.

"Sissies!" said Varshika.

"You guys go in." said Nath. "I'll help the girls and join you later."

He proceeded towards the car with the girls.

"Hi Varshika!" said Nath. "It's nice to finally meet you. How was the trip?"

"Bad," said Varshika in an irritated tone. "Had a fight – they wouldn't let Cuddly with me, insisted that she had to travel in the cargo hold. Poor thing! She must be so tired."

Some twenty minutes later, all were seated in Sri's living room, except for Sri and Guru, who were lazing on the sofa half asleep. The elders enjoyed freshly baked buns with hot tea while the girls and Nath talked excitedly in one corner.

"Good thing that today's a Sunday. Now we all can rest and later in the evening, you kids can show Varshika around," said Sri's mother. "She will join school tomorrow. I have spoken to Principal Sandipani and although there are only three days left for the term to end, he insisted that she join from Monday itself."

"That'll be great" said Tina in an excited voice. "We could go to school together."

"Done," said Varshika.

"You're welcome to our house any time dear," added Guru's mother. "Remember you have three houses here and we are all like one big family."

"Thank you," said Varshika. "Please teach me the recipe of those delicious chocolates that Tina keeps mentioning."

Soon fatigue overtook excitement and everyone dispersed. Tina helped Varshika unpack. Both were thrilled as their bedrooms had windows facing each other. After unpacking, they bid farewell and being extremely tired, fell asleep as soon as they hit their respective beds.

At one past noon, Nath joined Tina and Varshika for lunch. Sri and Guru simply refused to wake up. Tina dared to pinch them, but even then they refused to stir. Either they were really very tired or could bear a lot of pain, for she wasn't gentle when she pinched them. Finally, the girls gave up and decided to take a tour of the village with Nath, who was as fresh as a sunflower.

"Welcome to your new home," said Tina excitedly as they proceeded to explore the village.

"I miss Africa," said a dismayed Varshika, "but Batatawadai Puram is so unlike other villages in India."

"Believe me," said Nath. "You will love it once you really get to know this village."

Batatawadai Puram was a green village, with neat houses, well maintained roads and sprawling farms. The region was hilly with very fertile soil. Houses were arranged in neat clusters interspersed by farms. Guru and Sri had been neighbours since birth. Nath and his mother had recently joined them. Though Nath has been their friend since childhood, he lived in a different part of the village, as his mother faced a lot of financial difficulties. However recently, they had inherited the house next to Guru and Sri's from a distant relative of Nath's father.

Their houses were at the end of a narrow lane surrounded by dense woodlands that blended with the thick foliage of the hills behind. They did not have any farm lands but grew a variety of vegetables in their backyards. The teens walked for about five minutes and reached the main road - a wide road, flanked by shops on both the sides. Walking a few minutes on this road, they reached the village square. Now, many villages in India have a village square with a statue of some famous personality, but this was unlike any other village square, for in the square was a gigantic model of a Vada Pav* carved out of marble and placed on a stone pedestal with the name "Batatawadai Puram" etched on it. The entire structure was about seven feet high. Surrounding the square were some administrative buildings, the police station, post office and a medical centre. They walked further down the road and reached a junction where the road divided into two.

"The road to the left leads to our school," said Nath. "Whereas the one on the right leads to a number of farms, a huge lake and ends at the forest. The last farm at the edge of the forest belongs to Gendamal. His daughter Riya is the captain of the school archery team."

"Wow! That's great," said an excited Varshika. "I too was on my school's archery team in Africa."

"Would you like to take the road to the left and see our school?" asked Tina. "Further down the same road are the houses of many of our friends, and finally the road leads out of our village to the neighbouring village."

"You guys decide," said Varshika. "Is the neighbouring village anything like ours?"

"No way," said Tina. "And I don't like some of the people there."

"Let's take the road to the right," suggested Nath. "Anyway, we have school tomorrow, and can show her that part of the village after school."

They returned home after surveying most of the village and found Guru and Sri having tea in Guru's house. Apparently, the duo had recently woken up.

"Well, it looks like the lazy ones have awoken just now," teased Tina.

"About time too," added Varshika. "Anyway I toured the village without you guys. Nath was kind enough to show me around."

"Hah!" retorted Sri. "Nath gave you a superficial tour. Wait till we give you the real tour. We have many secret places that no one knows about, eh Nath?"

"But, but should we take the girls there? Is it safe?" asked a nervous Nath.

"Come on," said Sri. "They are tough girls. We must show them the temple and the caves and ..."

"Don't ever speak to me," yelled Tina. "You have secrets that you have kept from me, haven't you?"

"No sis," said Guru apologetically. "We discovered those a few days ago, and do you think we have kept anything hidden from you? Nath is right. We do not yet know how safe those places are."

"Okay," said Tina. "But we too want to see these places."

* * * * * * *

The next morning the two girls got ready to go to school. There was a lot of barking, for Cuddly was now fresh and alert and didn't want Varshika to go. Coffee, on the other hand, barked excitedly since he wanted to meet Cuddly. Finally, he managed to jump across the fence that separated the two houses and reached Cuddly, urging her to play with him. Perhaps he wanted to give her a tour of all his secret places in the village.

As the school was a short distance away, the children usually went to school on their bicycles, but that day Tina and Varshika decided to walk to school, enjoying the pleasant weather. The boys decided to go ahead on their bicycles. Tina was dressed in her school uniform, but Varshika, who did not have a school uniform, was dressed in a blue top and jeans. She has a vest coat on and looked like an adventurer on a trek.

"Is this how you normally dress?" asked Tina.

"Yep," said Varshika. "I come from the bush and one doesn't know what one may need. My pockets are full of supplies – a swiss army knife, energy bar, salted biscuits, first aid..."

"You won't need all that here," said an amused Tina. "This is a very calm and safe village, although we've had our share of adventures."

They reached the junction on the main road and took the road to the left. It was a very wide road and had cottages on either side. Soon they reached a huge building. Varshika was impressed, for it was one of the largest schools she had seen. It was three floors high and had a very huge play ground. There were a number of bicycles arranged in neat rows outside the school. A number of boys and girls dotted the huge grounds. The air was filled with excitement. Tina had mentioned that their exams were over and school would shut down for the mid-term vacations in three days. Very little would be taught in school and students would rather be busy in the try outs for the various teams and auditions would be held for the annual program that they would have in the month of December.

They were about to reach the huge gate when three girls accosted them.

"Well, well, well," said Saniya. "Who's the new wimp?"

Now, Saniya was from the neighbouring "Bondai Puram" and was extremely jealous of Sri and Guru.

"What are these," asked Varshika, "the 'Powder Puff' girls???"

Saniya, who was a foot taller than Tina and Varshika, moved menacingly towards Varshika and grabbed her by the collar with both hands.

"Watch it wimp, or I will rearrange your face."

"I wouldn't do that if I were you," said Varshika with clenched teeth. "I will count to three, then..."

"Then what will you do?"

"Not me, but old Samuel here might."

"Who's Samuel?" asked Saniya.

"My Black Mamba," hissed Varshika with clenched teeth, as she pulled a hissing and slithering snake from her bag. The creature's black mouth and mesmerizing eyes were enough to scare the wits out of the boldest person and Saniya was far from bold. "You don't want me shoving him down your throat do you?"

Saniya let out a shriek and took a few steps back. She swooned in Manya and Tanya's arms.

"Now listen, you losers," said Varshika looking directly at the other two. "If you girls ever cross my path again, I will feed you to my Tarantula." Saying so, she took out a spider the size of a coconut shell from her bag.

The two girls gave out an ear piercing shriek, promptly dropped a limp Saniya with a loud thud and rushed into the school.

Fifteen minutes later, both Tina and Varshika were seated in Principal Sandipani's office while he paced up and down.

"Do you girls have a good explanation???"

"Sir, they were the ones who provoked us," said Varshika politely.

"Firstly, smuggling dangerous creatures into the country... threatening to shove a snake down the throat of a fellow student... threatening to feed fellow students to a critter... um agreed that the creatures are absolutely safe... um I guess the spider must be defanged and the poison glands of the mamba removed... but this..."

"Now, why would I do a cruel thing like that?" asked a genuinely bewildered Varshika.

"You mean... you mean... they..."

It took a lot of effort on Sandipani's part to control the rising bile in his stomach and not throw up.

"Surely your mother did not get you these creatures..."

"No way," said Varshika deep in thought. "They were gifted to me by my Dad. Believe me sir, these creatures are divine. They will help save the world one day."

"And, may I know how you are sure of that?"

"Dad told me, the day he gifted them to me," said Varshika with the hint of a sigh, "the day he left for his important work. It's been six months now..."

"I don't care. You will never ever bring such critters to my school... and never ever threaten to kill anyone... you got me?"

"Ok sir, you have my word," said Varshika, reluctantly.

23

"I was just going through your report card... you almost got thrown out of your previous school for insubordination... easy to believe. Hmm... interesting... it says that you are a very bright student, an excellent dancer and outstanding archer... very difficult to believe. You will spend the rest of the day at the tryouts with Tina... and eh... welcome to Wadaipuram High."

"Thank you sir," replied Varshika politely.

"Listen carefully, you two," said Sandipani seriously. "Consider this your last warning. I've had enough trouble with Guru and Sri, now I don't want my problems compounded by their sisters teaming up. You may go now..."

They left the office in silence. But as they were out of the Principal's earshot, they heard loud cheers. Their names were being chanted.

"What's the raucous?" said Tina.

As they reached the school grounds, they were surprised to see a group of students led by Guru and Sri, roll out a red carpet in front of them.

"Enough with the theatrics," chided Tina. "And where did you get the red carpet from?"

"Way to go Varshu, way to go," said an elated Sri. "That's my sister, guys."

Varshika rolled up her eyes and moved on while Tina followed her rather amused.

"Shall I take you to the archery team?" asked Tina.

"Sure!"

They made their way to one end of the huge school ground. There were a number of targets arranged in a neat row with six students practicing with their bows. They seemed really good but were distracted by the approaching girls.

"Hi there Riya!" said Tina to a girl who moved with authority. "This is Varshika, Sri's cousin and I brought her..."

"I know," said Riya without much enthusiasm. "I also heard of your little adventure. But archery is a serious sport. If you want to join the archery team, you have to prove yourself. We are 'national level' players and are dead serious about our sport."

Everyone in the team stopped whatever they were doing and listened intently. The atmosphere was tense.

"I too love archery, and am ready to prove it. I challenge the best of your archers to a duel. Best of three shots... okay?" said Varshika confidently. "And please do not misunderstand my gesture. Neither am I conceited, nor over confident. I just want you guys to know that I have been trained by bushmen and am good... really good."

"Done," said Riya. "Beat me and you have our support. Rohan will lend you his archery kit."

Without a word, the two got ready for the faceoff. Riya offered Varshika to go first, but she politely refused. After concentrating briefly, Riya shot her three arrows in quick succession, managing to hit the centre of the target in each case. Everyone cheered for her. At fifty meters, it was a really good score. Now Varshika took her position. In quick succession she too shot three arrows. Initially no one realized what had happened, but when they approached the target, everyone was spellbound, for Varshika had split each of Riya's arrows into two by her arrows. Tina began clapping loudly, followed by the entire team.

"That's fab... I mean really fab," said an astonished Riya.

25

"I not only welcome you to the team, but offer you the captaincy as well."

"Aw, come on," said Varshika. "You are a great captain and a truly good human. Moreover, I will make a lousy captain. I'm not as disciplined as you guys, neverthless I would love to join the team."

"Welcome to 'The Wadaipuram Archery Team'!"

"My pleasure!" said Varshika.

"If you ever need me... ever," said Riya "do not hesitate to call me... um and those girls deserved what they got."

Tina and Varshika left with broad smiles. They felt really good from within.

"What other hidden skills do you have eh?" asked Tina, nudging Varshika with her elbow.

"Not more than you, but yes, a few odd ones," said Varshika with a mischievous smile.

"But what about Samuel and eh... the spider?"

"Jackson," said Varshika. "The Tarantula is 'Jackson'. You won't believe the trouble I had to take to get them here safely."

"But why did you get them here in the first place?"

"Dad told me to do so," said Varshika, "something about warding off evil. He sincerely believes that there would be an apocalypse. I don't believe in all the mumbo jumbo I hear, but he was so sincere and I love him so much, that I obeyed."

The next two days passed without any major incident.

October 14th, 7 am

Somebody gently prodded Varshika who lay on her bed fast asleep. She had a pillow over her head instead of under it. Her left hand hung loosely on the side of the bed. Clothes were strewn all over the room. On the study table stood two glass tanks with secure covers. Samuel, the black mamba was absolutely still in one of the tanks whereas Jackson, the tarantula moved about restlessly in the adjoining tank.

"Leave me alone Sri," she yelled. "I am not going to wake up, at least till noon, so get lost..."

Someone pulled open the curtains, flooding the room with sunlight. Varshika groaned and slowly opened her eyes...

"Happy birthday to you..." they sang in a chorus.

Varshika instantly sat up, trying to focus and adjust to the sudden brightness, looking around in amazement.

"You guys remembered...?" she asked rather flustered.

"Now wake up sleepy head," said Tina, "and get ready in a jiffy. We have a great day planned for you."

"Aunt Monika had phoned a few moments ago and will be calling in another fifteen minutes," said an excited Sri.

"What about dad?" asked an equally excited Varshika, "Was he there too?"

"I believe not," said Sri, "but aunt told me that he will surely be calling you on my cellphone. Here, keep it for today."

He tossed his cellphone to her.

"We're waiting for breakfast," said Nath, "so please do

27

hurry up."

Varshika joined them in fifteen minutes, looking pretty, dressed in blue jeans with a floral top and of course her patent vest coat. She rushed to the phone when it rang.

"Hi Mum! Thank you... love you too... yes, dad called me a few minutes ago... yes, yes I'll enjoy ... you take care... bye mum, love you."

After speaking to her mother and being wished by her uncle and aunt, Varshika came to the dining table. Sri, Guru, Nath and Tina were already seated and waiting for her. Tina looked cute in a polka dress, her hair combed neatly. She had dainty shoes on. Guru and Sri looked their usual selves, with high waist jeans and t-shirts, sneakers and unkempt hair. Nath, on the other hand looked smart, with a clean shirt, well ironed pant and highly polished shoes. Even his spectacles seemed new. His hair was neatly combed.

"When are you guys going to learn to dress?" asked Varshika, looking at Sri and Guru. "You look as if you have just returned from a battle field."

"What's wrong with our clothes?" asked Sri. "And you speak as if we are about to meet a beautiful princess in distress."

Everyone had a hearty laugh. Sri's father had baked a chocolate cake that was on the table. There were thirteen candles on it.

"How does it feel to be a teenager?" asked Tina.

"Great," exclaimed Varshika. "Hopefully now people will start treating me as an adult."

"Fat chance," teased Sri.

"So, what have you guys planned for me?"

"A day in your life, that you will never forget," said Guru. "We will first explore the neighbouring town... then... then..."

"Then what?" asked Nath, a little alarmed. "Hope you are not going to the temple?"

"We're doing exactly that!" said Sri. "They are a part of the gang and deserve to see it."

"Whoo! Whoo! Whoo!" went the girls.

"Can we at least take Coffee and Cuddly along?" asked Nath.

"Sure man," said Sri, "and take a chill pill, will you? Nothing's going to happen."

"That's what you guys always say..." complained Nath.

They left half an hour later. Each one had a bicycle, for Tina had lent her's to Varshika while she rode her father's cycle. The dogs trotted alongside. The roads were deserted and soon they passed their school. After riding for another five minutes, they came to the end of the village. A narrow road led them out of the village. As they approached the next village, the contrast in the surroundings became visible. The quality of the road rapidly deteriorated. It was clearly visible that the farmers here were not as well to do as those in Batatawadai Puram. Garbage was carelessly strewn around. Soon they reached a very huge farm that was markedly different from the surrounding farms. The owner seemed to be very rich and apparently wanted to flaunt his richness. Something on the farm caught Tina's eye and she stopped. Nath and Varshika stopped to find out what was going on, but Guru and Sri who were a bit ahead were unaware that the others had stopped and continued riding on.

"What's the matter Tina?" asked Varshika.

29

"Something is seriously wrong here, Varshu." replied Tina. "Look at the workers. Don't they seem strange? I've never seen these people here before, although I have been here a number of times."

"They do look a bit strange," commented Nath, "but what are you trying to imply?"

"I can bet they are zombies," said Varshika in a serious tone.

"Get out of my property!" said a shrill voice.

Saniya had reached the edge of her farm. She was standing with her hands on her hips, looking at the trio with immense hatred in her eyes.

"We're standing on a municipal road," said Tina, "and since when do you own a municipal road?"

"Didn't I warn you never to cross my path?" asked Varshika furiously.

"What will you do now, eh?" asked Saniya, stammering a bit. "Will you feed me to these dogs?"

"We don't feed our dogs garbage," said Guru who had just reached the spot. "They are a part of our family and eat home cooked food."

"You mean to say I'm... I'm..."

Everyone began to laugh aloud.

"Get lost, or I'll call the cops," she said hysterically as she stomped off.

"Now, what was that all about?" enquired Sri.

"I think, they have zombies on their farm," said Varshika seriously.

"Now, that's a bit too much Varshu," said Sri. "Agreed, they are the scum of the planet, but they don't have the guts to do something like that."

"Do you think these workers are bonded labourers of some sort?" asked Nath.

"I can bet they are zombies. They looked exactly like zombies. Let's get closer and I can prove that they are the undead."

"Ok, you're on," said Guru, "we'll visit them tonight at around eight, when everyone is indoors. But, if you are wrong, you will treat us with ice cream for the rest of the vacations."

"You're on," said Varshika as she spat on her hand, "let's shake."

"Uggh!" said Guru, "I'm not spitting on my hand and shaking. You'll have to take my word."

"Sissies!" said Varshika.

"Why spoil your day?" said Sri. "Let's enjoy. There's a lot more to come."

"Then let's go straight to the secret temple of yours," said Tina.

"First, let's make the dogs comfortable." said Guru. "C'mon sweeties, come here, come here..."

The two dogs approached him with enthusiasm. They looked tired and were panting. Guru placed a bowl on the ground and poured cold water in it. The dogs lapped it, making a loud sound. The group then returned to their village and silently rode towards Gendamal's farm.

It was around ten when they reached Gendamal's farm. The teens were drenched in sweat, so decided to park their bicycles at the edge of the huge farm and rest awhile. Guru mentioned that they would have to proceed further on foot, as the temple was deep inside the forest.

"So when did you guys discover this secret temple of yours?" asked Tina in an envious tone.

"I'd say, the temple wanted to be discovered," said Sri. "We were here some eight days ago to deliver a parcel to Riya's dad when Guru felt a sort of pull in that direction."

"I can't explain it," said Guru pointing towards the forest. "I just felt a surge of energy in that direction and before I knew it, I was drawn towards it."

"He was running like a madman," added Nath, "and we like fools, running and shouting behind him."

"Where is this temple located and what's so special about it?" asked Varshika.

"It is located about four kilometers in the forest on that hill," said Guru pointing towards a hill that was easily visible, "and you will have to see it, to believe that it is unique."

Tina now turned to Varshika.

"Looks like, you really miss your dad?"

"Coolest dad in the world," said Varshika lost in thought. "He was always there for me, cooked tasty dishes and had a lot of fun with me."

"What is his profession," asked Guru. "I know that your mum is a doctor, but have never had the opportunity of meeting your father."

"He is a part time professor of anthropology at the university and also a naturalist. We are close and spent a lot of time together. Moreover, he always planned his expeditions to coincide with my vacations so that he could take me along. Many a times, other learned people joined us on these expeditions and we enjoyed heated debates on a variety of topics ranging from the supernatural to the Vedas."

"But, I thought he is an African," muttered Guru.

"No way," said Varshika, "do I look one bit African? He is of Indian descent, but his ancestors had settled in Africa a long, long time ago. However many of his best friends are African, in fact some are African chieftains."

"Your parents seem poles apart," said Tina.

"You bet," said Vashika. "Mum is a very serious, at times boring sort of person, engrossed in her work. On the other hand, dad is a cool dude, loves dancing, cooking and both of us love animals. Do you know that we are pure vegetarians?"

"I don't believe this," said Sri. "Then you are like Nath, Guru and Tina. But what do you feed your snake and spider?"

"Samuel eats eggs, while I fed Jackson dead insects. I do not kill any creature to feed them."

"Hey guys," said Nath, "don't you think that we should be on our way? We have to be home in time for Varshu's surprise party... ulp."

"You have planned a party for me?"

Tina looked daggers at Nath.

"I'm gonna kill you."

"Sorry!"

Soon they were on their way to the temple. Guru and Sri led the group followed by an excited Tina and Varshika. Nath, sulking a bit, followed them some distance away. He felt bad that he had accidently revealed their big secret. The dogs, who were probably very tired by then, followed him without much excitement. The narrow path that led them into the forest, now almost disappeared. They were finding it difficult to navigate through the dense foliage and received occasional scratches from the number of thorny bushes. However they enjoyed picking berries - a bit sweet, a bit sour. After walking for about three quarters of an hour, they came to a clearing. The path ahead inclined steeply. It was a narrow path with steep slopes on either side.

"Now, watch your step guys," warned Guru. "One slip and you are a goner. The drop is some three hundred feet."

Tina looked down. It was a sheer drop and looking down made her dizzy. Soon they reached a rounded hillock and heaved a sigh of relief, for now the path seemed absolutely safe. They walked towards the top of the hillock. It was covered with huge trees that were hundreds of years old. The thickness of the barks gave a rough indication of their age. Amidst those trees, they caught a glimpse of a temple that lay in ruins and looked pretty dilapidated. The stone structure was hidden from plain view by the creepers and trees that had taken root in the cracks in these huge stones. In fact, some of the trees now gave support to the structure. They cautiously entered the temple through a huge opening. May be, a magnificent door had adorned this opening, a long time ago, but now all that was left was an opening, broken and damaged. The inner walls had a number of carvings, depicting mythological stories. The huge stone idol was badly damaged and one could not make out the deity. Varshika shone her powerful flashlight on every nook and corner. The architects must've been impressive, for not a square inch was left bare. Intricate designed adorned every nook and corner on the structure.

"Magnificent!" said Tina with awe. "This is a rare discovery. We should immediately inform the others. The temple may be centuries... no millennia old. We'll be famous."

"No," said Guru, "there's more to this temple than mere history. Wait till you see the entire temple."

"What else is there to see?" asked Tina.

"Follow me," said Guru, "and watch your step."

He led them behind the idol. The outline of a small door was barely visible in the darkness. Guru switched on his flashlight and led the way. The others followed cautiously, for the steps were steep and winding. The dogs whimpered but they too followed. As they descended, the dampness visibly decreased and the teens felt a whiff of cold air. They had entered a wide passage. To the left was a magnificent door that led them into a huge structure while the passage continued ahead. The teens entered this huge structure.

"Nath, will you do the honours?" said Sri, handing him a lighter.

Nath cautiously lit, what seemed to be an ancient torch and brightness flooded the structure. Sri, who was taller than Nath, now pulled out the torch from the niche in the wall that held it and proceeded to light other torches. Soon the entire structure was brightly lit up. The girls stood with their jaws agape, for they had seen nothing like this ever before.

"Temple, within a temple," beamed Guru. "Have you seen anything more spectacular than this?"

It was indeed a spectacular structure that had probably been carved out of a single rock. Like the temple above, every square inch had been sculpted, but unlike the structure above, the teens couldn't understand the intricate patterns. A script unknown to them covered every wall. Beside the script were figures carved in the stone, figures of supernatural creatures, demons and gods. They seemed to be engaged in a fierce battle. Surprisingly the carvings also depicted flying objects, sending beams on the fighting figures below.

"Did they have flying saucers then?" muttered Nath. "This one here seems so similar to one, seen over America in the late sixties. I have a picture of it in my book of supernatural mysteries."

Tina was drawn towards a huge statue, right at the centre of the subterranean temple. It was about eight feet tall and depicted a lean, muscular deity seated in meditation. She kept looking at his intense eyes and seemed mesmerized by them. They were kind and powerful eyes, radiating energy. The deity's palms faced upwards and rested at the centre of his joined feet. They had a strange looking object in them.

"What is the strange object in his palms?" asked Tina to the others who had by now gathered beside her.

"No idea," said Guru, "but somehow it seems important. It may be a diamond."

"Diamond," exclaimed Varshika. "Are you implying that the object is a diamond?"

"I'm not a hundred percent sure, but it may be a diamond or at least rare stone."

"Well, it's surely not a diamond," said Varshika, peering closely at it, "but is unlike anything, I have ever seen before."

"That's why we have not told anyone yet," added Sri. "Who knows what will happen if everyone comes to know of this temple. Moreover it seems so pure that we did not want to spoil it by making it known to the entire world. Don't you feel calm and contented, just standing in the proximity of this idol?"

"Yes," said Tina, "I can feel a positive energy surge

through me. You guys are right. We must not desecrate this place by making it known to the world. And yes, I believe you guys - it wanted to be found by us."

"I was wondering," said Varshika, "did the torches remain in working condition for so many millennia, for this temple is not centuries old but millennia old."

"No," said Sri. "We fixed those for you guys. We wanted you enjoy the beauty of this structure in the kind of lighting that our ancestors might have viewed it in."

"...And don't forget to mention that it was I who made the fuel for these torches," chuckled Nath.

The gang explored the structure for some more time. They couldn't figure out if the structure was originally on the surface, or it was intentionally built below. Later they explored the rest of the subterranean temple. There were a number of rooms filled with carvings from floor to ceiling and had strong stone doors. Apparently, no metal was used in the construction. What these rooms were originally meant for was a mystery. They were so fascinated that they did not feel like leaving. Tina seemed to be in a deep trance ever since she had seen the huge statue however it was Guru who noticed the time.

"Guys...we need to hurry," said Guru. "It's almost three past noon and we must go now."

"Is it that late?" asked Varshika. "Then we must hurry back. We have another appointment at eight."

"C'mon," said Guru, "can't we leave that for another day? Let's enjoy today."

"No way," said Varshika firmly. "I can prove that they are zombies. That household is keeping zombies as labourers. Isn't it cruel?"

Not a word was spoken on the way back. Tina walked mechanically, lost in thought. The others, including the dogs, were too tired to do anything else but trudge along the sandy road. When the gang finally reached home, they were indeed a sight, with soiled clothes, ruffled hair and scratches all over their bodies.

The teens enjoyed Varshika's birthday party and gorged on the delicious dishes prepared for the occasion. At half past eight, much to Nath's dismay, Sri asked the elders if the gang could hang out for a couple of hours but avoided mentioning their exact destination. Though it was late, the elders readily agreed, for the kids in Batatawadai Puram spent many a night gazing at the stars, in the mini observatory, in their school.

Thus the gang set on their mission to find the truth about the strange workers on Saniya's farm. To avoid drawing any attention, the dogs were left at home.

"Hope you have a lot of pocket money stashed somewhere?" teased Guru, simultaneously winking at Sri.

"We'll see," said Varshika.

"Nobody does anything stupid," warned Sri, "this is just a reconnaissance mission. If we find anything strange, we report it to the authorities tomorrow."

"Do we have to really go?" asked Nath. "What if we are caught? I don't like lying to my mother."

"C'mon," said Varshika, "don't you have any sense of adventure?"

"...And don't you like ice cream?" added Guru. "Think about it... free ice cream for the rest of the vacations. But did you guys pack anything for now? We may get hungry. What about those tasty salted biscuits that you usually carry?"

Varshika grimaced.

"Haven't you guys already eaten more than your tummies can hold?"

"Don't worry," said Tina, "I have plenty of those salted biscuits in my back pack. But what's with you and salted biscuits Guru?"

"Just developed a taste for them." said Guru again winking at Sri. "But why on earth are you so glum, sis?"

"Nothing," she replied, "yet overwhelmed by the experience in the temple. We must keep it a secret."

"Then let's shake on it," said Varshika.

"No way," said everyone firmly.

The gang reached Saniya's farm at half past nine. Getting in was easy as the boys knew every inch of the farm. After all, they had played many a prank on Saniya in the past. The boys were sure that the farm had no dogs and was safe. However the stench of filth and pigs was overwhelming.

Saniya's mother Maya was well known for extracting work out of the poor villagers in Bondaipuram. She rarely missed the opportunity of taking undue advantage of some poor farmer, badly in need of money. However the idea of keeping zombie labourers was a bit too far-fetched, even for a greedy person like her.

Once in, the teens made their way towards the huge barn situated in one isolated corner of the farm. The girls had noticed that the workers had been rounded up in a hurry that morning after their encounter with Saniya.

Keeping low, they tiptoed softly towards the barn door. However they froze in their tracks, when they saw a huge Rottweiler, right in their path, gnashing its teeth at them. It was growling at them so methodically, that the growl seemed like a running motor. Varshika beckoned the others to remain silent. Then to everyone's surprise she got up confidently and approached the dog, which, it seemed, was ready to spring upon her. She started whistling strangely as she approached the dog (that had a head bigger than hers), and on reaching it, started gently stroking its head above the ridge of its nose as she whistled her tune. The dog was asleep in five minutes.

"Wha...," Sri began to open his mouth, as she beckoned him to remain silent.

"Mesmerized," she whispered, "...as taught by my father."

Everyone looked at her, wide eyed, but not a word was spoken. They managed to enter the barn without further incident. What they saw inside sent shivers up their spines. About six of them sat huddled in one corner, with their heads in between their legs. Their clothes were tattered. The gang noticed that their legs were tied to each other with ropes. They sat motionless, with sightless eyes and bony bodies. One of them raised his head as the gang approached cautiously. It seemed as if he did not register their presence. Tears were streaming down his cheeks and he seemed ill. He seemed so young, just a boy. His face showed no emotions whatsoever.

"See, I was right" said Varshika angrily, "they are zombies."

"No," said Tina, "you are mistaken. These are bonded labourers - ill and starving. I'm going to get them out of here. It's inhumane... but are these guys, the same ones that we saw in the morning?"

"Watch out," warned Guru. "They may be dangerous. What if they bite?"

40

"Rubbish," retorted Tina. "Can't you see, they are hurt and abused. These are modern-day slaves."

The boys cautiously approached the so-called zombies and began to cut the ropes with a pocket knife. In a few minutes, they freed everyone and beckoned them to follow. However not one stirred.

"They're starving," said Tina as she hurriedly opened the packet of salted biscuits. She then handed two biscuits each to the workers. They kept gazing at the biscuits in their hands not knowing what to do. Tina had an idea. She sat in front of them and began eating one of the biscuits urging them to copy her. Watching her, a couple of them started munching on the biscuits, as if in slow motion. Soon everyone had begun eating the biscuits. Tina, who could now taste the salt on the biscuits that she had just eaten, was surprised to see the zombies get up one by one. Suddenly the air was filled with blood curdling screams. On eating the biscuits, the zombies seemed to have awakened from a deep slumber. They started approaching Tina walking slowly, with hands outstretched, like the zombies in the movies. The gang promptly let out louder screams, and rushed out of the barn. They saw the Rottweiler, up and alert in their path, but on seeing the zombies, it too sprang and ran away yelping.

"Now look what you guys have done," complained Nath.

"Shut up and run, if you value your life," said Guru. "It's the salt in the biscuits... I read somewhere that eating salt makes zombies blood-thirsty and they've eaten plenty of salt just now."

Sri and Guru jumped over the fence, and ran like they had never run before. In no time they were on their cycles and zoomed away.

41

"Maybe they won't follow," said Nath.

But he was mistaken, for the group of zombies, oblivious of everything else, did exactly that - follow them.

"Let's get the hell out of here," said Varshika, "then we'll figure what to do."

By the time Varshika and Nath reached their bicycles, the two boys had disappeared. By then, all the zombies were out of the barn, moaning and moving towards then.

"Where's Tina?" asked Varshika alarmed.

"She was right behind me," said Nath, "let's go back and look for her."

They cautiously moved towards the barn, trying to avoid the zombies. Meanwhile Tina, who had tripped on a wire outside the barn, got up and dusted her bruised body. She saw the zombies some twenty meters behind her and ducked into a small tool shed. She wondered where in the devil's name, had everyone disappeared, leaving her behind. The tool shed was partially lit up due to light entering a big window. In one corner, she saw an old man sitting with his legs drawn to his chest and head down. Hearing the noise, he got up unsteadily, approached her, grabbed her by both shoulders and shook her. He had glazed eyes.

"The relic has been stolen from our sacred shrine ... our planet is in peril... you have to find it... and then place it along with the other two in the altar...only you can... only you can..." said he.

Tina let out a scream, pushed the man and simultaneously ran out of the tool shed. She bumped into Nath, who had come back to look for her. Varshika was a few paces behind. They were happy to see each other safe but were taken aback to see the zombies just a few feet away, slowly moaning

42

and moving towards them.   With renewed vigour, the trio rushed towards their bikes.

"Where are these two?" asked Tina in a shaky voice, as they ran.

"Run away," said Varshika with disgust, "Cowards!"

They reached their bicycles, jumped on them and rode like hell. Five minutes later, they glanced behind, only to see the zombies at a distance running towards them.

"I don't believe this," said Nath. "How can zombies move so fast?"

"How many zombies have you personally known?" said Tina.

They reached the outskirts of their village and waited briefly. The zombies were nowhere to be seen. So they continued ahead, glancing back time and again, to see if the zombies followed. The road was deserted. They had almost reached their school gate when someone pounced on Nath and pulled him down. The girls screamed and rode with vigour, only to crash into someone. It was Principal Sandipani, who had probably been working late and was returning home.

"Have you girls decided to kill me," he cried hysterically as he got up and dusted himself.

"Yiiii...," screamed Sandipani, as he saw the zombies.

He must've run at the speed of fifty miles an hour, for all Tina and Varshika saw was a trail of dust.

"O God! We're dead," said one of the panting zombies, "that was Principal Sandipani."

The girls looked wide eyed at the sweating zombies, disbelief in their eyes. They also realized that it was none other that Guru and Sri who had pounced on Nath and at that moment were laughing their hearts out.

"Didn't we promise you a birthday that you would never forget in your entire life?" said Sri laughing uncontrollably.

"They're not zombies???" asked Varshika.

"Members of the 'Wadaipuram High Drama Club," said Guru. "We set it up when we went to freshen up before Varshu's party."

"Does Saniya know about this?" asked Nath.

"Why should she know anything?" said Sri, "and Guru, the dog was just perfect. Where did you get him from?"

"I thought that was your handiwork," said a surprised Guru.

"And what about the old man, who grabbed me?" asked a visibly upset Tina. "He really looked like a zombie and told me something about the planet being in peril."

"You guys set that up?" asked Guru looking at the zombies.

"No," said one of the zombies, "only six of us..."

"I'm going to kill you... yes I will... and feed you to Samuel... I'll make an exception this time," said Varshika as she rushed towards the duo.

They got up on their bicycles and pedaled away fast.

"Let's get them, Tina."

Both mounted their bicycles and pursued the boys, while Nath stood transfixed. The zombies looked at him quizzically.

"What should we do now?" asked one of them.

"Get the hell out of here fast," said Nath, "unless you really want to be turned into zombies by those girls. Knowing them, they are capable of doing just that."

Casting a look of fear at Nath, the six of them rushed away.

Nath cycled slowly down the road. He saw the girls pedaling furiously ahead, then turn a corner. The boys had probably taken the road to Gendamal's farm. Nath decided that it would be futile to follow them, and thought of returning home. However he became alert when he saw strange lights flash in the sky. A huge object was descending rapidly, and according to Nath's calculations, headed straight for Gendamal's farm. He pedaled hard and tried to catch up with the girls.

Varshika was the first to reach Gendamal's farm, for she has left Tina far behind, in her zest to catch the boys. Once she caught up with the boys, she decided that she would punch them hard, for playing such a prank on her... that too on her birthday. As she was looking around for the boys, she saw an object as large as a house land in the forest just beyond the farm.

"I know this is also your handiwork, you jokers," she called out as she ran towards the spot.

The object that resembled a hexagonal flying saucer was flashing wildly. She boldly approached, but froze when she saw the sheer size of the craft. A beam of light appeared from it in the form of an inclined plane and a form tumbled out and stood up with a lot of difficulty. Though it had a humanoid form, there was absolutely no doubt that the being standing in front of her was no member of the drama club but some kind of alien being, about five feet tall, with greenish coloured skin and a slim and muscular body.

She relaxed a bit when she saw the being's face, for it had a kind face. It had a huge head, with a narrow and tapering jaw and large blue eyes that showed extreme intelligence. The nose however, was very puny and small and the lips, well formed, but tiny. The ears were long and tapered upwards. It seemed in a lot of pain as it moved towards her.

"Arrrgh!" she shouted and took a step behind.

Guru and Sri, who reached the spot then, rushed from behind and grabbed her.

"Relax," said Sri, "he's our friend."

"King Xixorro from Xixipoo!" exclaimed Guru, "What a pleasant surprise dude?"

He approached the Alien to give him a hug. The Alien wildly swung his hands forbidding him to do so. He collapsed and then got up with difficulty.

"Don't touch me," he said, "I'm dying..."

Saying so, he once again collapsed a few feet from Guru. Tina and Nath, who had by then reached the spot, looked on wide eyed.

"You are friends with aliens?" asked a bewildered Varshika.

Nath, who was a couple of steps behind Tina, noticed that she was now swaying, as if in a trance.

"I see uncle Dhondiba...he, he is somewhere in the Himalayas... injured... aieeeeeh," she let out a scream, "he is surrounded by eight foot tall apes... monsters..."

Nath grabbed her in time, as she swooned. She was sweating profusely.

"Get some help!" yelled Guru.

Sri sprinted in a hurry towards the village square while Nath carefully laid Tina on the ground and followed. Guru fumbled for a moment for he was not sure what to do - to help the alien king or his little sister. He was a bit relieved on seeing Varshika take Tina's head in her lap. She did not utter a word and was probably too shocked. They would have to explain her, a lot of things. He remembered Xixorro's words of caution so decided not to touch Xixorro till help arrived. He too was overwhelmed by the sudden turn of events.

Sri and Nath arrived some fifteen minutes later with Principal Sandipani and Dr. Taranath Naik, the village physician. The boys briefly described the turn of events to the two elders. Dr. Naik immediately donned protective gloves and then proceeded to help King Xixorro. He remembered the first time he had met Xixorro*. The situation had not been very much different then. He approached King Xixorro and carefully began examining him.

Sri's father reached some five minutes later followed by Guru's father, who was panting heavily. Tina who was up by now, sat sobbing silently.

"What happened to Tina?" asked her worried father.

"She went into some kind of trance before collapsing," said Nath solemnly, "screaming something about Uncle Dhondiba being injured and lost in the Himalayas, and being surrounded by some sort of creatures..."

"O no, O God!" said Guru's father. "I just can't believe this. Some time ago we received a call from Mundu... remember Mundu, Dhondiba's caretaker. He phoned, to inform us that uncle Dhondiba has gone missing in the Himalayas. Dhondiba had undertaken a private expedition to the Himalayas and went missing. He also informed us that Dhondiba's friend Gopal, the security head at Astro Dreams, with the help of his bosses has

47

organized a rescue mission. They fear the worst. Uncle Dhondiba has been the main caterer of Astro Dreams for many years and the owners love and respect him. That is why they are spending such a lot of money, attempting a rescue mission. My wife is so upset. I was trying to console her when I received Principal's call so rushed here without informing her. Mundu is in constant touch with the people at Astro Dreams and will get back to me as soon as he has some concrete information."

"Can this be coincidence?" asked Principal Sandipani.

"No," said Tina feebly, "It was as if he was right in front of me... talking to me... asking me to rescue him."

"King Xixorro is awake," said Dr. Naik as he supported him up.

King Xixorro feebly waved to the group. He then adjusted the translator in his suit and began to speak almost in a whisper. However his translator transmitted the words loud and clear.

"Your planet is in peril," he said feebly. "The Asourbouts have arrived on earth."

"Wha... what?" asked Guru. "Who have arrived on earth and from where?"

"They are cyborgs... living robots from Xixipoo. They have come to destroy humans. They have been sent here by the evil princess."

"So they are metal robots with an exoskeleton of living flesh," asked Guru, "just like in the movies."

"No," said Xixorro, "the Asourbouts are cyborgs - nanobots inhabiting a cloned living body. In this case they have bodies that resemble humans. They even have a rudimentary brain. They work as a team and control the cloned body. These nanobots are in turn controlled by a super intelligent computer in Xixipoo. This *Master Computer* is unlike anything you have seen or heard before. It must've been designed by the Asourousse long ago, but somewhere along the way, it became self aware and intelligent and created these Asourbouts. It would be really difficult even for a smart doctor or scientist to distinguish the cloned cyborgs from a human on earth. However, on receiving the right command, these cyborgs can turn lethal. They are also in constant communication with each other and can think and act like one single being. Don't underestimate their abilities and powers."

"How many of them have landed on earth?" asked Principal Sandipani.

"Six of them." answered Xixorro.

"O that's all," said Sandipani, "we surely can handle six of them."

"Six of them have millions of nanobots within them and can easily destroy earth," said Xixorro, "and moreover they do not plan to attack earth with their lethal weapons. They do not want to destroy earth... only humans."

"And how do they plan to do that?" asked Sandipani.

"By infecting all humans with this deadly virus," he said with regret, "I have been tricked into carrying it to earth... I'm infected with it."

"No way," said Sri, "And how did they manage to do that?"

"We intercepted a message that a ship carrying Asourbouts was on its way to earth. I personally attacked the ship, but was ambushed. Though injured, I pursued their ship, but lost them when passing through the portal. I was unaware that they had infected me and I was supposed to be their

49

carrier. Though they are made of flesh and blood, they are not exactly living beings and possibly their bodies cannot sustain the virus. Now the virus matures inside me and if not sent back to Xixipoo immedaitely, they will extract it from me and infect all humans."

"But, wasn't Xixipoo a cold and dead planet when we last met?" asked Sri.

"Yes it was, but when we returned from earth to Xixipoo, we found it occupied by beings. The planet had begun to live. Some of the beings were very much like you humans, although a bit larger. They had brought back life to our planet, so we let them be. We did not confront them though they had occupied my city. We did not want anymore..."

He paused, trying to catch his breath. The doctor noticed that his condition was deteriorating and comforted him a bit.

"You mean these blokes are from earth?" asked Guru.

"No, maybe their ancestors were from earth... many millennia ago."

"So why do the punks want to destroy us?" asked Varshika, who seemed to have regained her confidence.

"Probably want to inhabit earth," said Xixorro. "But first, listen carefully, I am very weak and may not be able to help you."

He once again paused to catch his breath.

"Go to my spaceship and contact Queen Xixandra," he pointed to his ship. "She will help you. Tell her everything I told you. I am too weak to pilot my spaceship. She will instruct you how to send me back. Please hurry..."

The entire group, except Dr. Naik (who preferred

tending to Xixorro) went into the spaceship. They were surprised by what they saw, for it was nothing like the ones shown in the movies. It had a number of sections that seemed rather empty for a spaceship. As instructed by Xixorro, they went to a part of the spaceship that was the cockpit. Again it was a rather empty room with some six odd looking chairs. There was not a single gizmo or panel in sight. Following Xixorro's instructions, Sri sat on one of the chairs and drew a symbol in the air. At once a glowing holographic dashboard appeared. Sri drew another symbol in the air as instructed. Immediately a holographic image of an extremely beautiful woman appeared in front of them. She resembled a female version of Xixorro's species, except for the fact that she had four long fingers on each hand whereas Xixorro had only three. She had delicate facial features, a pale green skin and long golden hair.

"Queen Xixandra," exclaimed the two boys, "beautiful as ever."

"You boys will never improve," she said blushing, "so where is my husband? I need to have a word with him in private. Imagine running away without telling anyone and that too to earth."

They narrated whatever he had told them. On hearing them, she almost burst into tears but managed to compose herself a bit. She instructed them confidently, but the quiver in her voice revealed her concern for the sick king.

"You must carefully follow my instructions to the dot. The ship won't start unless King Xixorro instructs it to do so. It is tuned to his DNA. It will only obey his commands. We must over ride the system so that the ship can be controlled from Xixipoo, then carefully place him in the ship."

"Can't Dr. Naik save him? He has done it before." She

broke down and began to sob softly.

"Sorry, I'm being selfish," she said, composing herself again, "you must hurry. I need two of you here, to help me take over the controls of Xixorro's ship."

Guru and Sri volunteered to stay, while the others went down to help Xixorro. After wearing gloves, some of the others helped him into the makeshift stretcher that Varshika built, in a matter of minutes. Everyone felt bad for the alien king, who was sweating profusely and shaking voilently, but he had to be sent back to Xixipoo, for he carried a deadly virus in his being... a virus that could potentially destroy all humans.

"I have given him a shot of antibiotics," said Dr. Naik, "hopefully he will be able to fight the virus."

"My ship has the best diagnostic facilities," said Xixorro weakly from the stretcher, "however the virus couldn't be identified. It is a hitherto unknown virus, probably engineered by the Asourousse. The ship's robo-doctor has already pumped a number of antibiotics into me. The Asourbouts can infect the far edges of the earth in seventy two hours and can wipe out the entire human population in a month. The Asourousse have created an army of twenty thousand Asourbouts."

"So why didn't they send this army, instead of sending just six of them?" asked Sandipani.

"It's not that easy," he said, "the portal is unstable and presently is too small... only one small ship can pass through it at a time..."

"What is this portal that you keep mentioning," interrupted Sandipani, "what is its significance?"

He waved his hand as if telling Sandipani to stop.

"There is something very important that I need to convey before I leave. The Asourbouts seek three powerful objects from earth that have something to do with the portal. They must not be allowed to acquire these objects or..."

He passed out. Probably all the talking had been too strenuous.

"I feel so guilty sending him in this condition," said Dr. Naik.

The others looked on with sympathy. Nath was deep in thought, while Tina sat sadly. The turn of events hadn't made her forget her vision. She pined for her favourite uncle Dhondiba. Varshika on the other hand meticulously narrated the events of the evening to her uncle and Guru's father.

Meanwhile Guru and Sri were busy in the spaceship, being explicitly instructed by Xixandra. Suddenly the ship started with a loud hum and before the two could realize what was going on, the door closed.

"Now what did you do?" asked Guru annoyed.

"Nothing," said Sri equally annoyed. "And I'm not an alien engineer."

Without the slightest hint, the ship rose some forty feet above the ground and hovered. Guru and Sri lost their balance and landed on the floor of the ship.

"Who's controlling the ship?" asked a visibly surprised Xixandra.

"We thought it is you," said Guru with alarm.

"Someone from Xixipoo is controlling the ship, but it is not me," she replied. "Jump into those seats if you value your lives."

They did so without further delay and were surprised to find themselves being automatically secured to the seats and surrounded by a jelly like substance. The humming grew progressively louder. Everyone outside was surprised to see the spaceship rise.

"Now what have those boys gone and done?" asked Sandpani in an irritated tone.

The humming grew progressively loud till it was unbearable. Suddenly the ship disappeared in a flash of light, with the two boys in it.

"Help, Help!" shouted Sri's father running in the general direction of the ship, "our children are in that confounded space ship. Someone help them... please wake up King Xixorro."

He rushed towards King Xixorro who lay passed out on the stretcher and was about to hold and shake him when he was stopped by Dr. Naik, who just nodded, forbidding him from touching the dying king.

The others stood transfixed, not knowing what to do. Guru's father stood with one hand on his forehead, while Tina began weeping.

"If those guys go and get themselves killed or something, I'll just kill them," said Varshika. She was on all fours, crawling, banging her fists on the ground. "This, is one birthday, I'll never forget my entire life."

October 15ᵗʰ, 12.15 am (earth time), Space ship

"What the hell is happening?" asked Sri looking at the now fuzzy holograph of Queen Xixandra.

"The ship is on its way to Xixipoo. I do not know who is controlling the ship but we will regain control soon. My commanders are at it and the moment they succeed, we will send you back to earth."

"Are we really on our way to Xixipoo?" asked Guru. "It doesn't feel any different than in a cruise liner. Shouldn't we be feeling some kind of pressure or something?"

"The shielding gel is protecting you. Without it, you would be facing about 100 G's of force right now - hundred times the earth gravitational force - enough to cause your hearts to explode. Our ships attain very high speeds in a very short time."

"Three cheers to the shielding gel," said, a nervous Guru. "Hope you have some food on this ship?"

"Loads of it," she said with a smile, "but don't fret. Any moment now, we will regain control of the ship and you guys will be on your way back to earth. My holographic image will disappear for a while. I'll get back to you as soon as we succeed."

The boys waited impatiently for the next quarter hour for her to appear. They were comfortable in the gel but felt trapped. When she finally appeared again, she was not her cheerful self but looked terribly worried.

"I don't know how to break this to you," she said in a worried tone, "but, like it or not, you guys are on your way to Xixipoo. Hopefully you will reach us in two earth days."

"What's going on?" asked Sri. "Can't you guys fix the problem? My mother will kill me for leaving the planet without her permission."

"The communication system on the ship seems to have been sabotaged and the only personal communication device in the possession of King Xixorro isn't responding. The ship was aimed for Xixipoo, before the control and communication system was sabotaged. Looks like, someone badly wants you on Xixipoo. As of now, all communication with earth has ceased. However, with our help, you can control the internal functions of the ship but you can neither pilot the ship nor steer it."

"Great!" said Guru, "So we are being kidnapped by these hoodlums right under your noses, while you can do nothing about it and our parents haven't a clue about us and our planet has been invaded by these Asourbouts or whatever and there is a danger of a virus spreading, that can potentially wipe out the entire human race, as we speak. Could things get any worse?"

"Yes," she said nervously, "as of now, you guys can use only a part of the ship as there may be traces of the deadly virus on the ship. It will take five hours for the scanners on the ship to detect any traces of the virus. And, all the food is in that part of the ship that may be contaminated. Once you are out of the gel, you will have to confine yourselves to the small space that you are directed to, by the ship's computer."

"What about the loo?" asked Sri, "I really need to use it."

"Don't worry. The quarantine quarters on the ship have a good bathroom and some emergency supplies of food. Our best scientists are trying to regain control of the ship before you land on Xixipoo. I will not let you fall in enemy hands, I promise. Now just repeat the words I say and the ship's computer will guide you to the quarantine quarters once you are out of the gel. My holographic projection will appear there and I will update you on all that has been going on in Xixipoo. But rest for a few hours."

The boys followed her instructions and spoke the words. At once they heard a sweet voice.

"Greetings, Earthlings! I am Xixalmac, the ship's main computer. Follow me to safety. You must discard all your clothes before entering."

"No way!" said Sri, "I'm not moving around naked with aliens watching."

"Sir, you are alive and well right now, but if you do not follow my instructions precisely, you may soon be dead. Sorry for being rude, but you must understand that the chances of you being infected by the virus are very high. Your bodies have not yet been breached by it, but if you continue to be adamant, that may happen soon. There is no known cure for the virus and death is painful."

"Clothes coming out," exclaimed Guru, "I'm convinced, and if Sri has any brains, he'll follow suit."

The boys passed through a narrow passage, where they were decontaminated. They tried out a number of clothes, but ultimately had to settle for robes, as no other clothes fit them. The Xixipians, being small did not have clothes that would fit the boys. However, they were elated on entering the quarantine quarters, for it resembled a suite in a five star hotel. When Sri asked for the loo, a door appeared out of nowhere and he was ushered into the most luxurious bathroom he had ever set his eyes on. Similarly, when Guru asked for a bed, a very soft looking bed just appeared out of the floor. Soon the boys were fast asleep, their worries forgotten. Apparently it hadn't struck them that their families would be worried sick about them. The extreme luxury had made their senses dull.

October 15ᵗʰ, 12.20 am (earth time), Gendamal's farm

Xixorro stirred, blinked and glanced around. He saw the kind principal, the fathers of the boys and the new girl around him, peering anxiously. The doctor seemed to be comforting Tina, who was crying uncontrollably. He saw the fat owner of the farm lamenting as he became dizzy once again and passed out.

"Why always my farm?" asked Gendamal. "Why does every frigging spaceship, alien or zombie end up on my farm?"

"Don't over react dad," said Riya. "This is only the second time aliens have landed on our farm and no zombie came near the farm. Moreover they weren't real zombies. They were guys from the drama club, set up by Sri and Guru. Nevertheless it would be best not to involve mother in this mess. She may drive us out of the farm this time. As it is, she doesn't like our archery team practicing here."

"In fact, let this matter not spread beyond this group," said Sandipani, joining their conversation. "There may be utter chaos, if the word spreads about the deadly virus."

"And how exactly do we explain the sudden disappearance of the boys," said Varshika rather boldly, "their respective mothers will want to know their whereabouts."

"We can't stop the news from spreading, but merely stall it for a few days," said Guru's father. "We can tell their mothers that they left for the Himalayas with the search party. In fact we can lie that we were called here today, because a small plane sent by 'Astro Dreams', landed here, on

59

their way to the Himalayas and the boys volunteered to go."

"Do you think, they'll forgive you for letting the boys go alone?" asked Varshika. "Won't they be suspicious? What if Mundu tells them otherwise?"

"I'll talk to Mundu right away and as it is, I am joining the rescue team. I had asked Mundu to talk to them when we spoke earlier."

"I'm going with you," said Tina adamantly, "I have seen him and may be able to direct the rescue team to him."

"I'm going too," said Varshika assertively, looking at her uncle for approval.

"I think I'll help here," said Nath.

"What's going on? Where is my ship?" asked a weak voice.

Xixorro had regained consciousness and was frantically searching for his ship. Though weak, he was attempting to sit up in the makeshift stretcher. Dr. Naik placed a comforting hand on his chest and helped him relax. Sandipani then went on to explain the situation to him. With some difficulty Xixoro sat up. He took out a small device attached to his suit, fidgeted with it for a couple of minutes and turned to the others.

"We have lost all communication with the ship and my planet. I have this final communication. The ship was directed to Xixipoo and all controls sabotaged. That means someone wanted me stranded here. But it is strange that all communication has ceased, though my communication system is working perfectly. Looks like, someone on earth has blocked all communications with Xixipoo."

"That's bad, isn't it," asked Sandipani.

"On the contrary, it is good, because the Asourbouts

60

will not receive any instructions from their master in Xixipoo, so they will lie low for some time. Mind you, they will be keeping an eye on us and may strike if the failsafe is activated."

"What does that mean?" asked Sandipani.

"When all communication with them stops, these robots go into some sort of hibernation, but a backup program gets activated in them. This system has a record of the last instructions given to them and they will destroy themselves if necessary, to get their task done. In this case their task is to destroy humans, by spreading the virus multiplying inside me. If I am close to death, their failsafe will be activated and they will ruthlessly attack you to obtain the virus from me."

"So we are safe for now," said Sandipani. "Moreover it is imperative that we keep you alive and try to find a cure for your ailment. But we have some unknown allies on our side, who have helped us by blocking communications."

"Is there any information about the boys in the spaceship?" asked Guru's father eagerly. "What were they doing when you received the last communication? Were they scared?"

"They are safe," said Xixorro. "The last information shows Guru and Sri safe in the quarantine quarters on the ship. Guru is loafing on the giant bed, devouring grapes at a speed that even the ship's main computer is astonished and Sri... eh, Sri is in the bathroom... dancing naked in the shower singing his heart out..."

"Thank you King. I guess the description is sufficient," said Sandipani. "So, for now, they are safe."

The girls giggled, while Nath stood baffled. He failed to understand, how his friends could keep their cool... no, not only keep their cool but behave in a scandalous manner in the face of death.

The antibiotics seemed to have had some positive effect on Xixorro for he seemed a wee bit better. Presently, Principal Sandipani beckoned everyone to assemble around him. King Xixorro remained seated on the stretcher, for it would've been impossible for him to stand up.

"Now listen carefully," said Sandipani, as if he was addressing his students. There was no doubt, that many of those present were indeed his students. "We have a situation here that we need to tackle. As I mentioned earlier, the news of the recent events should not leave this group. Considering the multiple threats and dicey situations that we face, it will be best if we split up and each group be given a task. I do not want to seem melodramatic, but the fate of our planet is in our hands."

"I completely agree with you," said Sri's father, "Guru's dad can proceed to the Himalayas..."

"With us in tow," said Tina and Varshika in a chorus, "as Tina may be of valuable help in locating Uncle Dhondiba and I, her escort."

"Ok," said Sri's father, very reluctantly, "you will be under the strict vigilance of Tina's father, and mind you, one slip and you are grounded for life. I've had it with Sri and his foolish pranks, now I do not want to complicate things further with you going and doing something else."

"Yes," said Tina's father. "We are going as observers, I repeat OBSERVERS ONLY. We stay put and if Tina gets one of those visions, she will recount what she sees to the rescue team. Neither are we, mountaineers, nor have we had any formal training in mountaineering... you girls cool with that?"

"Yes Sir!" said both.

"So it is agreed that Guru's father with the girls will be going to the Himalayas. Meanwhile Riya's father and Sri's father will use their resources to try and locate the Asourbouts or whatever those devils are called," said Sandipani turning to the two gentlemen. "You guys can set up camp here, at the edge of the farm and scout the surroundings. Dr. Naik and I will take up the responsibility of trying to determine the nature of the virus in the body of Xixorro and keeping him safe."

"But, shouldn't Xixorro be put in quarantine in some highly advanced research centre?" said Guru's father. "Don't we need scientists and medical professionals to take care of him?"

"We do," Sandipani said, "but cannot risk taking him to any hospital. We will have to arrange for all that right here."

"But how will that be possible?" said Guru's father.

"I'll talk to my friend, Ishwar. He is the mentor of Batatawadai Puram and has always helped us. We will have to take him into confidence. Being a billionaire and resourceful person, he can arrange for a laboratory with modern technology to be set up, in a matter of hours. I will call him right away, but we need a safe place for Xixorro."

"Not on my farm," protested Gendamal. "I am ready to cooperate in all other ways, ready to assist Sri's father, but please set up the quarantine somewhere else."

"We can take him to our secret temple," said Nath, who had been silent for a long time now."

"What secret temple?" Sandipani asked, rather suspiciously. "Now don't tell me, you guys have more secrets hidden from us?"

"We do," said Varshika. "The temple in question was discovered by Guru and Sri and is located about four

63

kilometers in the forest on a hillock. I believe, it will be the most ideal and safe place for the king. We can take you there."

"But, isn't it holy?" asked Tina. "Hadn't we decided not to take anyone there and desecrate it?"

"No Tina, maybe the temple was found by the boys for this very reason and didn't Guru tell us that he was drawn to it?"

"Let's not waste time," said Nath earnestly. "I'll show them the temple and then we can make arrangements to transfer King Xixorro there."

"Just had a word with Mundu," said Guru's father as he got off the phone. "He mentioned that the rescue team has reached the Himalayas. The owners of Astro Dreams have lent one of their private jets for the rescue effort. They managed to rope in four of the best mountaineers of South India, to try and locate Dhondiba. They will be glad to have us there, but it is left to us, to reach the rescue-team before they attempt the rescue."

"Then you should not waste any more time," said Sandipani. "Go and pack your bags. I will talk to Ishwar and arrange to get you to the Himalayas as soon as possible."

"I have a suggestion," said Nath with a little reluctance. "Since you have assigned each team some task, will you allow Riya and me to be your coordinators? I can set up a communication centre in my house and we can coordinate the communications between all. Moreover you will need someone to ferry goods, say from the village to the temple and maybe samples from the temple to the research laboratory. We can contribute in that way."

"That's a brilliant idea Nath," said Sandipani. "This way each group can concentrate on their tasks while you keep us updated on each other's activities. However you don't need to establish a communication centre at home as it will raise too much suspicion. I will arrange for communication equipment. You just monitor and coordinate the messages between us."

"How I wish Mr. Bose were here," said Nath in a dejected voice. "Maybe, he could have found a cure."

"Come on Nath," said Sandipani sympathetically, "you know very well he is a nutcase and is locked up in some asylum in Calcutta."

"You are wrong Sir," said Nath assertively. "I have told this before and am repeating it – he is not a nutcase but a brilliant scientist."

October 15th, 2 am (earth time), Outskirts of Calcutta

The other inmates of the 'Sister Nancy Home for the Mentally Challenged' were fast asleep, except for the four inmates who were prowling about in the warden's office. The group was led by an extremely short, bespectacled man, with unkempt hair and a long beard. He wore clothes that were probably from the nineteenth century.

"Do I really look like a scientist, Mr. Bose?" asked the stout man behind him enthusiastically.

Mr. Bose turned around with some irritation and looked at the three inmates standing behind him. The fat man was dressed in a striped half sleeve shirt that was probably two sizes too small. He had a black pant on and a long white lab coat. The man standing beside him was tall and broad. He looked every inch, a security guard - his navy blue uniform well ironed and starched, highly polished military boots and a bunch of keys neatly attached to his belt. He kept twirling a stout baton. The fourth person in the room was very old and walked with a distinct limp. He was bent and looked like an experienced doctor with a stethoscope around neck.

"Yes you do," he said kindly. "But you mustn't make any noise. We have been assigned an important mission and must not fail. The fate of the planet depends on this mission. Now let me find the Warden's official seal and the keys to the ambulance. I hope you remember the plan. We have to execute it perfectly. So, while I search for some important things, you rehearse your parts. Biswajeet, if you are half the driver that you claim to be, then we should reach our destination in the next seventy two hours. The world may think you are mad, but I know you are geniuses. If you want to save your planet, please help me get to my destination."

"You don't worry, Mr. Bose," said the tall man. "I'll get you to your destination, even if that's the last thing I do. But, where are we going?"

"To a village in the Sahyadris... and I thank you kind people for helping me out."

Not another word was uttered. Mr. Bose finally found what he was looking for. He scribbled something on a letterhead and affixed the official stamp of the warden on it. Then he carefully placed everything back in their rightful places. After stuffing a wad of cash in his pocket, he beckoned the others to follow.

The asylum was a very old building, in need of repair. It was close to a century old and the architecture was probably Victorian. They walked through a dimly lit passage and reached a huge door and could hear muffled voices on the other side of the door. Probably a couple of guards were still awake chatting with the matron who had finished her rounds at midnight. By then, all the inmates were fast asleep due to the effect of the sedatives given with their supper. She would go from bed to bed tucking in the inmates and ensuring that no one fell of their beds. She was a kind lady, unlike the other staff who were, rather rough on the inmates.

Mr. Bose placed his finger on his lips indicating the others to remain very silent. Then he pointed to a door to the left that led to the store room. They went through the dingy store room careful not to make a noise. At the far end was a door. Mr. Bose took the bunch of keys from Biswajeet and after some effort found the key to the door. The door opened into a narrow path. It was the far end of the hospital. A couple of vehicles lay rusting in one corner. There were vehicle parts and tires strewn about. It was probably the section where the hospital ambulances and other vehicles were repaired. Mr. Bose had been assisting the hospital mechanic for the past few months and was aware that he had been secretly trying to refurbish an old ambulance. He led them to a vehicle covered by a canvas cloth and carefully lifted the cloth, revealing a very old ambulance, probably abandoned and forgotten by the hospital authorities. Reaching his pocket, he fished out a key that he handed to Biswajeet.

"Get us out of here."

Biswajeet got into the driver's seat, inserted the key and turned it. The ambulance started with a hum. Though it looked ragged and old, the engine purred like a brand new vehicle. The others got into the ambulance. Mr. Bose ordered the fat man to lie down and pulled a cloth over him and carefully arranged instruments to look as if the fat man was a patient. Biswajeet had by then, put the vehicle in motion and drove along a narrow path. They reached a small non-functional, locked gate at the very end of the premises. Mr. Bose once again got down with his bunch of keys. Five minutes later they were out of the premises and on a dirt road that led them to a back road out of the city. The road was deserted except for occasional mongrels whose aim in life was to bark and chase every vehicle that passed. After a short bumpy ride, they reached the highway that would lead them out of the city and eventually out of the state. It was there that they were stopped at a police check post. The police man who approached them was of medium height with a huge paunch and a moustache that resembled a tooth brush. He opened the back door of the ambulance.

"So what are you guys doing in the dead of the night?" he asked gruffly. "May I see your papers?"

"Sure sir," said Mr. Bose. "We are transporting this mental patient to another hospital with better facilities. He recently turned violent and bit thirteen other inmates. He thinks he is a werewolf."

"Is that so?" asked the policeman taking a step back.

"Yes sir," said Mr. Bose. "Please go through these official papers. He may be contaminated or something. Hence we are shifting him in a hurry."

He waved the letter in front of the policeman who was reluctant to accept it.

"I will not delay you further. You must hurry. Your papers seem authentic."

They did not encounter any more obstacles for the rest of the night and were well on their way to their destination. By the time, the staff at the mental asylum discovered their absence they would be in another state.

October 15ᵗʰ, 9.00 am (earth time), 30,000 feet above sea level

Tina awoke with a start. She looked around her, rather confused by the unfamiliar surroundings before realizing where she was. She had been asleep in the reclined seat of an airplane. Casting a wide glance around her, she saw Varshika curled up and fast asleep on the two seats adjacent to hers. A narrow aisle separated their seats. Her father too was fast asleep in the row behind. He was snoring in a rather rhythmic manner. The two bodyguards who had joined them were sitting rather expressionless in the seats just behind the pilot.

She recollected the events of the previous night and felt a pang in her stomach as she remembered her brother and Sri, who were on their way to Xixipoo against their will.

After Guru and Sri had disappeared in the spaceship, the others had split up into various teams. One team had transferred king Xixorro to their secret temple. Ghasitaram, the school cook (who had been summoned by the Principal), Guru's father and Dr. Naik had taken turns to carry the king in the stretcher made by Varshika. It must've been a strong one for it stayed intact. Nath and Tina led the way. It had taken them, about two hours to reach the temple as it had been very difficult navigating in the dark and that too with the ailing king on a stretcher. They had managed to reach the temple at about half past two and transferred the king to the subterranean temple. Once settled, Dr. Naik had checked his vital signs. Satisfied that he was stable, the lean old doctor had sat down beside him. The others decided to return to Gendamal's farm and transfer equipment requested by Dr. Naik.

Meanwhile some of the others had been waiting for the team of scientists and their equipment at Gendamal's farm.

Principal Sandipani had phoned Ishwar and explained the entire situation. Considering the seriousness of the situation, Ishwar had promised to help them. He had assured Sandipani that he would immediately dispatch a couple of trustworthy scientists with the necessary equipment.

Varshika and her uncle (Sri's father) had then gone home, to help pack equipment for the journey to the Himalayas. There Sri's father had done some smooth talking to convince Guru and Sri's mothers that the boys had left for the Himalayas. He had cooked up a fantastic story blending some of the facts with pure fiction, but managed to convince them. The ladies had initially been unwilling to let the girls travel to the Himalayas, but were convinced when Sri's father assured them that they would go only as observers to help the rescue team locate uncle Dhondiba.

However Sri's mother had flatly refused to let Varshika go without the permission of her parents. Varshika had then begged her aunt to speak to her father rather than her mother. Surprisingly, after hearing the story narrated by her aunt, Varshika's father had not only given her permission to join the team but also advised her to be extra careful and convinced the others not to worry. Sri's father had also convinced the ladies that Guru's father would be there to care for the kids and at that very moment they were coordinating with the rescue team.

When Tina, her father and Nath had arrived, Varshika had almost finished packing for all of them with the help of her aunt and Guru's mother. The two men had a tough time convincing the ladies not to accompany them and had also managed to convince them that Sri's father and Nath would

71

spend a lot of time away from home as they would communicate with the rescue team from the outskirts of the village where there was a communication antenna and some radio equipment (courtesy Ishwar). It was rather difficult to convince Nath's mother (who had joined them later) that he would spend a few days away from home trying to help Sri's father with the communication equipment. She initially had flatly refused, but been convinced by Sri's father, who promised to take great care of Nath.

Finally Varshika had begged her aunt to take good care of Cuddly. She was aware of her aunt's fear of reptiles, hence had requested Nath to take care of her other pets. After a teary farewell, they had left for Gendamal's farm.

They had reached Gendamal's farm at four in the morning to find a helicopter waiting for them. The same helicopter had dropped two scientists (with a load of strange looking equipment), who had rushed to the temple immediately. Since they would not fly for a couple of hours the trio had decided to make one quick trip to the temple. It took them three quarters of an hour to reach the temple. There they had been ushered into the subterranean temple by Principal Sandipani. The team there must've been very busy, for they had converted one room into a makeshift hospital. King Xixorro was quarantined and lay on a comfortable bed in a transparent plastic-like enclosure and had a number of wires clamped to him. A machine on a trolley monitored his vital signs. He waved feebly. Another large room had been converted into a sleeping quarters with a number of sleeping bags neatly arranged on the floor. A third room was being converted into a lab and another small room into a communications centre by the scientists. They had left the main sanctum of the subterranean temple, housing the deity, untouched and only occupied all the other rooms. That was because Tina had insisted that they maintain the sanctity of the main sanctum.

Principal Sandipani and Nath had come to see them off. Sandipani had wished them luck and assured that he would keep in regular touch. Incidentally the communication equipment sent by Ishwar was so advanced that they could comfortable communicate with each other without the fear of their communication being intercepted. He had also promised that they would try to locate the Asourbouts and keep an eye on those devils. Tina, Varshika and Nath had finally gotten some time alone with each other.

When alone, Varshika had earnestly requested Nath to take good care of Samuel and Jackson, for he was the only one who could be trusted to take care of them while she was gone.

Nath had assured that he would feed them as instructed by her and also mentioned his intention of placing them in their tanks on a table in the communication centre that was being set up in the temple. He further requested the girls to be careful and not do anything rash or stupid.

They had hugged each other, then the two girls and Guru's father boarded the helicopter. A twenty minute flight had taken them to an abandoned airfield where a twin-engine plane had been waiting for them. Two men dressed in military-like uniforms had escorted them to the plane. They were part of the personal security of Ishwar and were assigned to protect the three. They had assured Guru's father that they had been instructed not to interfere in his work but would be there in the event he or the kids faced any danger. Tina marveled at the lengths to which Mr. Ishwar went, to help the people of Batatawadai Puram.

The plane had a plush interior and could seat sixteen passengers. They had been introduced to the pilot who assured them that he would get them to their destination in a little over four hours.

Tina had been so lost in her thoughts that she did not notice Varshika come to her side.

"Got some rest?"

"Not much," Tina said. "What about you?"

"A bit," Varshika said as she stifled a yawn. "How long do you think will it take for us to reach the rescue team?"

"My guess is that we should land in about an hour," Tina said looking at her watch. "Let's talk to the security guys. Looks like, they are in constant touch with the pilot, who obviously is in touch with the rescue team sent by Astro Dreams."

The two of them approached the gentlemen and inquired about their present status. The men were a bit taken aback by the bold questions put forth by these small girls but were extremely courteous. The girls learnt that arrangement had been made for the plane to land on a small airstrip right at the foot of the mountains and they would reach in an hour and a half. There they would await a team who would lead them to the base camp in the mountains. They would probably have to trek some eight hours, as the base camp was some twelve kilometers away from the airfield. The men advised them to get some rest as they would have a tough day ahead.

Taking the advice of the gentlemen, the girls returned to their seats and were fast asleep in no time. The plane took more than the estimated time to reach the destination and some two and quarter hours later the plane landed rather roughly on a makeshift airstrip right at the base of the mountains. The girls had to be woken up just before the plane landed as they were fast asleep, probably due to the exhaustion from the events of the previous day.

They bid the pilot good bye and thanked him before

they alighted from the aircraft. They were immediately awestruck by the beauty and magnificence of the rugged mountain ahead. Its snow covered peaks glistened in the sunlight. The girls noticed that their teeth were chattering due to the biting cold winds. Soon they were greeted by two rugged looking mountaineers and a man whom Tina found familiar.

"Good morning Tina," he said cheerfully, "hope you haven't forgotten me?"

"Mr. Gopal, what a pleasant surprise?" Tina said, accepting his extended hand. "You look different?"

"Shaved off my bushy moustache," he said laughing aloud.

"Let me introduce you to the others," Tina said in excitement, pointing to the others. "This is my Father, Dr. Madhusudan and this here is Varshika, my best friend and Sri's cousin and they are er..."

The two gentlemen grinned and stepped forward as one of them spoke.

"I'm Ram Singh and this is my colleague Rahim Ali, ex commandos – we are here to help the team if they need any assistance."

"Great," he said rather surprised, "but this is a rescue mission... any way, do you guys have any mountaineering experience?"

"Plenty," replied Rahim, "we're good at mountain warfare – served in Siachen for five years."

"Well," said Tina trying to break the ice. "May I introduce you to Mr. Gopal, head of security at Astro Dreams and also a good friend of Uncle Dhondiba."

Gopal handed them special Gorka Suits which they got

into without further delay, for they had begun to turn numb. With the protective suits on, everyone was visibly more comfortable and the mountain goggles protected them from the harsh glare. Ram Singh offered to carry the backpack with basic supplies. However his partner convinced him that it would be better if all the elders took turns to carry it.

"I suggest we have a light snack and rest a bit, before we begin our journey to the base camp," Gopal said in a serious tone, "...and mind you, the climb is going to be tough... especially for amateurs. The search team will begin their work tomorrow."

"Can you fill in the details?" Guru's father asked.

"I will tell you everything I know, on the way to the base camp."

Varshika and Tina exchanged glances.

"Looks like we have a tough journey ahead," Varshika said, as they got ready to leave.

October 15th, 4.00 am (earth time), Africa

Simba approached the hidden temple in a hurry. It was imperative that he conveyed the latest news to the high priest. He looked around and saw brush on both the sides. He was not concerned about wild animals, for he had grown up in the bush and knew the habits of all the animals, but was a bit concerned about militia – looters of the dark. He put his hand inside his coat pocket and felt the cold steel of his automatic pistol. That reassured him a bit. A number of thoughts crept into his mind. Only six months ago he was one of the youngest research students in the university, doing his PhD and now he was involved in this business, his family secret being revealed recently. His clan had protected the relic for millennia and now it had disappeared from the temple. His grandfather, the king of the region had ordered him to set everything aside and devote his entire time to find it, for according to the old man, the shifting of the relic was a precursor to an apocalypse. He obeyed because he loved his grandfather very much.

Simba had practically been raised by his grandfather as he had lost both his parents in an accident, when he was a toddler. The only other person in the world, whom he loved almost as much as he loved his grandfather, was his mentor and guide at the university. He was sad to have abruptly discontinued his doctorate program, but promised himself to complete his studies once this business got over.

He saw the temple at a distance. Outwardly it lay in ruins and nobody ever ventured near it, but Simba knew that below that temple lay another magnificent subterranean temple and that was where he would find the high priest. He panted heavily (since he had been running all the way), and made his

77

way into the temple and then carefully through the narrow passage behind the idol. Simba had to be careful as he navigated through the passage, for he was well over six and a half feet tall. He passed through a labyrinth and reached the inner sanctum of the temple. It was brilliantly lit by torches. The walls were covered by intricate patterns and carvings. The high priest had mentioned that the patterns were an ancient code that he was trying hard to decipher. Simba found the high priest seated at the centre of the large room, book in hand, copying the patterns.

"Ah Simba!" said the priest in a pleasant tone, "glad to see you. What news have you got for me?"

"With deep regret, I wish to inform you of the demise of your uncle, the high priest Ramghoolam. He was found a few miles away from a village nestled high up in the Sahyadris. It seems that he had gone completely insane before his death."

"Hm," said the high priest with genuine pain in his eyes. "Was the relic recovered from him?"

"No Sir,"

"That's because he had not taken it. Someone else has."

"I am aware sir," Simba said with a slight tremble in his voice. "Your guess was right."

"I have been having visions of the relic lately. It is somewhere in the Himalayas."

"You are right again." Simba said surprised. "That scoundrel was last spotted at the foot of the Himalayas. Perhaps he seeks the other relic. He has a band of murderous mercenaries with him."

"Then we must reach the Himalayas fast," said the high priest with impatience in his voice. "How soon can we reach?"

"Everything has been taken care of. We will leave in a couple of hours and should reach in twenty two hours. We will be accompanied by six of the best warriors of our clan."

"Give me half an hour," said the high priest. "I have some personal business to attend to and then we will be on our way."

October 15ᵗʰ, 1 pm (earth time), Space ship

"Wake up, sleeping beauties," said a sweet voice to Guru and Sri, who were sprawled on the gigantic bed.

However the two continued to sleep, unperturbed. The voice got louder and then the air was filled with loud beeps.

"Get lost Tina," Guru said, "I need rest. You won't believe the nightmare I've had."

The beeps got louder and both the boys woke up and looked around rather confused.

"Gosh," exclaimed Guru, "I'm really here. It isn't a nightmare."

"No it isn't," said the holograph of Queen Xixandra. "You are on your way to Xixipoo and it's time for your lessons."

"What lessons?" Sri asked with a quizzical expression. "I want to sleep. My vacations just began. I don't want any lessons."

"May I remind you dears," she said with a sweet voice, "...that you are not travelling to a neighbouring country but to a far corner of the galaxy and your life may depend on the knowledge you acquire now. So please freshen up and get ready for your lessons."

The boys were all alert now and got ready in a jiffy. A warm shower and a change of clothes made them feel cozy. They were surprised to find clothes that fit them, for when they had gone to sleep, all the clothes on the spaceship were too small for them and they had to contend themselves by wearing robes. As if reading their minds, the holographic image spoke.

"Hope the clothes fit well? The ship's computer has been busy for the past twelve hours, modifying things on the ship to suit your needs."

"Thanks!" mumbled Sri.

"You are welcome sir," spoke a female voice.

"I have some good news and some bad news," said Xiandra's holographic image. "We have managed to gain control of most of the functions of the ship. Scans reveal that the ship is free of all pathogens. So you may now move freely around the ship."

"That's great," Guru said enthusiastically. "So are we on our way back home?"

"I have not told you the bad news yet," said the hologram. "We can control most of the functions of the ship except steer it. The controls of the ship seem to be jammed and you are definitely on your way to Xixipoo. The other bad news is that all communication with earth has ceased. It seems that something strong is blocking all communications."

"I know," Sri said, "It's those devil Asourbouts. They must've blocked the communications."

"We checked," said the hologram, "It is something much more powerful that is blocking all communications. We are certain that even the Asourousse are not able to communicate with Xixipoo."

"You mean earth is destroyed," Guru asked rather alarmed.

"Don't be silly," said the hologram. "Only communications have ceased and that could be good for earth."

"How come..?" Sri asked.

"If communications with earth have been blocked, then it means the Asourbouts will receive no commands from their master at Xixipoo. In that case, they will go into a sort of hibernation-mode. They will not attack earth unless a failsafe is activated."

"What kind of a failsafe?" the boys asked in unision.

"Unfortunately King Xixorro is the only one who would know that. He was the one tracking them." she said, almost in tears.

"That means there is hope" said Guru excitedly. "I'm sure our friends at Batatawadai Puram will figure a way out."

"Now listen carefully," she said in a severe tone. "We have less than twelve hours to teach you as much as we can about our planet."

"What happens after twelve hours?" Sri asked.

"You enter the portal," she said in a matter of fact manner. "The portal has such high energy, that the ship would disintegrate without protection. To pass safely through the portal, we will raise a number of energy shields around the ship. However those shields would reduce our communication abilities by more than ninety percent. It will take you eight earth hours to pass through the portal. But once you have passed through the portal, we will have to watch your backs, for you will be in our part of the galaxy. It is very likely that you may be attacked. So, now is the right time for you to learn all that you can."

Two chairs appeared out of nowhere. Once the boys occupied these chairs, they reclined. The boys remembered their recent experience in a planetarium where they had enjoyed a similar show, however things were different here.

Firstly they did not feel the chairs. It was as if they were weightless and floating in space. Then the entire surroundings transformed right before their eyes. Everything seemed so real that the boys forgot they were on a spaceship. Instead they felt that they were actually flying around the planet Xixipoo. They spent the next four hours experiencing such a virtual reality that no one on earth would have ever dreamed to experience.

Guru and Sri learnt that Xixipoo was slightly larger than earth. But unlike earth, its axis was not tilted. A day on this planet was equivalent to about twenty two earth hours and the duration of day and night was always the same, eleven hours of day followed by eleven hours of night. However, it remained bright for a long time after sunset. A year comprised of about four hundred earth days. The duration of about twelve minutes was called a Xilamha while ten such Xilamhas were called a Xiklaak. The day comprised of eleven Xiklaaks. The planet appeared yellowish in colour from space, since most of its surface was covered by vast deserts. There were eleven deserts in all and some of them were as large as the continent of Europe. These eleven deserts were like eleven continents on Xixipoo and were the only habitable places on the planet, the rest of the planet being inhabitable. Some of these inhabitable regions were extremely hot regions where lava flowed freely and the air was polluted with poisonous gases and then there were other regions with such temperature variations that life could not exist. The polar regions of Xixipoo were permanently frozen with temperatures as low as minus 120 degree Centigrade.

The planet did not have oceans like earth but was dotted with large water bodies. These were called the Xixoases. It was in these Xixoases that life thrived. Two of these eleven deserts had a very large number of water bodies.

The boys learnt that more than ninety percent of living beings occupied those two deserts. One of the deserts, known as Xixidorra was located close to the equator of the planet while the other desert, known as Xixibamba was located at higher latitude, some one thousand miles away from Xixidorra. Xixidorra was the home of Queen Xixandra and her tribe while King Xixorro's vast kingdom was located in a magnificent city in Xixibamba.

The narrator's voice changed while Xixidorra was being described. It was the voice of queen Xixandra. She proudly described her homeland while the boys listened enraptured. A large part of Xixidorra comprised of rocky and hilly terrain. The day time temperatures reached 50 degree Centigrade while it went forty below zero at night. The Xixoases here froze at night. The region never experienced rain but the water that evaporated during the hot day condensed in the form of frost as the temperatures dipped. Thus at night the desert floor was covered by a layer of frost. The frost dissolved and percolated, once the sun rose. The climate remained the same throughout the year.

Xixidorra had some peculiar plants and animals. The dominant plant here and elsewhere on the planet was a thorny bush that had thick tubular leaves and black berries the size of pepper. The Xixipians called it Xibora. This bush could grow at astounding rates and the boys were informed by Queen Xixandra that they could cover an area of a couple square miles in a week. It was the staple food of most of the creatures and the berries though bitter were extremely nutritious. The leaves had antiseptic properties. The boys were informed that the Xixipians had modified and successfully introduced a number of species from earth like onions, carrots, yam, potatoes and a number of tubers which were now their staple food. Unfortunately large leafy plants brought from earth couldn't survive the harsh climate.

The animals were weirder. A number of insects had evolved to survive in the extreme climate of Xixidorra. There were millipede-like creatures, a foot long and covered with some sort of armour. They rolled themselves into a tight ball when the weather turned extreme and could crawl at astounding speed. They devoured all the dead and decaying matter and were the scavengers of the desert. Then there were beetle like insects that extracted the juice of the Xibora and converted it into a honey like substance. The desert was home to a couple of bird species. One species resembled the common hen although twice its size. They had very long and powerful legs that enabled them to run at speeds exceeding twenty miles an hour. Their plumage was denser than our average hen and they had a very tough beak. They could fly short distances and lived in the cracks and crevices of the numerous rocks in Xixidorra. They laid enormous eggs that the Xixipians relished. Xixidorra has some mammal-like species. The prominent species was a creature that resembled a lamb. These creatures were covered in very thick fur and instead of horns, had a dome shaped bone on their forehead. They had very strong and sharp hooves and the boys learnt that they could dig burrows to protect themselves from the extreme climate. The other mammal-like creature that the boys found fascinating was a fox like creature. They were tiny and fast and had razor sharp teeth, but what was fascinating about them was that they could glide from one giant rock to another, as they possessed folds of skin between their forelimbs and hind limbs. Most of these creatures ventured out a couple hours before sunrise and a couple of hours after sunset when the weather was bearable. During these hours they were in a frenzy to feed on whatever they could obtain.

The boys were curious to know about the dwellings of

the Xixipians living in Xixidorra. Queen Xixandra mentioned that all the original inhabitants of her planet were presently living in her city since the magnificent city of King Xixorro was now occupied by the Asourousse. Queen Xixandra's city, called Xixarappa was located more than a mile below the surface. Xixarappa lay beneath a flat top mountain with steep sides and ledges. The mountain was the sole tall structure in the relatively flat terrain at the centre of Xixidora desert. The boys looked wide eyed as they were given a virtual tour of Xixarappa. The flat top of the mountain seemed to open and they were led into a deep shaft. After travelling through darkness, they entered an underground city. They were told that the city was located in a natural hollow formed in the rocky structure. The city was about four miles long and a couple of miles wide. Though everything looked natural, Queen Xixandra mentioned that every square inch was artificially made by them. It was a well lit city and one could not distinguish between the natural light at the surface and the artificial light in the city. A gigantic waterfall emptied all its water into a river that meandered all around the city. The entire city was lush and green with many plants that resembled those on earth. There were a number of odd looking structures, which they learnt were the living and working quarters of the Xixipians. Queen Xixandra mentioned that all their food was grown in these structures and the plants elsewhere in the city were left untouched. One of the structures housed spaceships and other strange looking crafts and vehicles. The Xixipians travelled from place to place in egg shaped vehicles that hovered in the air.

The voice of Queen Xixandra then began to describe Xixibamba. This desert seemed like Eden compared to the other places on the planet. It was located on a plateau and was surrounded by high peaks. The region was blessed with a number of Xixoases and was relatively green. One could compare it with some of the semi arid regions on earth. It had a number of shrubs although thorny ones and with scanty leaves. The temperature variations were comparatively less with a high of about thirty eight above zero and a low of about twenty below zero. This was the only region of the planet where it occasionally rained. The most spectacular feature of Xixibamba was the palace of King Xixorro that was now occupied by the Asourousse. It was a magnificent structure with bricks made of colourful crystals. The boys were shocked to know that these bricks were diamonds, a relatively common substance on Xixipoo. Guru mentioned that he would love to take a couple of bricks back home. The voice of Queen Xixandra mentioned that palace was probably carved from a single giant diamond and it was impossible to spy on the palace even with their modern technology. Somehow the structure could block signals. That was the very reason, they did not learn about the plans of the Asourousse till the very end.

The boys were jolted back to reality when the scenery around them rapidly changed. They were once again in the confines of the spaceship and realized that many hours had passed.

"You must be tired," said Queen Xixandra's hologram. "Eat and rest a while. Then we will continue our lessons. Our next lesson will be about survival on our planet and then finally we will get you acquainted with the Asourousse."

After a delicious meal, the boys rested a couple of hours. They were overloaded with information and badly needed some rest. Then, as before, they were woken up, to take some more lessons.

This time the lessons were different and harsher. The boys could actually feel things around them. First they were given a virtual tour of the desert and brought face to face with some of the dangerous creatures. When a two foot worm attacked Guru and bit him in the arm, he really felt pain. It was as if his arm was on fire. He began to yell loudly, but was assured by Queen Xixandra that he felt virtual pain. Guru wondered what real pain would be like, if virtual pain, pained so much. He swore that he would smash any stupid creature that attacked him. Then they were given the virtual taste of many plants and taught to judge whether a plant was safe or not by mere examination. They were also taught basic survival methods in the desert if they were lost. Sri was alarmed and wanted to know why they were being taught those lessons.

"Won't you get us, once we reach Xixipoo?" he asked Queen Xixandra.

"Of course dear," she assured him, "I bet my life that I will get you once you land, but you must not forget that the spaceship is being steered by someone else and if such a situation arrives, you must be prepared."

"Please ensure that such a situation does not arrive," said Sri.

The session continued for a couple of hours without any more interruptions. Then Queen Xixandra's hologram appeared once again.

"This is the last lesson," she said. "Please be attentive while we teach you all that we know about the Asourousse. They seem to be extremely smart and powerful beings. We know very little about them and request you not to go by their polished looks."

The session began once again. The boys were told that when King Xixorro and Queen Xixandra arrived back to Xixipoo from earth, it was already occupied by other creatures. In their quest to destroy each other, the Xixipians had left their planet, believing it to be cold and dead, but they were wrong. The first thing they noticed was that they were not the only survivors but some two hundred Xixipians belonging to both the races of Xixorro and Xixandra had survived by hiding themselves. They decided to gather everyone together. Since the Asourousse had occupied Xixibamba, the Xixipians decided to occupy Xixarappa for the time being. King Xixorro had conducted a meeting of all the surviving Xixipians and explained what he and Xixandra had learned from the people of earth. The others were impressed by the people on earth and their philosophy, so they decided to end their animosity once and for all and live peacefully. Xixandra and Xixorro were unanimously chosen Queen and King and soon got married in an elaborate ceremony. They also repopulated Xixarappa with some of the species of plants and animals obtained from earth. Thus the Xixipians initially concentrated all their energy and technology in making Xixarappa magnificent. It was only after their lives had become stable that they decided to explore their planet and the strange new visitors.

The Xixipians cautiously spied on the new arrivals on their planet and were shocked when they realized that the new arrivals were not new, but had been living on their planet for about fourteen years maybe since the time the Xixipians had left their planet while trying to annihilate each other.

The Xixipians decided not to approach these beings, lest it resulted in another big war. Frankly, they were tired of war and wanted to coexist peacefully. However, they kept tabs on the other inhabitants, although discreetly. They soon realized that the Asourousse were the dominant species and decided only to concentrate on the activities of these beings. They learned that the Asourousse had technology comparable to theirs and were not very different from the humans. They did not mind, that the Asourousse had occupied the erstwhile royal palace of King Xixorro in the desert of Xixibamba and were contented living in Xixarappa. However, with each passing day they received more and more disturbing news of the activities of the Asourousse.

One day one of their drones was shot down by an Asourbout and the Xixipians realized that their presence was known to the Asourousse. After that, for no apparent reason, the Asourbouts began attacking them. They immediately went into stealth mode and hid away in their city of Xixarappa. They started studying the Asourousse more closely and realized that they although they exhibited certain characteristics of humans, they were basically evil. Further studies revealed that all the Asourbouts were linked to one extremely intelligent computer. Whereas the Xixipians had advanced computers, not one was comparable to this Master Computer possessed by the Asourousse. The Xixipians realized that the Master Computer had used whatever they had left behind, before leaving their planet to create the Asourbouts, so it was basically Xixipian technology, but if the Master Computer could simultaneously exist in the bodies of Asourbouts, then it could eventually control their computers. So they reprogrammed all their computers in such a way that the Master Computer could not get into them. The Xixipians then tried to locate the Master Computer, but soon realized that the location of the super computer was only known to the king of the Asourousse - Mooisausooura.

The boys now came face to face with a being around seven feet tall. He looked as if he was from one of the famous epics of the Hindus. He had a body that resembled a super-villain and was clad in clothes that may have been worn in very ancient times. Every inch of his body was muscular and he looked like a bull.

"Do the Asourousse wear clothes like this?" asked a

90

baffled Guru.

"No," said the voice of Xixandra, "this is the holy attire, only worn during very important occasions."

The being began to transform right in front of their eyes. He now resembled someone from a science fiction movie.

"And this is their normal attire," said Xixandra's sweet voice. "He is the only one who knows about the whereabouts of the Master Computer."

"But why are you obsessed with this Master Computer?" asked Guru.

"...Because it has declared war on us... and you as well."

"I don't understand," said Guru. "Why has it declared war on us?"

"My guess is that your planet is far better than Xixipoo," said Xixandra. "The Master Computer must've somehow been able to connect to earth through the portal and analyzed that the conditions there are much more suitable than here. The only obstacle, in the path of the Asourousse, is the human race. Hence it must've sent the Asourbouts to destroy all humans, so that the Asourousse can occupy earth unopposed."

"What is Mooisausooura's role in all this?" asked Sri. "Is he calling the shots or is this Master Computer calling the shots?"

"We have not been able to figure that out, so far," said Xixandra. "But the Asourousse are definitely keen on invading earth. There is one more being who is a part of this puzzle."

"And who's that?" asked Guru.

"An Asourousse princess," said Xixandra. "She is always

kept hidden and we have only gotten a glimpse of her so far. The only person who visits her is Mooisausooura. She may be his daughter. But I can assure you that she is evil, for whenever he visits her, something bad happens. In fact we have begun to believe that she may be the one calling the shots. We call her 'The Evil Princess'..."

October 15th, 12 Noon, Himalayas

Varshika glanced around, trying to absorb the details of the terrain. Tina was right behind her. They would begin their ascent in half an hour. After a light breakfast, they had been given instructions about the journey ahead and what to expect during the climb. The girls had volunteered to carry some of the equipment, but the elders stubbornly refused to let them carry any equipment. Instead they were repeatedly warned about the perils ahead and the possibility of a number of ailments including mountain sickness. After breakfast, while the adults packed and checked the basic equipment, the girls were allowed to do some exploration albeit within the perimeter set up for them.

The magnificent Himalayas sprawled ahead of them as far as the eye could see. Their snow covered peaks were mesmerizing. The region was one of the relatively unexplored regions of the Himalayas, due to the difficult terrain and treacherous peaks. Turning their attention from the Himalayan peaks, to the terrain below, the girls were shocked to know that they were by no means close to sea level and were already at a high altitude, for the terrain below was dotted with small rounded but desolate hills. They strained their eyes to spot tiny villages nested between the hills but strangely there were none. As far as they were concerned, there was not a living soul below – not even birds or the occasional animal. It gave them the creeps that they were possibly some of the few people in this desolate rugged terrain and if they needed help, it was far - far away.

It was Gopal's call that drew them out of their thoughts.

"C'mon girls, time to go," he said gently. "Hope you are up to it?"

"We, most certainly are," Tina said with renewed energy.

"Join us in prayer," he said "for the journey ahead is full of perils."

They gathered at a small temple that the girls had not noticed so far. The deity was a single saffron-smeared stone and resembled an ape. A saffron flag at the pinnacle of the temple fluttered in the wind. After a brief but sincere prayer, the team set out on their journey, to the base camp, to join the others, in their search for Uncle Dhondiba.

The first hour of the journey was especially hard for the girls, for they slipped, on more than one occasion and had bruises all over them. The altitude and rugged terrain seemed to affect Dr. Madhusudan the most and he threw up on many occasions. The others were worried that he would slow them down but in a couple of hours he seemed better and they trudged ahead, tired but determined. The elders were also worried about the girls but they seemed more steadfast than the rest. It seemed that they were pushing themselves to their limits and then a bit more. They walked in a single file with Gopal and his two colleagues in the lead followed by Dr. Madhusudan, Tina and Varshika. Ram and Rahim were at the rear and seemed well coordinated. They were all attached to each other by nylon chords, lest someone lost his footing or fell into a crevice.

Although most of their journey comprised of trekking along a well formed path, it was the occasional steep climbs over huge rocks that sapped them of their energy. They encountered huge boulders and had to overcome these to reach their destination. The team stopped at regular intervals to let the novices catch their breath and sip very small amounts of water.

They reached the snow line in the fifth hour of their journey and from there the journey became, slow, perilous and excruciating. The girls were informed by Gopal that the base camp was only two kilometers away but it would take the best part of three hours for them to make it there. Moreover the weather seemed to take a turn for the worse. It was biting cold and their thick coats offered little protection from the wind that felt like daggers piercing them. Now, covering a few feet ahead, in one go, seemed like a challenge. The girls faltered a couple of times and refused to budge, but Gopal gently reminded them of Uncle Dhondiba, who at that very moment was probably freezing in the very same conditions and praying to be rescued. That thought fired up the girls and they moved ahead with new resolve, although their fragile bodies protested.

All that while Gopal was filling in the details about Uncle Dhondiba while Dr. Madhusudan, Tina and Varshika listened patiently. They learnt that a fortnight ago Uncle Dhondiba started having visions and felt he was being summoned to the Himalayas. He could vividly describe the location although he had never been there before. He had conveyed the details of his visions to his good friend Gopal who had tried his best to dissuade him from acting impulsively. They had argued bitterly when Gopal told Dhondiba not to put himself in peril on account of a stupid dream. He had pointed out that Dhondiba was not in shape to undertake such a journey. However Dhondiba seemed like a man possessed and had taken off a week ago. On reaching the Himalayas he had phoned Gopal and mentioned that he had hired two guides to take him to the place that he has seen in his visions and though initially reluctant, they had finally agreed to accompany him when he offered them a large sum of money.

Then three days ago Gopal had received that dreaded phone call from one of the guides that Uncle Dhondiba had gone missing. It seems that amidst their journey, they were caught in an avalanche. One of the guides was badly injured and Uncle Dhondiba had simply disappeared. The other guide tried his best to locate Dhondiba but had given up when the weather turned dreadful. He had subsequently informed the authorities and Gopal, since Gopal's number had been registered by Dhondiba as an emergency number. That was when Gopal organized the search party with the help of the bosses at Astro Dreams.

They reached the base camp at around eight in the evening and the girls were so exhausted that they had to be carried to their tent. On the way to their tent they noticed that Gopal had indeed organized an efficient rescue team. Tents were neatly pitched and the people around seemed to know their business. The girls knew practically nothing about mountaineering, but were impressed on hearing that the camp had a dedicated communications centre and medical tent.

Three quarters of an hour later after sipping steaming hot tomato soup, warming their aching legs and relieving themselves, the girls were fit enough to meet the others, although briefly. They felt like celebrities, for they were the centre of attention. Everyone was curious to meet the tiny girls who have braved the elements to reach the base camp. After warm handshakes and hugs, Gopal insisted that the girls get some rest. He wanted Tina well rested and alert before the rescue team left the next morning, for he sincerely believed that the details of the location seen by her in her vision could help them reach Dhondiba on time.

On the way back to their tent, the girls briefly visited

the communications tent where they could speak to Nath, who was in the communication centre set up in the temple. He informed them that nothing much had happened in the past eighteen hours. King Xixorro's condition continued to be critical and the scientists were so far baffled by the nature of his ailment. However, Dr. Naik and the scientists had managed to keep him stable. So far they had failed to locate the Asourbouts, although Principal Sandipani along with Sri's father and Gendamal had scouted the area around Gendamal's farm. Thoroughly exhausted, the three of them were resting.

He also informed them that he had visited their houses and spoken to Tina's and Sri's mother. They were yet under the impression that their children were on their way to the Himalayas trying to help the rescue team. They had no idea that Guru and Sri had disappeared in a spaceship and were very far away from home. Nath had to lie to them that he had spoken to both the boys briefly when the girls had landed. Nath also informed them that the communication blackout continued and King Xixorro could not communicate with Xixipoo when he tried to do so during a brief spell of consciousness.

By that time Tina's father reached the communication tent. So Nath informed them that he would connect them to Tina's house. Probably Sri's and his mother would be there. He informed them that he would deliberately cause disturbance in the line so that the communication would be brief, lest the ladies wanted to speak to Sri and Guru. Accordingly Dr. Madhusudan spoke to his wife and also to Sri's mother. He lied that the boys were safe and were having their dinner along with the other mountaineers. He also lied that it was very difficult to communicate due to the frequent blackouts on account of the bad weather there. The girls then briefly spoke and assured the ladies that they were safe. Nath then told them that he had some ideas of his own regarding the

Asourbouts and he would try to locate them the next day. He assured Varshika that her pets Samuel and Jackson were safe with him and the dogs were safe at home although very quiet. After wishing him luck, the girls returned to their tent.

Once in the tent, the girls zipped themselves up in their sleeping bags, after zipping the tent shut. Once cozy in their sleeping bags, they realized how tired they were and how badly their bodies needed rest.

"I miss my father," Varshika said. "This tent reminds me of our many adventures in Africa although it was a lot warmer there."

"I am sorry to involve you in all this," said Tina.

"C'mon girl," said Varshika, "A wild elephant could not drag me away from this. What are friends for? And we are more than friends, I believe."

"Yes, we are soul sisters, but I feel bad that you have to face all this on our account."

"Don't be sorry," Varshika said. "It is destiny. We have been brought together for some purpose and each one of us has our role to play. I only hope the boys are safe."

"So do I, so do I."

"Now let's get some sleep. We will need our energy. Hope you have some more of those visions of yours and they can help the team locate your uncle."

"Good night!"

Varshika drifted into deep sleep almost immediately. She started having weird dreams. She dreamed that she had snuggled up to her father. Both were in a tent in the African bush on one of their many expeditions. It was warm but pleasant. She felt cozy and secure in the arms of her father.

"Daddy, I've missed you so much. Why did you have to suddenly leave?"

"Each one of us has to take a test to prove our worth. I am taking mine right now. You will soon have to take yours," he said solemnly.

"I know," she mumbled. "But how do you know of the situation that I am in?"

"Because, you are my little lioness and I love you more than anything else in this world. A time will come when you will have to take a leap of faith. Trust in the lord and do not falter."

"But, but...,"

Suddenly the weather began to change drastically. It was getting awfully cold in the tent. It was literally snowing. Varshika began to freeze. She felt snow on her face. Outside the wind was howling.

She woke up with a start and looked around her, then glanced at her wristwatch. It was quarter past midnight. She realized that she had been dreaming, for she was no longer in the African bush but in a tent in the Himalayas and yes, it was freezing in there since the tent flap was open and snow was blowing in, right onto her face. She quickly looked to her right to see if Tina was okay. The sleeping bag beside her was empty as Tina was not in the tent. Varshika was thoroughly alarmed. May be Tina had gone out to relieve herself. So stupid of Tina, sneaking out like that without informing her. She hurriedly put on her shoes and slipped out of the tent. Everyone seemed to be asleep. She contemplated calling someone, but decided against doing that. Maybe it was a false alarm. Maybe Tina was close by and would be there presently. The wind was howling and it was snowing heavily. As she scoured the surrounding area, she noticed a figure walking in a trance, quite some distance away. It was Tina, probably sleep walking. But she had moved quite far away from the camp and was heading for the cliffs. Varshika had to hurry. She considered raising an alarm but what if she lost sight of Tina? So she hurried in the direction of Tina.

Tina was still moving towards the cliff, so Varshika tried to increase her pace, but Tina was fast – really fast. She was baffled by Tina's behaviour. Was she really sleepwalking? How could she move so fast and what in the devil's name had possessed her? Weren't they tired to the bone? From where was that girl getting the energy to move so fast in such bad weather conditions? Varshika reached the base of the cliff some ten minutes later, only to find that Tina had begun climbing the treacherous cliff. Was that girl out of her mind? Even the expert mountaineers used sophisticated equipment and this crazy, stupid girl was climbing using nothing but her bare hands. Varshika glanced back at the camp. It was far away. She had travelled quite some distance. She yelled at Tina, but the girl was climbing steadfast, oblivious to the surroundings. Finally Varshika decided to follow. She tried to take the path taken by Tina and slipped and landed heavily on her back with a groan. She had to think fast for Tina was getting smaller by the moment, meaning that she was ascending at a fast rate. Varshika once again focused all her attention to her present task and began ascending. This time she managed to climb, although very slowly. She decided not to look down lest she chicken out.

Varshika managed to catch up with Tina some half an hour later, that too because Tina decided to rest a while, on a flat ledge. She grabbed her and shook her violently.

"What in God's name are you doing? Is this a suicide mission? Are you completely mental?" said Varshika furiously.

"Huh!!!"

She shook Tina once again, more violently. That seemed to break the trance.

"Stop doing that," Tina protested. "I was merely following instructions."

"What instructions? Whose..."

Varshika couldn't speak one more word because her blood froze. Right behind Tina was an ape like creature, covered with snow-white fur, close to nine feet tall with huge but surprising gentle eyes. In one swoop, it picked up Tina in one hand, held her like a mother holding a baby and leaped onto the rocks above. It must've leaped some twenty feet and Varshika stood with her mouth agape at the ease with which it carried Tina. She could only helplessly watch the creature carry Tina away high up into the mountains. She tried to scream, but no sound left her mouth. Suddenly she felt herself being hoisted into the arms of something furry and warm. Another of those huge creatures had her in its arms. With ease, the creature began ascending the mountain with Varshika held tightly close to its bosom. There was nothing that she could do.

October 16ᵗʰ, 7 am (earth time)
Batatawadai Puram

Nath opened his eyes, stretched a bit and looked around. The surroundings were unfamiliar. His own bedroom at home was airy and bright whereas the room where he lay now was cold, stuffy and dull. He sat up in the makeshift bed and looked around lazily and remembered that he had stayed awake till three in the morning, monitoring the radio equipment, eagerly awaiting some communication from Guru or Sri. Then the Principal had ordered him to take rest. He recollected his conversation the previous night, with Tina and Varshika. The rescue team would be on their way. He softly prayed for Uncle Dhondiba and his friends Guru and Sri.

Something caught his attention to the left. The tarantula was moving about restlessly in the glass tank. It was probably hungry. Nath had spent more than three quarters of an hour collecting dead grasshoppers and other insects from the forest floor near the temple in a paper bag. He went near the tank, carefully opened the lid and emptied the contents of the bag. The spider moved quickly towards the dead insects. He hoped the meal would keep the spider quiet for the next twenty four hours, for he loathed the creepy creature. The only reason, he even kept the creature was because he had promised Varshika to do so. He carefully secured the lid of the tank and turned his attention to the adjacent tank. The black mamba lay still. Probably it was still too cold for it to stir. However, he carefully placed an egg inside the tank using a long pair of iron tongs and hurriedly closed the lid. He promised himself that he would never again volunteer to look after such dangerous creatures, but for now he had to take care of the creepy duo and would do so till Varshika arrived.

Picking up a bottle of water he made his way to the top. The sun shone brightly and the leaves in the forest rustled in the gentle breeze. Various birds chirped loudly as they hopped from one branch to another eating the ripe fruits. A turf war between two groups of langurs (bonnet macaque monkeys) was in full swing and one of them landed a few feet from where he stood, startling him. After shooing it away, he washed his face and though tired, felt a sort of energy surge into him. He approached Sandipani, who was pacing about a few feet away.

"Good morning Principal Sir," said Nath.

"Ah Nath, you're awake."

"Yes sir," said Nath obediently. "Is there anything that I can do now?"

"There most certainly is," said the Principal. "But I need you to go home for a couple of hours, freshen up and return. Your mother is awfully worried and I promised to send you home as soon as you awoke."

"Is there anything that I need to carry to or bring back from the village?"

"Yes if you don't mind, please get the groceries required by Ghasitaram," mumbled the visibly embarrassed Principal, for he did not like accepting favours from students. "He is a blabbermouth and I would not like him going to the village and accidently blabbering out everything, thus creating unnecessary panic."

"Surely sir," said Nath. "What is the matter? You seem visibly upset."

"Nothing good is happening right now. The two scientists have been up the whole of last night in their makeshift lab, but have no clue about the virus. This virus is unlike anything seen on earth and they fear the worst. They are exhausted and asleep. Also King Xixorro is not showing an iota of improvement in his condition. Dr. Naik is exhausted tending to him. Gendamal and Keshava spent the whole of yesterday trying to locate the Asourbouts, but all in vain. We have no clue, what they look like and what to look for, in them. Then last night, without the slightest hint, all communications with the base camp ceased. Our equipment is fine and I believe that the bad weather there, may be responsible, but still am worried. It is all so depressing."

"Don't worry sir," said Nath empathically. "Everything will be alright. The most important thing is that we are all together and isn't Mr. Ishwar doing his best to help us. We shall overcome the obstacles and triumph in the end. We always have. Now I'll be on my way but promise to return soon."

Nath quickly moved into the temple. He too, was depressed and apprehensive, but did not show his emotions. He yet wished Mr. Bose would somehow reach there and help them. Contrary to what everyone thought, he knew Mr. Bose well. He was not a nutcase as believed by everyone. He was a brilliant scientist and had extensive knowledge. His habits may have been a bit queer, but that did not make him a nutcase. Nath walked down the steps and reached the subterranean temple. Instead of walking straight ahead, he turned to the left and entered the huge door leading to the main sanctum of the temple. The place was brightly lit up by the torches modified by him. That part of the temple did not have electric light for the Principal had forbidden the others from entering the main structure of the temple or disturbing it in any way, so though they had brought a portable generator, that region was left untouched. The rest of the subterranean temple was well lit up by electric lights.

He stood with folded hands in front of the huge deity. Those gentle eyes seemed to radiate energy. He silently prayed – prayed for strength, for success and for the evil to be defeated. Then he refilled the torches with fuel and went to the other part of the temple. As he walked through the wide passage, he came to the room he had been sleeping in, the communication centre. It was empty. He carefully went in and tinkered with the radio equipment. He did not hear the familiar hiss – all he heard was static. But he was not worried, for it was quite possible that communications had been cut off due to the bad weather conditions in the Himalayas. Hadn't the girls told him about the bad weather the previous night? He only hoped that the weather was not so bad, that the rescue efforts would be hampered. Walking further ahead, he came to the quarantine area and peeped in. Dr. Naik was asleep on a chair while King Xixorro seemed to be sleeping peacefully in his plastic enclosure. He could hear the feeble beeps of the medical equipment connected to the Alien King and decided not to disturb them. The next room to the right was well lit and had a plastic curtain on the door. He quietly moved aside the curtain and peeped in. A scientist was fast asleep in his makeshift bed while the other was peering into a microscope. On the table he saw equipment scattered around. Some were familiar objects like test tubes, centrifuge and various beakers while some equipment was unfamiliar. The scientist looked up, smiled but forbade him from entering. He waved and moved on. May be it was too dangerous to go in. He walked further ahead and entered the last room to the right. It was a huge, dimly lit room and could easily have accommodated a large number of people. There were a number of sleeping bags lined on the floor. Two of them had occupants – Riya's father and Sri's father were fast asleep in them. The other sleeping bags were empty. An electric table fan hummed beside them. Glancing around he noticed that the far end of the room was being used to store equipment. Ghasitaram, the school cook was nowhere in sight though he saw vegetables and other kitchen equipment neatly stacked in one corner. Hence he moved out carefully so as not to awaken the occupants and hurried along the wide passage only to bump into someone heavy.

"Ow!" said Ghasitaram. "Where were you? I've been searching for you."

"And I've been searching for you."

"I found the lower rooms too claustrophobic and hence decided to set up my kitchen a little distance away from the temple in a small clearing in the forest."

"Oh!"

"Don't worry!" said Ghasitaram. "I have taken the Principal's permission. Follow me."

They walked silently to the temple above and then exited it. Principal Sandipani was yet pacing about, so they decided that it would be best to avoid him. They took a path adjacent to the temple that led to the rear. The rear looked different from the front of the temple. The front had elegant carvings, but the rear end was a huge rock some forty feet high. It was part of the huge rock that formed the temple but was left in its original form. Anyone approaching from the rear end would not believe that the rest of the rock had been carved into a magnificent temple both above and below the ground. Ahead were some more huge rocks that were not part of the temple. They were separated from the main temple by a narrow path. Nath also realized that the temple had only one entrance. There was only one way in and out. The path they had taken, led to a glade in the forest. It was there that Ghasitaram had pitched his kitchen tent. Using rocks for

106

support and firewood from the forest, he had made three stoves that had vessels on them and a bright fire below. The delicious aroma made Nath's mouth water. Ghasitaram must've sensed that Nath was hungry for he offered him breakfast that Nath gladly accepted. He sat on a boulder and devoured the breakfast as he studied the terrain. Nath noticed that the clearing was a small one and immediately after the clearing, the forest became dense. He also noticed that the land sloped downwards. Thus the temple was on a peak that was at the highest point in the area. Ghasitaram handed Nath a list of items required by him. Thanking him profusely for the filling breakfast, Nath left.

He reached the front of the temple and took the path back to his village. It was a path sloping gently downwards and the forest was dense on either side. Soon he reached a narrow path with a steep drop on both the sides. The path joined the peak where the temple lay to the other part of the mountain leading to their village. It was about twelve feet wide at the narrowest point and some thirty feet wide at the widest point. The drop was a good three hundred feet on either side. Nath was curious and peeped down the valley on the left. The sheer drop made him feel dizzy. A little ahead he saw a stout tree right at the edge of the path. He held on to the tree and peered below once again. This time he saw a ledge some six feet below. The ledge was about seven feet wide and some ten feet long. Nath wondered if he could climb down to the ledge just to admire the uninterrupted view of the forests below, but developed cold feet at the last moment. He realized that if he couldn't climb back up, he would be stuck there for a very long time, so decided to continue on his journey back to his village.

After some time, he came to a familiar clearing that lead to Gendamal's farm. There he saw Riya tending to her cows. She cheerfully waved when she saw him, so he decided to chat with her for a while.

"Hey Riya!" said Nath enthusiastically.

"Hello Nath. You look pretty tired. Any positive news..?"

"Alas no!" said Nath. "What's been going on in the village?"

"Oh the usual boring stuff. Many families have left for the vacation, so the village is practically deserted. My dad and Sri's father searched every nook and corner of the village and then scouted the perimeter of the village. They did not find anything unusual and were pretty sore about it."

"Yeah, I know," said Nath in a matter of fact manner. "They were fast asleep when I left the temple. Anything else unusual, that you noticed?"

"No, but have you heard the latest news about Saniya's Mom from Bondaipuram?"

"Who cares," said Nath. "What has she gone and done now?"

"She has converted a part of her pastures into a camping site. She has pitched a few tents and is renting them out to campers."

"Has anyone gone and checked out the place?" asked Nath.

"Are you silly? We have better things to do."

"I am going home now to freshen up. Then I have a few errands to run but I will check out the campsite before going back to the temple," said Nath seriously.

"Your wish, but believe me, it is a sheer waste of time."

Nath shrugged his shoulders and left. He reached his home in fifteen minutes and found it locked, so went to Guru's house next door. As expected, his mother was in Guru's house along with Sri's mother. She hugged him tightly.

"So, what has my pumpkin been doing?" she asked.

"Please don't call me that," said an embarrassed Nath. "I've been monitoring the communications and weather in the Himalayas. It was I, who put the call from Tina through, last night."

"Thanks," said Guru's mother. "But why was the line so unclear? I could barely hear them. Imagine our boys – having no time to speak to their mammas. I just hope those rapscallions are not up to some mischief?"

"Yeah!" said Sri's mother. "You better connect them to us, once you reach your communications centre, or whatever you call it. I am really worried about those two – they and their knack to get into trouble."

"They are fine," Nath lied. "I spoke to them yesterday when Tina and Varshika landed. They are extremely enthusiastic about the whole 'search and rescue' and are trying to be a part of the action."

"You mean, they are actually taking part in the rescue operation."

"No, no," said Nath regretting what he had said a few moments ago. "Do you think the elders would let them? Now can I go?"

"Can't we come to your, eh, communication centre and speak to them?" said Guru's mother.

"No," said Nath firmly. "The equipment is sensitive and expensive. The engineers do not want Mr. Ishwar's equipment damaged. I will keep you updated - I promise. Now may I leave?"

"Don't forget to take a thorough bath and wear clean underwear, my pumpkin," said Nath's mother.

"Mom, please!" said Nath, rather irritated. "If you haven't noticed, I'm adult now."

He left in a huff, with the ladies looking at him with expressions on their face that was hard to describe. His mother looked on with pride in her eyes.

"My little boy is growing up into a strong young man."

After a brief shower, Nath filled his backpack with some essentials and went to the market on his bicycle. There he purchased whatever Ghasitaram had requested him to. It was quite a load but instead of riding towards Gendamal's farm, he took the road out of his village towards Saniya's village. Soon he was out of his village and moving towards Bondaipuram. The surroundings abruptly changed from neat to untidy, for the inhabitants of Batatawadai Puram took extra efforts to keep their village clean. He was puffing and panting, for it was really hot. On seeing Saniya's farm at a distance, he parked his bicycle by the side of the road and cautiously moved towards the farm on foot ensuring that he was not visible and moved towards the so called campsite. It was an extremely untidy campsite, with tall grass, filthy pigs moving around, feeding on the garbage strewn around carelessly. One could've easily gotten hurt. There were ten tents pitched in two neat rows of five each. Some efforts had been made to keep the area around the tents clean. He spent the next half hour studying the campsite and its inhabitants, though out of sight the entire time, then abruptly moved towards his bicycle and rode as fast as he could to Riya's farm. He yelled for her, when he reached within hearing distance. She came out rather surprised.

"I think I've located the Asourbouts," he said breathlessly.

"Where are they?" she asked with wide eyes.

"Camping," he said.

"Now please," she said. "I know you guys hate Saniya and her mother, but why would they harbour Asourbouts?"

"Because Saniya's mother is both stupid and greedy," he said firmly. "And she doesn't know that the campers are the Asourbouts. She must've readily rented the campsite for a large sum of money, without verifying the people or in this case the Asourbouts."

"How can you be sure that they are the Asourbouts?" demanded Riya.

"Because there are six of them..."

"So?" said she with her hands on her hips. "They could be six campers. It may be just a coincidence."

"... looking exactly the same," continued Nath in a slow and deliberate manner. "Is it normal to see Sextuplets camping, in a Godforsaken camp site, that too filthy and pig infested. And though they look human, there is something amiss."

"Are you a hundred percent sure?" she said. "And if you are, then what should we do?"

"I am almost certain about them," he said. "We will have to keep an eye on them."

"What do they look like?" she asked thoroughly alarmed.

"I have taken a few photographs," he said.

"Oh God, we are in trouble now. They are highly advanced cyborgs. They would have surely detected your electronic camera."

"Do you think I have the word 'stupid' written on my forehead?" he said annoyed.

"No," she said taken aback. "On the contrary, I think you are one of the smartest in our school."

"Then don't fret," he assured her. "I did not use any electronic device. Instead I used a very old manual camera, gifted to me by Mr. Bose. It has a roll of film, that I want you to develop for me."

He handed her a roll of film.

"Who will develop it for us?"

"Try Mr. Rego," he said. "He is a retired photographer and will surely be able to develop the film for us."

"I will have it developed by evening," she said earnestly. "Then I will keep an eye on the Asourbouts."

"Please be careful," he pleaded. "They are not human and will not hesitate to cause harm to anyone who comes in their way. I also wonder how they are monitoring King Xixorro?"

"May be, they are spying on you at the temple," she said alarmed.

"No," he said. "I'm sure they know about the whereabouts of King Xixorro, but have not come anywhere near our temple. If they are camping, so casually, so far away from him, then they must be having some way by which they are remotely monitoring his health. We will have to investigate."

He took her leave and proceeded towards the temple. He would have to inform the others about what he had learned. Once Riya delivered the photographs, they would be able to study the Asourbouts. Then they would have to monitor those devils and wait for the inevitable. Deep in thought, he entered the forest.

October 16ᵗʰ, 2 am (earth time) Himalayas

Varshika had lost all track of time. Her guess was that they had travelled for almost an hour, but there was no telling for how long they had travelled, maybe time itself had stopped. Moreover visibility was poor. She believed in looking at the *bright side of things* and the bright side was, at that moment both of them were snug in the arms of those huge, furry creature, else they would have perished in the dreadful storm. How those creatures withstood the harsh climate was yet a mystery. The creatures slowed down and cautiously entered a ravine, so she managed to get a glimpse of Tina who seemed safe for the moment. She could only guess what lay ahead in store for them. The creatures seemed to be moving much slower and more cautiously through these ravines. To Varshika, they seemed to be moving in circles and that frightened her a bit. Dreadful thoughts began to creep into her mind. What if they were approaching the lair of those creatures? What if the creatures were flesh eaters? That would be the end of the line for them. She glanced over the creature's shoulder and once again caught a glimpse of Tina. Surprisingly Tina seemed calm and composed. It was getting brighter by the minute and seemed as if dawn was fast approaching though dawn was a couple of hours away. Then the creatures slowed down and began walking. Once they stopped, they gently placed the girls down. Varshika looked around, but couldn't believe her eyes, for they were at the gates of a city.

"A city in the Himalayas," Varshika shouted above the wind.

"It is the 'Holy City'."

"How do you know that?" asked a bewildered Varshika.

"Because," said Tina, "these holy beings have been communicating with me."

"They have?"

"Yes," said Tina. "We've been exchanging thoughts."

They entered the huge carved gates that had been cut out of a rock and looked around, awestruck. The city was located in what seemed to be a crater. It must've been a kilometer and a half long by half a kilometer wide and appeared to be made entirely of ice. Only closer examination revealed that it was made entirely of stone and covered with thick layers of ice, some of which was so ancient that it was blue. In fact it would've been more appropriate to call it a temple complex rather that a full-fledged city, for at the centre was a magnificent temple and the other structures around it seemed to be the structures accompanying the main temple. This structure was similar to many ancient temples found in other parts of India, especially South India.

They followed the creatures along a narrow path towards the centre of the city. Along the way, the many beings that were busy performing various chores, paused momentarily to bow to the girls and continued with their work.

After walking for some time, the four of them entered the outer sanctum of the temple through a Gopuram (gate pyramid) and looked around. The main structure of the temple with a huge courtyard caught their eye. The temperature here was a degree or two above freezing although it must've been thirty below freezing outside. A huge being approached them in a very dignified manner. The two creatures that had brought them, to the city, abruptly stopped and stood in attention. When this creature came near, they immediately touched his feet and moved away to the background.

"Touch his feet," said Tina. "He is one of the seven high priests."

Both the girls touched his feet.

"Please tell us sir, why have we been brought here?" said Varshika boldly.

He gestured her to kneel down. She obeyed without complaint. Then he placed both his palms on her head. A spasm of energy seemed to pass through her body. She was dumbstruck for about a minute, but later could hear a number of voices around.

"How do you feel now, little one?"

Varshika had definitely heard the words, or rather felt them, but no one had spoken.

"Do not be surprised. We are conversing via our thoughts."

"But how is that possible? Unlike Tina, I do not have any special abilities," said Varshika.

"You do not need to speak. We can converse via our thoughts. Moreover though the world has beings communicating using different languages, the language of thought is universal."

"How did I achieve this ability?" asked Varshika via her thoughts.

"Your energy flow was not proper. There were many blocked pathways. I merely cleared them. You had the potential in you. I merely showed you the path."

"Thank you." Varshika said via her thoughts.

"Who are you and why have we been brought here?" Tina said via her thoughts.

"We are known to you by many names. Some call us 'Bigfoot', and others call us "Yeti' and still others call us 'Migou', but we prefer being called the 'Vanars'."

"So, you do exist. It is not a myth." Varshika exclaimed.

"We will answer all your questions. But you must cleanse yourselves before entering the inner sanctum of the temple. After cleansing yourselves, please leave all your clothes out here and wear only these robes. My girls will show you the way."

Two more Vanars approached the girls. They were as tall as the others but had a distinct feminine look. They smiled sweetly and led the girls, through a narrow passage outside the main temple to one of the adjoining structures. Here they saw a number of rooms cut in the rocks. Water was flowing from the top of these rooms like tiny waterfalls.

"Are these what I think they are?" said Varshika.

"Yes, they are bathrooms," said Tina. "I am definitely not going to bathe in this freezing weather and get killed."

The two Vanars smiled and pointed right into the rooms. The girls peered at the interior of these rooms and realized that the water that was falling was steaming hot.

"The water is close to boiling. We will enjoy a steaming hot bath." Tina said.

"But they have no doors," said Varshika.

The girl Vanars once again gestured Varshika to wait. One of them went close to one of the rooms and pointed to a door like structure. It was made of woven fibres that looked like hemp. Inside, the girls saw saffron robes, neatly hung besides what appeared to be towels.

After a refreshing bath and change of clothes, the girls were lead back to the main temple. They had the saffron robes on and strangely were not freezing. Instead they felt calm and relaxed. They were taken to the high priest who welcomed them with a smile.

"*Welcome to the 'holy city'. You are amongst the few privileged ones who will lay their eyes on our city. I will take you around our city and show you how we have existed here peacefully for millennia, guarding the sacred temple. Later you shall meet the Abbot of the temple, for he is in deep prayer right now.*"

"*And my uncle Dhondiba?*" asked Tina.

"*You already know that he is safe here. However he is not conscious. He was badly injured on his way here. Had we not found him on time, he would've perished. You may see him now. The high priest will decide on how he has to be transported back to your camp. But that is secondary. You have been brought here because you have been chosen for something very important. The Abbot shall explain everything once he has finished praying. Now let's go and see your uncle.*"

They were led through a narrow passage to a chamber. There, lying on a bed made of the same hemp like material was uncle Dhondiba. He seemed to be sleeping peacefully. His breathing was calm and his chest heaved up and down in a rhythmic manner. Tina rushed to him, hugged him and kissed his forehead. However he did not stir.

"*Will he be alright?*" asked Tina.

"*He has to be kept this way till he is taken to one of your hospitals. He will be in hospital for a long time but will recover completely. Do not worry about him. I can understand your sentiments and how you would like to spend more time with him here but you have been chosen to perform some important tasks - extremely important tasks.*"

Both the girls were relieved that Uncle Dhondiba had finally been located and was safe. Though, relieved, they were reluctant to leave uncle Dhondiba. Finally with a heavy heart, they decided to tour the 'Holy City' with the high priest.

"*Do you know that we are located right above an active volcano?*"

"*No way,*" said Varshika. "*What if it erupts?*"

"It can, but it won't. We have controlled it for many millennia."

"How is that possible?" asked Tina.

"This is possible due to the powerful relic or 'Astra' that is present in the temple. It was made by the 'The Great Lord' himself. It is the energy of the Astra that keeps the Holy City going."

"Why has the holy city never been discovered by man?" asked Varshika.

"That is because of the temple and relic that lies within. It magnifies our mental abilities and with those abilities we make our city invisible to humans. A lost mountaineer may occasionally catch a glimpse of our city, but using our ability, we make it disappear like a mirage. Moreover we can wipe out the memory from his brain. This city is neither visible from land nor air. Let me show you our city."

The girls followed the high priest around the 'holy city'. As they had previously observed, it was a small city built around the temple. They were first given a tour of the temple. On entering the inner sanctum of the temple, they found it to be similar to their secret temple at Batatawadai Puram. It had the same intricate designs carved on every nook and corner on the structure. However there were some basic differences between the two structures. Whereas the temple at Batatawadai Puram was constructed underground and was dark, this temple was bright and at ground level. It required no artificial lighting. Moreover it was many times larger than the one at Batatawadai Puram. The Vimana (central tower) of the temple was some thirty meters high. It lay above the innermost sanctum of the temple that housed the deity.

They solemnly bowed before the deity. It was a larger version of the deity in their temple at Batatawadai Puram. The high priests then pointed out to chambers on either side.

"These are prayer chambers. These chambers are used whenever a high priest or the Abbot needs to pray or contemplate. There are seven such chambers. Sometimes, one of us may go into a trance and be in the

chamber for a number of days."

"Without food and water?" asked Tina

"Yes. Don't you feel their presence? Close your eyes and concentrate."

The girls solemnly closed their eyes and could literally feel the vibrations.

"Six high priests have been in deep prayer ever since we sensed danger to our planet. It is they, who have blocked all communications to earth, thus preventing those machines from communicating with the planet of their origin."

"Thank you," said Varshika.

"You don't have to thank us little one. We are merely performing the task assigned to us all those millennia ago. However I cannot tell for how much longer they will be able to sustain themselves, for the task is draining all the energy from them."

He then took them to the back yard of the temple. It was much bigger than the front yard. At the centre of the yard, was a huge well. It had been covered by a huge slab of stone that may have weighed a ton. He pointed towards it.

"That there is the 'well of life'."

There were four very huge Vanars close to the well. They stood in attention when the high priest and girls approached. He looked towards them and nodded. They immediately rushed to the well and with a lot of effort, shifted the stone so that the inner part of the well could be viewed. The high priest directed the girls towards the well. They peeped in together and saw a reddish orange glow some two hundred meters below. The blast of hot air almost knocked them off their feet.

"You guessed right. It is the volcano."

He then again looked at the Vanars and nodded. They

immediately ran out and returned with huge blocks of ice, carefully dropped the blocks into the well and shifted the stone back into position over the well.

"These here, are the keepers of the 'well of life'. Only the strongest, amongst the Vanars are chosen for this job. Their job is to feed the well at fixed intervals of time. The ice on touching the volcano will get converted to super heated steam. This steam will rise and enter the temple through an intricate network of stone pipes. The steam keeps the place warm, heats our dwellings and enables us to cook whenever we have to."

"So, the water used by us for bathing came from here?" asked Tina.

"You are right. The steam passed through meandering stone pipes, so when it reached you, it had been converted from steam to very hot water. The water, after use, is again made to flow through a meandering network of pipes, so that when it is released from the city, it is very cold and immediately gets converted to ice."

"How do you sustain yourselves in such harsh conditions?" asked Varshika.

"We are the servants of 'The Great Lord'. We have been obeying his instructions for millennia and guarding the sacred relic in this temple. It is our sense of duty towards our Lord, due to which we yet exist as a species else we would have become extinct millennia ago. Our basic necessities are quite different from yours. We do not need clothes even in these harsh conditions because our body is covered in thick fur that evolved over millennia. We have lost our tails. Our diet is limited. We only eat fruits and occasionally vegetables. Most of our food grows here in the city itself. On some occasions, the younger Vanars are sent to the lower parts, to collect fruits or vegetables. The temple provides us the little shelter that we may need. The energy radiated by the relic, gives us the power to tune into the minds of humans, thousands of kilometers away. Hence we spend twelve to fifteen hours a day meditating and learning about the world through you humans."

They walked further ahead and came to the sloping walls of the crater. Here they observed various cave-like structures cut into the walls at different heights. The region was dense with vegetation and pathways in between the foliage led to each opening in the walls of the crater. The girls were surprised to see luscious fruits hanging from the plants that were growing directly on rocks.

"Those above are the humble dwellings of the Vanars. The Abbot, priests and other temple servants, live in the temple itself. The younger Vanars usually perform the tasks of growing and collecting food, keeping the city clean and serving the elders. Then, when they come of age, they are initiated by any one of the seven high priests and are given the divine knowledge. According to their abilities and virtues, each attains position."

"When do the young Vanars come of age?" inquired Tina.

"When, they attain the age of about fifty. The energy radiated by our temple coupled with our lifestyle and food habits increases our lifespan considerably. We can live for many centuries. The Abbot is well over five centuries old."

The girls marveled at the size of the fruits. They seemed luscious.

"Would you like to taste our fruits?"

Both of them nodded eagerly, for they were indeed hungry. The high priest looked around. Immediately a couple of young Vanars rushed to the spot, carefully plucked a couple of fruits and handed one each to the girls.

"Please eat. Then I will arrange for you to dine and rest awhile. When the Abbot is ready, he will call for you. In the meanwhile you can interact with the Vanar youth."

He looked around and nodded. Immediately a number of Vanars leaped out of their dwellings and reached the spot in a jiffy. Many of them were girl Vanars. Probably they were eager to meet other girls. As soon as the high priest left, an attractive girl Vanar approached Tina and Varshika. She was eight feet tall with snow white, soft fur, almond shaped eyes and prominent curved eyebrows. Her palms were very light pink in colour and she gently shook hands with them.

"My name is Tara. I am in charge of the young Vanars. Would you like to see our dwellings? But first I would like to introduce you to some of my companions here."

"Sure" said Varshika.

They spent the next fifteen minutes being formally introduced to each other. The girls realized that these Vanar youth were so much like them, full of life and enthusiasm. Then they were eagerly led to the dwellings. While climbing the shear rocks was an easy task for the Vanars, the girls were panting and puffing by the time they reached the first dwelling. This dwelling was the dormitory of the girl Vanars. The boys had their own dormitory. The girls were told that when a Vanar baby became a youth, he or she had to live in the dormitory along with the other youth. Here they were given the basic training in various skills and prepared for the initiation. This was the 'fun and care-free' phase of their lives. The girls learned about the lives of these youth and how they spent their time. By the time they were called for a meal, the girls had befriended many youth and even remembered a few of their names. There was Pragnya, who was a scholar, then Chaturbhuja was very strong and a particular Vanar named Kamaroopin had the ability to change his form. It was he who was sent to the lower reaches of the Himalayas, most of the times to collect fruits and vegetables because of his uncanny ability. Then there were others like Nala, Nila, Taar and Dwivida who befriended them.

The girls were enjoying the company of the Vanars so much that they failed to realize the fact that many hours had passed since they had disappeared from the base camp. When that realization dawned upon them, they were worried and requested an audience with the high priest.

"I know why you have come. Do not fret, for the Abbot shall

123

meet you soon after lunch."

"But, our parents will be terribly worried by now," said Tina.

"Your father and everyone at the base camp are surely worried, but they cannot convey the message to your folks at home, because we have blocked communications from the base camp. After the Abbot has spoken to both of you, we shall return you and Uncle Dhondiba to a location close to your camp. Now please have something to eat before you meet the Abbot."

They were taken to the hall adjoining the temple. Here a number of Vanars were seated in circles on the floor and were eagerly looking at them. Many of them smiled and the girls reciprocated. The Youth were seated in the outer circles and the elders in the inner circles. The central region, meant for the high priests was vacant, as all the high priests except one, were in deep prayer, trying to save the planet. The girls sat with Tara and some other Vanar youth. Lunch was served to them in huge cup like structures made of leaves. Food consisted of a variety of fruits and boiled vegetables. However before they could start their meal, the high priest, who had been interacting with them, stood up. Everyone looked at him enraptured.

"Dear Vanar Brethren, our planet is in peril. These two brave girls, Tina and Varshika shall be entrusted our most valuable possession, the Astra, entrusted to us by none other than the great Lord. Using this Astra these brave-hearts will try to save our planet. Please pray for these brave girls, for though so young and tender, they are being entrusted with such a colossal task. Also pray to the great Lord to protect this city, for without the Astra, we too are vulnerable."

With folded hands, everyone began to pray. Then the high priest signaled them to stop.

"Relish this meal, for it is on a rare occasion that we share our meals with humans, though over the millennia, they have been sharing their food with us."

After the meal, everyone got up and left in an orderly manner. The Vanar youth hung around for some more time with the girls. Then it was time for them to meet the Abbot. Tara gently hugged Tina and Varshika and bid farewell with tears in her eyes. The high priest then led them into the inner sanctum of the temple. The Abbot was seated on a slightly raised structure with pillows on either side, for support. He probably had been very strong in the past, but now was bent with age. His face was heavily wrinkled but his eyes sparkled mischievously.

The high priest instructed the girls to approach the Abbot and left. The girls approached him as if they were approaching their school Principal. He looked at them and smiled.

"No need to fear me, little ones. You can boldly approach me."

He then looked at Tina.

"Ah Tina!" he said. "So finally we meet. It was I who projected that image and don't regret it. You are indeed the chosen one and have all the qualities of your uncle Dhondiba and then some more. Come to me."

She bowed and touched his feet. He tenderly blessed her. Then he turned his attention to Varshika.

"Ah! Whom do we have here? It is Varshika, the unique one, the wild one, who finds it very difficult to obey authority. I knew a young Vanar who was exactly like that... but a very long long time ago."

Varshika blushed and then spoke.

"O great one, being an ordinary girl, I'm blessed to have met you."

"Ordinary eh..? I can see a lot of energy flowing in a wild frenzy. Come to me."

She approached him and bowed low. The moment he placed both palms on her head, she felt as if a lightning bolt had struck her. The surge of energy was almost unbearable. Physically, she was in a lot of pain but mentally she felt calm and tranquil. Then he motioned them to sit down. Varshika and Tina sat down in front of him with folded knees.

"Tina, fate has chosen you to be the guardian of the Holy Astra. However, before I hand over the Astra to you, I want you to know the legend of the great Lord. This legend has been passed on from one generation to the other, so some details may have been lost in translation. However, I will narrate all that I know.

Many millennia ago, there existed an eighth continent on earth. It was the smallest but the greatest continent at that time, for it was inhabited by superior beings. It was located far away in the great ocean. The beings that inhabited that continent were different from the ones found on the other seven continents. Those beings had a humanoid form but were far more intelligent than the beings found on earth today. The continent had two kingdoms, the northern kingdom and the southern kingdom that were separated by a mountain range. In due course of time the beings in the northern kingdom began giving importance to the pleasures of the body while the beings in the southern kingdom gave utmost importance to the pleasures of the mind..."

"Sorry to interrupt," said Varshika. *"I did not quite follow..."*

He looked at her and nodded.

"Pleasures of the body mean, giving undue importance to your body rather than your soul. Let me put it this way – the beings in the northern kingdom were addicted to luxuries. They did not eat to live, rather they lived to eat. They used far more than required by them, in order to live a luxurious life, harmed other creatures for their own benefit and believed that the planet existed merely to satisfy their needs rather than believing that they shared the planet with millions of other beings.

Pleasures of the mind mean, achieving the highest level of happiness, peace, love, compassion and contentment. That was what the beings in the southern kingdom wished to achieve. They were ready to undergo physical hardships to achieve mental pleasure.

With the passage of time, the beings of the northern kingdom and southern kingdom evolved into altogether different beings. The beings in the northern kingdom came to be called the 'Asuras' whereas the beings in the southern kingdom came to be called the 'Devas'.

Since the Devas gave importance to their minds, they achieved great mental power in due course of time. They had total control over their minds. Some of them even evolved such mental strength, that they could move matter with the energy of their minds and others could change their form for short intervals of time by rearranging their molecular structures. Then others could control the elements of the weather in their immediate surroundings by using their mental energy. Also there were few, who could reverse the effects of gravity and levitate themselves or other objects. Since they were so full of compassion, they never hurt other living beings and strove hard to maintain the balance in the environment.

The Asuras, on the other hand, developed scientifically, due to their superior brains and weakness for luxury. They built such machines that would make your present supercomputers look like toys. They had found a way to use gold to generate large amounts of energy in the presence of sunlight. This material was woven into their roofs. Hence the northern kingdom glowed in the sunlight and looked like a city of gold. The Asuras achieved all that the Devas had achieved, but by using what you call 'science'.

The Asuras lived extremely cunning, corrupt and indulgent lives. They only cared about themselves and were ready to betray even each other for personal gain. However they lived luxuriously at the expense of the surroundings. When they had exhausted the resources of their continent, they began exploiting the other continents. Then finally the Asuras began playing 'God'.

The universe itself exists because of a delicate balance between the good and bad energies. The bad energy is distributed evenly throughout the universe and the good energy that exists in clusters tries to balance the bad. It is the good energy that we call 'God' and God exists all around us and within us. So though we tend to be basically bad, the good within us tries to prevent us from doing bad. However the Asuras concentrated such bad energy within them that the good inside them became negligible.

When the Asuras achieved highest excellence in science, they decided to become immortal. They began experimenting ways to live forever. Firstly, they modified their genes to filter out any irregularities or shortcomings. So within a span of a couple of generations they had become almost flawless beings. Then they began experiments on regeneration and were successful to a great extent. They began to live for many centuries. But even that did not make them immortal. So finally they devised a method to clone their bodies. Then they transferred their thoughts and memories to a super computer and transferred it back to the newly cloned body.

However, every coin has two sides. The cloning experiments started going very wrong as the entire memory couldn't be transferred to the newly cloned bodies. The newly formed creatures began developing severe abnormalities. Some grew very huge and strong. They craved more food. They came to be called the 'Rakshasas'. Then others developed a craving for flesh – especially human flesh. They came to be called the 'Pishachs'. Soon many other evil creatures evolved.

The period became the darkest period in the history of our planet. Those evil creatures began occupying the other continents and committed atrocities on the beings inhabiting the other continents. The ones to suffer the most were the ancestors of the human beings. They were rounded up and reared like cattle, only to be consumed later. The women and the weak humans suffered the most.

When evil crosses a limit, the good energy has to counter it, in order to restore the balance. Since, we are inferior beings and do not have the capacity to understand the good energy in its natural form, the energy has to enter our form and convey its message to us. However, it has to enter a special being – one who can withstand the energy. If that energy were to enter a common being, the being would vaporize, as our bodies are too fragile to accommodate such a large amount of energy. But rarely, a few of us are born with bodies and minds strong enough to accommodate that energy.

In that era, the good energy entered the body of a brave young prince – our great Lord. He was the son of the king of the southern kingdom. He was both, physically and mentally beautiful. He was extremely handsome and good looking but was very loving and compassionate. He loved all creatures and took great efforts to protect the weak. Right from a very young age, he fiercely opposed the atrocities committed by the evil beings. The great one, sent envoys to the kingdom of the Asuras, humbly requesting them to change their ways. He requested them to show compassion to the planet. However his pleas fell on deaf ears.

When his requests were turned down, he undertook a journey to the other continents and began helping the oppressed creatures. It was on one of his many expeditions that he met the Vanars and our great ancestor pledged to be his servant for eternity, though the great Lord took him as a brother. These actions of the great Lord did not go well with the Asuras and they began troubling the Devas. The Devas, on account of their mental abilities were unperturbed. This angered the Asuras even more and their king, who was an extremely arrogant but smart being decided to personally hurt the young prince.

The prince then sent a final message to the great Asura king to change his ways and bow down to the power of the good. He warned the Asura king that his excessive pride would lead to his fall and that one shouldn't go against the laws of nature. Everything that is born has to die, so that others may be born. This cycle of birth and death has to continue for the universe to exist.

The Asura king retaliated by launching a very powerful bomb on the kingdom of the Devas. A weapon of such massive destruction had never been launched before. However, the great Lord, assisted by our great ancestor, managed to turn back to weapon. It finally exploded over the kingdom of the Asuras and set their city on fire. The intense heat caused the gold on their roofs to evaporate and it rained gold. Thus began the greatest war in all history.

The war was fought on all the continents. The Devas, merely using the power of their minds, countered all the weapons of the Asuras. When it became apparent that the Asuras were losing, the Asura king launched a final weapon. He launched a weapon into the sun itself. The resulting burst of energy from the sun was to be directed by a special device onto the kingdom of the Devas and annihilate it. However the Asura king had underestimated the consequence of his action. The burst of energy from the sun was so great, that it would've converted the entire planet into one giant ball of fire.

The great Lord then did his best to dissipate the energy into the surroundings, by opening a portal in space, yet a great deal of energy reached the planet. He finally directed that energy into the eighth continent so as to save the other continents. That resulted in great earthquakes that tore the great continent to pieces. It sank forever into the ocean in seven days.

The great Lord killed the Asura king single handedly and put an end to his evil reign. He ordered the Devas to round up all the evil creatures. The punishment for such atrocities was, most certainly, death, but the great Lord being compassionate decided to banish the evil ones to another part of the universe through the portal that he had opened.

The Devas had fought fiercely in order to protect the planet but the Great War almost consumed earth. The dust and fumes resulting from the war blocked sunlight and the earth began to freeze. The Devas felt responsible and they too left the planet through the portal. Our great ancestor was so pained by the war that he decided to spend the rest of his days in penance. His tribe loyally followed him to the Himalayas.

Our great ancestor requested the Lord to close the portal, lest the evil ones returned. However the great Lord was reluctant, since the portal was the only way back to this part of the galaxy, if the Devas ever wished to return. To protect the planet, he created three Astras and requested our great ancestor to build three temples, to keep those Astras. The Astras would shield our planet from prying eyes and they have been doing so for millennia.

The temple you are standing in is one of the three temples. The second temple was constructed deep in the continent of Africa. It held the second Astra. The whereabouts of the third temple were kept secret. Only recently did I realize that it is the one located close to your village.

You are aware that our planet is in peril. Those evil creatures have landed on our planet and threaten to wipe out mankind. We will have to close the portal. However, nobody exactly knows how, for it was the Lord who created the portal. The mystery lies in the temple near your village. I have been in deep prayer for a long time now and every time I seek guidance on closing the portal, I have a vision of your temple. Hence I believe that the secret to closing the portal lies within that temple. That must be the reason why those machines have come to the temple. Maybe they want to find a way to fully open the portal so that an invasion of earth will be possible.

Your uncle was the chosen one, but fate had now chosen you

Tina, as the guardian of the Astra. Therefore I now entrust you with the holy relic. Take it to your temple and place it on the altar. The alien king is very ill and I fear the worst. If the failsafe is activated then the Astra will be the only line of defence between you and the machines. Therefore it is imperative that you reach the temple soon.

Mind you, this is a very powerful relic and only the chosen ones may touch it. Anyone else touching it will surely perish. So be very careful with it. Moreover, I am also asking you to hurry up because the Astra is the lifeline of the Holy City. This city cannot last long without it. The super volcano below the city will erupt without it.

"But, then how will you exist if you give it to her?" asked a worried Varshika.

"Don't fret, little one. As soon as the Astra is taken from its pedestal, I will go into deep prayer and keep the volcano under control until the Astra is returned back to its place. This frail old Vanar still has a few tricks left in him.

Without a further word, he got up and beckoned to someone. The high priest, who had been standing just outside the door of the inner sanctum of the temple came in and bowed. The Abbot tenderly touched his head. He then looked at the girls who abruptly stood up.

"Let us bow before the great one and humbly beg of him to reveal the Astra, for it has been hidden here for millennia. It is somewhere in or on the idol, that is the reason why nobody except the Abbot touches the idol."

The Abbot stood right in front of the huge idol, with the girls to his right and the high priest to his left. The four of them then went on their knees and bowed. The entire temple seemed to be reverberating with energy. When they opened their eyes and looked at the idol, one object caught their eye. It was shaped like a conch shell, was glowing and seemed to be radiating energy. Had it been there before? Nobody could tell, although it must've remained unnoticed for many centuries. It seemed to be made of a material hitherto unknown to mankind.

131

The Abbot stood up, once again folded his hands in front of the idol and carefully picked up the Astra with both hands. He handed it to Tina, who was yet on her knees. Tina could feel each cell in her body tingle. She was so overwhelmed that tears began to flow from her eyes. The surroundings seemed to dissolve and she felt as if she were in the core of the sun with energy radiating from around her. The Abbot gently placed a hand over her shoulder and urged her to rise. She rose unsteadily and slowly looked around her. Gradually the temple came into focus. Varshika was standing beside her, wide eyed.

The Abbot then took the Astra from Tina's hands and carefully placed it inside what seemed like an ancient money purse. He secured it, by pulling both the strings and once again handed it to her.

"Go in peace little ones. May the Lord protect you from all peril and may you prove your mettle and worth. "

He then looked directly at the high priest.

"Trust you will ensure that the little ones and the injured man are delivered safely near their camp. I will now go into meditation and should not be disturbed until the relic is returned to the temple."

They looked at him one last time before they left. He smiled at them weakly. His eyes were slightly moist. Then they followed the high priest out of the inner sanctum of the temple.

"I have arranged for you to be taken back to a spot near your camp. Four strong Vanars will accompany you. Two will carry your uncle Dhondiba, who is wrapped in a special cloth and the other two will carry you. I have instructed them to place your uncle in a small cave very close to the camp. He will be safe there. You two can then proceed to the camp and summon help. You will be handed your clothes and the equipment carried by your uncle. It may come in handy. May the Lord be with you."

He led them to four Vanars who were waiting with folded hands. The girls approached them boldly. They were not scared anymore. After bidding them goodbye, the high priest went back into the temple. The girls knew that they had a long journey ahead.

October 16ᵗʰ, 11pm (earth time) Spaceship

A jolt threw them off their beds.

"What the..." Sri cursed as he looked around. Guru was lying, a few feet away, half on the floor and the other half on the bed.

The hologram of Queen Xixandra appeared.

"You are out of the portal and in our part of the universe."

"How far away are we from Xixipoo?" asked Sri.

"Two hours away."

"Have you guys gained control of the ship yet?" asked Guru, composing himself a bit.

"Not yet," said the hologram with a hint of despair. "But don't worry, you guys. If we do not gain control in the next hour, I am getting my ship ready, to be beside you when you land."

"Hope they don't blow us up?" said Sri rather alarmed.

"Don't be a fool," said Guru. "If they wanted to blow us up, why bring us here? They could've done it on earth. They want us alive."

"That's what I am scared of."

"Don't worry," said the holograph. "I will get you out of here safely, even if that's the last thing I do."

"Get dressed and hurry up to the cockpit," said the holograph of Xixandra. "I need to give you a crash course on how to fly this ship."

"We're ready right now."

"Get dressed! The climate here is not at all like that on earth, and a couple of teens in nothing but shorts will attract all the carnivores from quite a distance."

"Sane advice," said Guru, "...getting dressed up in a jiffy."

"Does the ship have weapons?" asked Sri.

"Yes," said the queen's holograph, "but you need the king's DNA to activate them."

"Darn!"

The boys spent the next half hour getting dressed up in protective suits and gobbled a meal. They spent the next hour in the cockpit receiving last minute instructions about the craft. Then a huge screen appeared in front of them and on it they saw a huge yellow planet.

"That's Xixipoo? In real time, or is it a recording?"

"It's Xixipoo alright."

"Got control yet?" asked Guru.

"No," said the Queen. "But I am airborne and will be close to you in fifteen minutes."

The cockpit underwent a transformation as holographic windows appeared on all sides. Now it was possible for them to get a glimpse of everything that was happening all around them. Due to the holographic screens, it was as if they were seated in a glass room. Five minutes later they saw a tiny dot approaching them, getting larger by the minute. It was probably Queen

Xixandra's craft. Then three more dots appeared at different positions. At that moment, Xixandra's holographic image appeared. She seemed in the cockpit of a craft.

"Brace yourselves, we have company."

"What do you mean?"

"There are three more crafts approaching you and I do not know if they are friendly or hostile. You will be in their firing range in the next five minutes."

Sri immediately jumped into the pilot's seat as Guru looked on. The gel like substance covered him.

"Who put you in charge?" asked Guru crossly.

"Don't be an idiot!" said Sri even more cross. "I am taking precautions, just in case we gain control of the craft. Moreover I am a much better rider than you."

"Says who?"

"Remember last year's cross country race in Batatawadai Puram?"

"Yeah," said Guru, "we stood last."

"Yes," said Sri. "That was because of the unique circumstances that we faced then, else I would have won."

"That's unfair," said Guru. "I too had a very good chance of winning."

"But what's wrong if I maneuver the craft? You can handle the weapons."

"No problem," said Guru, "But if you crash this craft or get us killed because of your stupidity, I will rip your heart out."

So Guru got into the other seat and was covered by the gel like substance. The four crafts had become visible and it was obvious that they were moving towards their craft. Then, without the hint of a provocation, two of the crafts started attacking the third one. There was a lot of shooting and when a stray shot almost hit their craft, it shuddered. The queen's holograph appeared once again.

"One of the crafts is friendly and two are hostile. I am entering the fray, trying to help the friendly craft."

The boys saw the complex maneuvers of the four crafts as they engaged in battle. The fight continued for some time. The two hostile crafts concentrated their fire on the craft of Queen Xixandra, but she dodged each shot with skilled maneuvers. After all she was the best pilot in all of Xixipoo. With their attack-plan foiled, the enemy changed tactics. One enemy craft turned to the boys craft and attacked it, but the other friendly craft came to their aid. The boys tried to jump off their seats. However, whoever was controlling their craft was almost as skilled as Queen Xixandra. Their craft too began maneuvering skillfully. Then the ships computer spoke.

Weapons control has been handed to you. Defend the craft.

"Yesss..!" said Guru. "Some alien butt is going to get kicked."

Two joysticks appeared on the seat beside his hands and quick instructions were given. He could spin his chair to get a view of the crafts around and worked in synchronization with whoever was maneuvering the craft. Guru remembered the numerous times when he and Sri had played with his Xbox. He was the unbeaten champion of Batatwadai Puram. Now it was three against two with Guru shooting at the enemy craft.

137

Everything seemed to be going on well when disaster struck. The queen's craft got hit and was on fire. But before descending, she managed to blow up one of the hostile crafts. Now it was two of them versus the remaining enemy hostile craft.

The enemy was skilled, and attacked the two crafts vigorously, but the one controlling their craft had an edge over the enemy. So they managed to dodge the enemy, every time they were attacked.

Then Guru struck gold. He managed to hit one edge of the enemy craft and they went into defensive mode. A second direct hit almost pulverized them, but before bursting into a flame, two bright lights shot out of the enemy ship towards them. However, in the nick of time the other friendly craft came in between and took the hit, thus sacrificing themselves in order to save the boys. Their craft exploded in a bright glow. After the glare subsided, the boys peered, but the craft had just vanished – vapourized.

We are hit! We are going down. Control of the ship has been transferred to you. You will have to land the ship. I have been given coordinates where to land, and will guide you.

"Yesss...yesss..." said Sri, as he heard the ship's computer.

Sri spent the next few minutes piloting the craft, being closely instructed by the computer. The ship was badly damaged and on the verge of breakdown. The ever increasing temperature indicated that it was ablaze. However, Xixipoo was getting visibly larger with every passing minute. Initially it appeared like a giant yellow ball but soon various landforms became visible. Finally the ship's computer spoke one last time.

"You will land in precisely four minutes. The ship will get destroyed shortly after that, so run as soon as we land. Take only whatever is essential."

The boys waited anxiously as the minutes passed. They were in the atmosphere of the planet and the ship seemed on its last legs. Descending rapidly into what seemed like a very huge desert, they desperately looked around for any signs of life, but there was none. Soon they were close to the surface and could see a vast range of rocky, mountains ahead but the ship was still moving fast. Then without the hint of a warning, the ship slowed down abruptly and landed. A foamy gel like substance (probably some sort of fire retardant) surrounded the ship. And just like that, their magnificent journey ended.

The kind of danger, they were in, dawned upon them when the gel shield disappeared. It was as if they were in an inferno. They jumped out of their seats and rushed to the open door of the space ship. On the way, Guru managed to grab a huge piece of cloth, bigger than a double bed sheet.

"What's with the cloth?" asked Sri.

"Just in case the weather turns bad..."

They rushed out and ran as fast as their feet could carry them, away from the ship and towards the mountain. Once outside, they missed the luxury of the space ship, for the climate was harsh – really harsh. It was colder than they could imagine. When they were a safe distance away, they turned and watched the ship disintegrate.

The boys scanned the surroundings, for it was reasonably bright though the sun was not up. That was because Xixipoo had three moons and incidentally that night all the moons were shining brightly. So though it was night on the planet, it appeared like dawn on earth.

"I feel so bad for the beings in that unknown ship who sacrificed themselves to save us and also our spaceship," said Guru. "It was as if Xixorro's ship was a living being, what say Sri?"

But Sri was not paying attention. His attention was fixed on something far behind. A huge wall was building up, almost reaching the sky.

"It is a sandstorm – a monster sandstorm. Let's get out of here and find shelter."

"Look at those caves," said Guru, pointing to some caves in the mountain. "If we could reach there..."

They began running towards the caves. Guru opened the cloth and both the boys took it over them and ran. The wall of sand was fast approaching them. It threatened to overtake them and if that happened, they surely would perish. They ran as fast as their feet would take them, but were tiring out, firstly because of the biting cold and secondly because the percentage of oxygen in the atmosphere was probably lesser that that on earth.

They barely made it to the caves and ran straight in. It did not occur to them that they were on a different planet and there could be dangerous creatures lurking in the depth of the caves. They just kept running. Surprisingly the small cave seemed to be getting larger and brighter as they moved into its depth, and they stopped when they reached a huge brightly lit structure.

"Where are we?" asked Sri.

"No clue," said Guru. "But I bet, this structure is man-made, or alien made or whatever. Look at the number of exits."

They jumped when something came crashing in. However they were relieved that it was Queen Xixandra. She was close to five feet tall and beautiful as ever. She rushed to them and gave each a hug.

"Am I glad to see you guys? I thought you were goners."

"We thought the same. Where's your ship?" asked Guru.

"It got destroyed! I managed to salvage a small transport vehicle from the ship and followed you guys here."

"We still can't figure who brought us here," said Guru.

"I did!"

Everyone spun around to see who had spoken. She looked stunning in her suit and must've been the age of Guru and Sri. She walked confidently towards them as Guru watched with wide eyes.

"Greetings queen Xixandra!" she said politely, bowing a bit.

"You are..."

"The Evil Princess!" exclaimed Sri, before the queen completed her statement.

The queen looked sternly at Sri and was about to open her mouth to say something when the princess gestured her to stop.

"Hi guys! I'm Amindita, but you can call me Amy, and I am not evil."

"We owe you an apology," said the queen, "I can feel goodness radiate from you."

Guru kept staring at the princess. His heart was pounding and head spinning.

What a beauty! I could get lost in those beautiful eyes. And look at how toned her body is. I wonder if she is an athlete. And just look at those lips – pinker than a rose. She looks so stunning, though she is all covered in that jumpsuit sort of thing. I wonder how...

She abruptly turned angrily and walked towards Guru.

"Know how hard I hit?"

"No."

"Want to know?" she asked clenching a fist.

"N-Nope," said Guru taking a few involuntary steps backwards.

"Then stop staring at me and passing those stupid comments."

"Wh-"

"She is a Sarpousse," warned the queen.

"And what the hell is a Sarpousse?" asked Guru.

"She has the ability to read the minds of people close to her."

Guru, you fool, you blew it. One girl you liked and she can read minds. Yet I wonder how that huge buffalo Mooisausooura can be related to her. She's such a beaut...

She glared at him, but then turned to the queen.

Blew it, blew it.

"We must hurry," she said with urgency in her voice. "The Asourbouts may attack any moment. I have brought these two suits for the boys."

She handed one suit to Sri and the other to Guru, still glaring at him. The boys looked at the strange material of the suit and felt it between their fingers. They had never seen such a material before. It was as light as air, but strangely very tough.

"And put these in your nose," she said, handing each of them, cotton like devices, "they will deliver the precise amount of gases that you need."

I am not changing in front of the ladies, at least not in front of my future girlfriend. I wonder if it is safe to go behind those rocks…

"The rocks are absolutely safe and you can keep your clothes on, just wear the suit above your clothes" she said sharply, "and let's hurry, or you won't have any clothes left on, if the Asourbouts capture you."

Fool! Fool! Can't you keep your mouth shut or rather your thoughts shut.

Amy looked at Guru, a slight smile on her lips then walked to the queen. Sri glared at Guru. He knew, something was going on between the Alien princess and Guru, but couldn't figure what exactly was happening. He was fed up of the mind-reading garbage and wished Guru told him something. However Guru meekly walked towards a clump of rocks, some distance away. Sri took cue and walked towards the other side of the cave, suit in hand. By then Amy had reached the queen.

"Ma'am," said Amy earnestly, "I want you to know that I had no hand in the attack on your people. In fact, till a few days ago, I was virtually a prisoner. The four, who protected me and took care of me, for the last fourteen years, are not with me anymore…"

"Don't worry sweetheart!" said the queen. "I can read your soul and am absolutely confident that you are very pure. The four people, you talked about… were they the ones in the craft that tried to protect the boys from the robot crafts?"

"Yes," said the princess sadly. "It was with their help that I managed to escape from captivity and even bring the boys here. It was from here that we were controlling the boys' craft."

"But their ship turned into a huge ball of fire," shouted Sri from the far end.

"Shut up!" shouted the queen. "For once, let me handle things."

"I know they are..." said Amy, tears building up in her big eyes.

But she didn't have time to complete her statement. Something exploded a few feet away, from the ladies and they were thrown to the ground.

"Run!" shouted the queen getting up. "The Asourbouts have found us."

She ran to where Sri was changing and grabbed him. Amy, in the meanwhile ran towards Guru.

"Follow me," she said, wiping a tear from her eye. "...and do exactly as I say. Your life may depend on it."

The queen looked behind her shoulder to see if Amy and Guru were following her and Sri, but they seemed to be going in the opposite direction. Then she saw an Asourbout running towards her and Sri. She lifted some sort of a weapon and fired. The Asourbout disappeared in a huge ball of fire. One more explosion rocked the cave.

"Where do we meet?" shouted the queen on top of her voice.

"Where life and death converge..."

"I have Sri with me. You and Guru take care."

By then Amy and Guru had entered one of the caves. They heard one gigantic explosion and as Amy turned around, she saw a huge ball of fire following them.

"Run with all your might Guru," she said.

The cave had many twists and turns and the two ran as fast their feet could carry them. The tunnel suddenly divided into two branches in a fork. They paused for a moment, trying to judge, which of the two paths were safe. The princess was aware that the path to the right would lead them out of the caves. She also knew a place, where a couple of transport vehicles were stashed, but was not sure if it was safe anymore. So she peered into the left entrance cautiously. An explosion threw her off her feet and she cried out in pain. Guru ran to grab her, but she turned and waved to him.

"Don't touch me," she said, pain in her voice. "Run through the other cave. I will be with you in a moment."

"Whoa!" said Guru, "Just trying to help."

Without paying much attention to Guru, she slipped on, what looked like a glove to her right hand, and got up unsteadily. She cautiously approached the left entrance and pointed her hand in the direction, sending two bolts of light inside. An explosion rocked the place. Then she turned to Guru and gestured him to run.

Both ran into the right entrance and kept running for the next few minutes. Luckily they were not followed. The tunnel seemed to be getting narrower by the minute and abruptly, they came out in the open. The sand storm was still raging on and visibility was limited to a few meters in all the directions. It was apparent that the princess knew what she was doing and so Guru followed her without a word. The path followed by them had a number of twists and turns and Guru was finding it very difficult to keep up with her.

Guru almost bumped into her when she abruptly stopped. He couldn't believe his eyes. Standing in front of them was a motorcycle-like device. It would have been more appropriate to call it a space motorcycle, for it had no wheels, but could seat two. The princess removed the glove from her hand, made some sort of adjustments in it and turned to Guru.

"I will have to fly the craft. So you wear the weapon. I have adjusted it so that it will fire if you point it to a target and bend your forefinger."

Guru took the glove and wore it on his right hand. Strangely it fit snugly. By then the princess had alighted the space motorcycle and seemed to be tinkering with it.

"Are you okay?"

"I'm fine," said the princess. "Just sit behind me, and don't touch me."

"C'mon," said Guru. "What with this touching business..."

She didn't reply, so Guru sat beside her, keeping sufficient distance between them. Something secured him to the craft and an egg shaped shield formed around the craft. Then, without the slightest warning, the craft took off. Soon they were moving rapidly some hundred feet above the ground, at least Guru thought so.

It was now obvious to Guru that the princess was not the one who had controlled their craft. Probably the four noble souls, who had perished trying to save them, were the ones who had controlled their craft and brought them to Xixipoo. Amy seemed a novice and Guru felt the bile rising in his stomach as she flew. He was about to say something when he saw a dot following them.

"We are being followed," said Guru thoroughly alarmed.

"I'll try to lose them. Hang on tight."

Before Guru could protest, she began spinning the craft

and going into loops. However the enemy kept pace and though visibility was poor, he could see the familiar dot following them.

"They're yet following us."

"Then I'll slow down a bit," said the princess. "If they are hostile, they'll surely try to attack us."

"Can't we just escape them," said Guru. "I don't feel so good."

She slowed down just a bit. As the craft came nearer, Guru noticed that it was similar to their own craft, but an Asourbout was piloting it and abruptly attacked them. Their craft shook violently and Guru lifted his hand to fire.

"Don't," shouted the princess. "The shield is up and any shot fired by you will ricochet back into us."

"Then lower the damn shield," shouted Guru.

"I will warn you and lower the shield for a few seconds giving you time to fire at the craft."

"Ok."

So they picked up speed and the princess began her maneuvers while Guru tried not to throw up. Then she warned him that she was lowering the shield and Guru sent a volley of shots towards the enemy. They missed by a mile.

"You don't have too many shots left," said Amy, "we can't afford to miss."

"Easy for you to preach," said Guru. "I can't bear your maneuvers and am going to throw up any minute now."

"Ugg!" said Amy. "Please wait till I lower the shield... shield down."

Guru turned and royally threw up, even as the craft spun and as luck would have it, the barf landed on the occupant of the craft that was following them. The vomit must've landed on a crucial spot on the Asourbout, because it lost control momentarily – time enough for Guru to get a perfect shot. The craft disappeared in a ball of fire.

"Yippie!" shouted Guru. "See, what I can achieve if I am at ease."

She nodded for an answer and Guru felt piqued. After all, hadn't he destroyed an Asourbout? He wondered why she was not impressed by his feats. Maybe, she thought it below her dignity to interact with a mere earthling like him. She continued driving and seemed to be focusing on the path ahead. They travelled at high speed for the next hour or so and may have covered hundreds of kilometers. The sandstorm had cleared out or rather they had left it far behind. Guru looked around and saw a sprawling desert as far as the eye could see. It was a flat sandy desert, except for the few gigantic sand dunes that dotted the terrain after long intervals. As far as Guru was concerned, there was no sign of life below.

As time passed, the terrain below began to change. It steadily became increasingly rocky, with rocky peaks jutting above the ground. These appeared and disappeared below them rather fast, probably because they were travelling at supersonic speeds. Then Guru saw a huge peak dead ahead. Amy didn't seem to notice it and was travelling straight towards it.

"Watch out!"

"Uh," said Amy, who seemed only half awake.

However she abruptly became alert and the craft shot right up into the air. They were very close to the huge peak and missed the top by a whisker. As they passed the peak, Guru thought he saw something below, a huge man. But then he thought he must've hallucinated, for if he had indeed seen a man, that man had to be over ten feet tall. That was impossible, so Guru turned around just to confirm. He wished he had hallucinated, for there was a giant standing on the top of the cliff. He had a huge hammer in his hand and flung it with great force towards the craft. Before Guru had any time to yell or alert Amy, the hammer hit the craft and they spun around as they descended. Amy managed to land relatively softly behind a clump of huge rounded rocks. The duo were thrown off the craft as it hit the sand, skid out of control for another couple of kilometers on its own and exploded.

Guru got on to his feet in a jiffy, because he had landed in very soft sand and except for a few bruises, was okay. He rushed to Amy who lay sprawled in the sand on her back. It was then that Guru noticed blood on her jumpsuit, on the left side of her abdomen. He also saw some kind of a shaft sticking out of her jumpsuit. He realized that she had been injured, not then but probably when she had been ambushed in the caves at the junction. The shaft had pierced her then. He approached her. She was barely conscious and mumbling something, so he put his ear close to her mouth.

"It's a Rakshousse," she mumbled. "Leave me here. Run away and save yourself."

He went to touch her, in order to comfort her, but she raised a hand defensively.

"Don't touch me... Run away... You stand no chance."

Then she collapsed. Guru looked around confused what to do. He distinctly heard a whirring sound as something crashed into the rocks, sending a shower of rocks over them. He rushed to the clump of rocks that was the only protection they had and carefully peered towards the cliff. The

Rakshousse was still standing on the cliff with the huge hammer in his hand. He swung it once again towards the rocks. Guru ducked as the hammer came whirring towards the rocks. Then as before, it hit the rocks and returned to its owner, who caught it with precision. The creature held his hammer high and seemed to be laughing.

Something snapped inside Guru. He was not going to take such garbage from the Rakshousse or whatever that oaf was. He decided that it was time to kick some Rakshousse backside. Noticing that Amy was lying in a vulnerable position he rushed to her and dragged her to the safety of the rocks. He ensured that she was well in the shade, since it was extremely hot by then. Satisfied, she was safe for the moment, he turned his attention to the Rakshousse. The creature was getting ready to descend. Guru knew that would take a long time, probably an hour, for the cliff was really high, but he was so wrong. Taking giant leaps that would put the best of apes to shame the Rakshousse began descending the huge cliff.

Guru knew he had to act fast, if they were to survive. He noticed the weapon in his right hand and remembered that he did not have too many shots left. Every shot had to count. He aimed carefully at the creature and discharged his weapon. The creature was too fast for him and jumped sideways with surprising agility and began to descend even faster. It was as if Guru was seeing a character in one of the video games of the late ninety's. The creature kept appearing and disappearing.

There was no doubt that the creature was strong and agile, but Guru was smart. He aimed his weapon and fired to the left of the creature and then to the right, then again repeated the sequence. When he was convinced that the creature was trapped in a particular position, he kept on firing at the cliff above the creature – firing, till his weapon ran out of juice. He had exhausted his shots, but a smile appeared on his lips, for the part of the cliff above the creature gave way and tons of rocks came crashing on the creature, before it could escape.

"That takes care of the Rakshousse," said Guru to himself, namely because there was no one around and Amy was unconscious.

Guru then turned his attention to Amy. She lay on the sand, motionless. He bent to her and put a finger below her nose, relieved to find her still breathing. Then he gently touched her cheek and felt energy surge through his body. It felt as if he had received a jolt of high voltage. He couldn't understand the strange phenomenon, but concluded that it must have something to do with climate on the alien planet. He didn't bother much about what had happened, since he had urgent tasks at hand.

He carefully removed her blood soaked jumpsuit and was surprised to find that she had worn clothes that resembled ones worn on earth. She had a flexible flask attached to her left hip. Guru undid the flask and opened its cap. The clear liquid inside resembled water, but he had to be sure. So he brought the flask to his lips and sipped a little. However he did not swallow the liquid and kept it in his mouth for some time. When he was convinced the liquid was indeed water, he gulped a little. Putting the flask to Amy's mouth, he poured a little water in and was satisfied to see her gently swallow it. Her eyes opened a bit and she mumbled a few words that were inaudible and passed out again.

The pierced shaft would have to be pulled out of her body, but before doing that Guru needed something to stop the bleeding that would follow. He was lost in a desert – a desert located on some far off planet, about which he knew very little. The chances of survival were slim. Then he remembered the sheet of cloth that he had folded and tucked in between his back and the jumpsuit. He had hidden the sheet because he had not wanted to appear like a sissy, carrying a sheet. But at that time had instinctively felt that the cloth would come in handy and how right he was. He opened his jumpsuit and pulled out the huge cloth. It was bigger than a bed sheet, but extremely thin and light. Guru tore a strip from the sheet and divided it into two pieces, one piece he folded into a pad and the other he kept as a bandage. Now all he needed was something to prevent the wound from getting infected, but where would he get an antiseptic in the desert.

Guru tried hard to recollect what he had learnt about Xixipoo, on the spaceship and remembered the Xibora – a plant freely available on Xixipoo, whose leaves had antiseptic properties. He would have to venture out in search of the Xibora, but how could he leave Amy there? She lay there in the sand, injured and incapable of defending herself. What if more Asourbouts or Rakshousse attacked? But sitting there and doing nothing was not going to help. Their chances of survival were sharply declining by the minute. Guru decided that he would make Amy as comfortable as possible and travel in widening circles to locate the Xibora plant. However he would keep her in sight at all times.

Before leaving, Guru ensured that Amy was comfortable. He folded her jumpsuit into a pillow and placed it beneath her head. Then taking the cloth over him, he ventured out of the shade. The search was excruciating, but after three quarters of an hour, he located Xibora plant amidst some rocks. He collected as many leaves as possible and went to Amy. She was still unconscious. Guru put as many Xibora leaves as would fit in his mouth and chewed them to form a paste. This paste he put on the cloth pad that he had made earlier and kept it beside Amy. He slightly tore her shirt around the wound so that the wound was accessible. Then holding the shaft in his right hand, he pulled it out in one clean jerk. It must've caused terrible pain to Amy, for she momentarily opened her eyes, trembled violently, tried to get up and then collapsed. Guru felt bad for her. Blood poured out of the open wound and he had to act fast. He pressed the cloth pad with the Xibora leaf paste firmly against the wound and tied the bandage around her stomach. He also cleaned up the blood from around the wound and finally sat down with a sigh. He examined the wound some fifteen minutes later and was satisfied that the bleeding had stopped.

Thoroughly tired, Guru decided to get some rest, so he lay down beside Amy. He must've drifted off to sleep, for he had the most terrible nightmares and woke up in a cold sweat. He glanced around hurriedly and an involuntary shriek escaped his lips. They were surrounded by hideous creatures – two foot worms, all waiting to attack. He had not forgotten the virtual sting from the spaceship and was up in a jiffy and began running around and kicking the creatures. Initially they put up a fight, but Guru became all the more violent, so they buried themselves in the sand and disappeared.

Guru knew that they weren't safe there. The creatures would probably regroup and attack them. Amy was still unconscious. He felt for a pulse and was relieved to find one. They had to leave the place. It would be best to travel and hope that the Queen and Sri found them. He wondered if Amy had any sort of communication device, and even if she did, what difference would that make? Anyway he did not know how to use their devices, and what if the Asourbouts intercepted the message? Then it would be curtains for them. Still he searched her to see if she had any device that he would probably recognize. He found nothing. He then checked her water bottle and found very little water left, but that was not a problem as he knew the whereabouts of a stream and could refill the bottle. He wondered if he should stay put and wait for a rescue team, but decided against that. It would be better to travel rather than wait there and be eaten alive by God knows what.

He wanted to make one more trip to the stream to fill his bottle and wet the huge cloth, but did not dare leave Amy alone, lest the worms returned. So he lifted her and slung her over his shoulder, fireman style and began walking towards the stream. Once there, he ensured that they were safe and laid her down gently. There he refilled the water flask and thoroughly wet the huge cloth in the stream. He also collected a number of Xiboras and tied them in one of the jumpsuits. After securing the jumpsuit thoroughly, he ate a few Xiboras and found the taste awful, but that was better than starving.

Having collected rations, Guru once again checked on Amy. She stirred a bit, so Guru touched her reassuringly. She opened her eyes, mumbled a few words that did not make sense and passed out. Guru decided to move on, so lifted her and slung her on his shoulder once again, covered both with the wet cloth and began his journey into the unknown.

After travelling for many hours, Guru began losing hope. He was terribly tired, not because he was carrying the princess, for she was surprisingly light, but because of the terrible heat. Maybe he should have camped near the stream and Xibora plants, maybe he should've waited for Amy to get better, but somehow he felt that he had to keep travelling. The only other time he had felt the same way was when he had been drawn to their temple in Batatwadai Puram. He remembered his village, parents, friends and Tina. Was Tina safe? What if the

Asourbouts had caused them harm? They did not possess the advanced weapons that the Xixipians possessed. Had earth been destroyed? Then again he felt drawn in a particular direction and reluctantly walked in the direction one painful step after another. He knew that his strength was fast deserting him...

October 17th, 5 am (earth time)
Xixidorra Desert

They were travelling at breathtaking speed, faster than Sri had ever travelled before. The queen and Sri had been travelling like that for the past three hours and a lot had happened in those three hours. Firstly, after reaching a safe zone and pulverizing all the Asourbout crafts that had been following them, the queen had contacted her people. Dispatch teams had been sent in the general direction where the Princess and Guru had gone. The queen was confident that they would be found soon, for the princess had given her a clue where she was heading. She had mentioned that they would meet where life and death converged. There were a few such places on the planet and the one nearest to where they had met was some three hundred kilometers away. It was a strip of land, a few kilometers wide and fifty kilometers long, bordering the habitable zone and the dead zone on the planet.

"We will reach Xixarappa soon," said the queen. "It appears that our scientists have perfected the device that will help us defeat the Asourbouts once and for all."

"That's great," said Sri. "Any news of Guru yet..?"

"None, so far," said the queen, "and we better find them fast, for we cannot deploy the device unless they are found."

"What device?"

"One which will cut out communication between the Asourbouts and their master," said the queen, "one that will probably fry every electronic device on the planet."

156

"What...?"

"That's the only way..." said the queen, "the Master Computer is getting powerful by the minute and has to be stopped, if the planet has to be saved."

"But who could've created such a computer?" asked Sri. "And you say that they were already on the planet when you returned?"

"Yes," said the queen, "and what is strange, is that there is no trace of the craft that brought them here. All the crafts that they presently have are the ones destroyed in our war. The Master Computer somehow refurbished them. Even the Asourbouts have been created, using our technology and devices that remained after we devastated our planet."

"Could they have been here all along?"

"Impossible!" said the queen. "We launched the final assault on King Xixorro and his people some fourteen earth years ago and I can assure you that our planet was cold and dead by then. After that we lived on our space ships and fought for about twelve years, mostly in space, almost destroying our entire race. Finally we reached earth..."

"You reached Batatawadai Puram," said Sri, "and luckily, you didn't kill Guru and me, so you are alive and married to the king."

"C'mon," said the queen, "I had not intended to kill you and Guru, just fired a warning shot."

"Yeah!" said Sri, "and blew a hole the size of a car, inches from where we were hidden."

"Thanks to you guys," said the queen suppressing her emotions, "I have a loving husband and family and our planet lives. I only hope he is alive..."

"Now relax and have faith," said Sri putting a hand on her shoulder. "King Xixorro is in Batatawadai Puram and I assure you they will find a way to save him. You will be reunited soon."

"Yes we will, and you guys will go home safely. I will not let those Asourbouts come in the way – not anymore. We have already lost a lot and I won't let bad things happen to our planet as well as yours."

Sri had comforted the queen with his encouraging words, but was finding it difficult to control his own emotions. He summed up his situation - he was on a far away planet, couldn't contact earth and was separated from the only person who could offer him any solace. He pined for his beloved village, his parents, friends and his cousin Varshika. He wondered what Tina and Varshika were doing at that moment. Were they trying to find a way to communicate with him, or were they tending to the ailing king? He wondered if his parents were safe. Had they gone to the police, and what of the Asourbouts? He had seen them in action and knew that they were capable of destroying earth. What if the deadly virus spread on earth?

Sri was so lost in thought that he did not notice the small speck in the vast desert. Only when the speck got bigger, did he realize that they were fast approaching Xixarappa – the city of the queen. It was exactly as seen in the virtual tour on the spaceship. They reached the flat top of the huge mountain. Xixarappa lay buried more than a mile inside the mountain. A huge hatch opened and they descended into darkness. Once they reached the city, it became bright as if they were out in the open. Xixandra neatly parked their egg shaped craft next to other crafts. There were a number of Xixipians waiting to receive them.

Sri was overwhelmed by the reception, for his

reputation preceded him. Word spread that the savior of Xixipoo had arrived and everyone was eager to get a glimpse of him. A couple of female Xixipians ran to him and kissed him on the cheeks. Sri did not recognize them but was later told by the queen that they were part of her entourage who had visited Batatawadai Puram. His mind went back to the time when King Xixorro and Queen Xixandra were sworn enemies and had pledged to destroy one another. He distinctly remembered how the king's craft had crashed near Gendamal's farm and how they had ultimately managed to broker peace between the two warring factions. The Xixipians had enjoyed their hospitality for an entire week before leaving for Xixipoo. Guru and he had been instrumental in ending the civil war that had ravaged the planet for nine hundred years.

They were ushered into a huge structure. This structure had royalty written all over it and Sri guessed that he probably was inside the palace of the queen. He had never seen anything so magnificent before. They were lead to a section where chariot like devices were neatly parked.

"Please get in," said the queen.

Sri got in and the queen followed suit. Once in, the queen gave the command and immediately the chariot rose up and started moving at a reasonably slow pace. It was similar to a hovercraft.

"Can I remove the device sticking out of your nose? You won't need it here," said the queen moving her hand towards Sri's nose.

Sri instinctively reached for his nose. He touched the device sticking out of his nose. The female Xixipians had probably dislodged the device when they had kissed Sri. The princess had given it to them before the Asourbouts had attacked. He wondered what Guru and the princess were doing at that moment and wished they were safe.

They travelled for a few minutes and were greeted loudly by all the Xixipians who saw them.

"How many of you are there?" asked Sri.

"About three hundred of us remain," said the queen, "but I would like you to meet two special Xixipians before we meet the scientists and start our work."

Sri looked quizzically at her, but she did not give any further clarifications. The chariot came to a halt abruptly and both got down. The queen now led Sri through a long passage and into a huge structure that resembled a kindergarten. A female attendant approached them and bowed to the queen. She gave Sri a quick glance and led them further in a room where toys lay scattered. A number of babies were crawling around. She led them to two babies playing in one corner.

"What have these two been doing in my absence?" asked the queen.

"This one managed to escape out of the nursery and the other one almost rode away in one of the chariots," said the attendant rather nervously.

"Sri," said the queen looking directly at him. "Meet the princes of Xixipoo – Xixisri and Xixiguru. The king and I named them after you guys, and mark my words they may very well turn out like you two."

"Wonderful," said Sri as he gently lifted the tiny babies in both his arms.

The babies looked at him and giggled. Then without a hint of provocation, one of them poked a finger into his eye.

"Ouch, I believe you," said Sri as he handed the babies to the queen who cuddled them affectionately.

She handed the babies to the nurse and turned to Sri.

"Let's go to the scientists and see what they have developed."

They went by hover-chariot to another part of the city. Whereas the residential area of the city had been clean and green, this part looked technical. They entered a huge structure and saw about a dozen Xixipians tinker with what looked like a huge sphere with a number of projections sticking out of it. They looked distinctly like scientists and Sri wondered if scientists looked alike, all over the universe. On seeing them, the chief scientist approached and slightly bowed in front of the queen. He then took Sri's hands in his own and shook it violently.

"Welcome to Xixipoo, boy! I am the chief scientist and my name is Xixiklaam."

"Has the device been perfected?" asked the queen.

"Yes ma'am," he said. "Once deployed, it will send pulses of powerful waves all around the planet. Anything that is essentially electronic will stop working – even all our devices."

"Get the device ready, but we will wait to deploy it until Guru and the princess are found."

"We cannot wait for long ma'am," said Xixiklaam. "The Master Computer has probably located us and as we speak, a fleet of warships with Asourbouts are assembling at Xixibamba. If they reach us, we will be massacred and our planet, as well as earth will be destroyed."

"What about the scouts sent by us? Have they found any clue?"

"They have identified the direction in which the princess and boy have gone and are following but it will be too

161

late if we keep waiting for them to locate the duo."

"But once the device is deployed, won't their crafts stop functioning? Then how will they reach Guru and the princess? Have they been able to establish any contact with the boy or the princess?"

"We have sent four crafts and three of them will cease to function once the device is deployed, but one craft will continue functioning."

"How come..?"

"Because ma'am, it is a mechanical device, like the ones found on earth. It travels very slowly but will not be affected by our rays."

"What about the princess' craft?" asked the Queen, "Will it cease to function?"

"I'm afraid so," said the scientist, "but she will have enough time to land if they have not yet reached their destination. It is true that they may be stranded, but more likely they would've reached their destination by the time we deploy the device."

"How long will it take for you to deploy the device?"

"About half a Xiklaak..."

Sri looked at the queen enquiringly.

"A Xiklaak is almost two earth hours," said the queen, "so we have an hour in our hands. By then we should be able to locate Guru."

"What if the device fails?" asked Sri.

"Then we perish," said the scientist. "From the information we have, they are expected to leave in a Xiklaak."

"Then go ahead and deploy the device," said the queen. "Do you have any more of those mechanical crafts?"

"Yes ma'am, we had built two of them. Let me show you."

He took them to another part of the structure.

"A World War I airplane," said Sri looking at what the scientist showed. "Guru is crazy behind these things. It has a petrol engine."

"Brilliant!" said the queen. "Get the device ready. Sri and I shall leave in this craft as soon as the device is deployed."

Preparation began in full swing, for deploying the device and also for the queen's journey. After a quick snack, the queen and Sri were given instructions on flying the airplane. They wore a special suit that would protect them to some extent from the elements and got ready to fly. Both the craft and energy device were hoisted to the top of the mountain. A tower like structure had already been erected to hold up the device. Hopefully it would cause damage to the Asourbout army and their crafts.

Sri and Xixandra reached just in time to see the device being deployed. Sri felt the hair on the nape of his neck stand and his body tingle, as the device began operating. A brief check revealed that all electronic devices in the vicinity had ceased to function. Xixiklaam mentioned that soon the energy radiated by the device would spread all over the planet by repeatedly bouncing off a charged layer in their atmosphere. What effect would the rays have on the Asourbouts and the master computer? Nobody could answer that with certainty - only time would tell.

After giving last minute instructions, the queen got into the cockpit of the tiny airplane. Sri occupied the copilot's cockpit behind her and they took off from the flat top of the mountain. It took the queen about ten minutes to get the hang of flying the small aircraft, but soon she began flying the craft as if she been flying such crafts her entire life. The Xixipians must've been brilliant scientists to make such airplanes in a very short span of time. The queen told Sri that there was one basic difference between the airplane they were flying and the ones used in World War I on earth. The Xixipians had used a composite solid fuel that slowly got converted to fumes. The airplane would not need to be refueled for thousands of kilometers and they were carrying sufficient extra fuel.

Thus Xixiandra and Sri set out on their mission to locate Guru and Amy. Sri instinctively felt that a lot more was about to happen...

October 17ᵗʰ, 4 am (earth time) Himalayas

Varshika knew that dawn was fast approaching. They had been travelling for some time now, but the circumstances were very different as compared to their ascent. Both the girls were conversing (via their thoughts) with the Vanars carrying them.

However the journey down was far more perilous as compared to their ascent. Varshika and Tina were being carried by a Vanar each whereas two Vanars were carrying Uncle Dhondiba in a makeshift stretcher.

Before they had left, the Vanars had fed some kind of liquid to Uncle Dhondiba. It was meant to put him in a deep sleep so that he, in his precarious condition would not be uncomfortable during the descent. After a teary farewell the group had left the holy city of the Vanars and had begun their descent to the so called civilized world. Varshika wondered if it would be right to call the human world 'civilized', for elsewhere there were beings so civilized that would put humans to shame. The Vanars lived a simple and pure life, took care of one another and selflessly guarded the planet while most humans spent each waking hour thinking of new ways to exploit the planet, in order to make their lives more comfortable.

They had spent most of the time chatting with the Vanars, who had been carrying them like babies – only when the terrain got very dangerous did the Vanars politely request them to remain silent so that they could concentrate on descending. Twice, during the journey the Vanars had requested to switch carrying the girls. Whichever Vanar was carrying Tina, seemed to be losing all energy in a short time. It must've had something to do with the powerful Astra that she had had, clutched so close to her bosom. The other Vanars too had had a tough time carefully carrying the limp body of Uncle Dhondiba, for they did not want him accidentally hurt. He was out cold and probably had no idea that he was undertaking such a dangerous journey.

Presently the Vanars stopped and looked at each other, then at the girls and pointed to something below. The girls strained their eyes to see what exactly the Vanars were pointing to. In the distance they saw tiny structures that looked like tents. It was their camp, but far away. The Vanars must've had very powerful vision to spot something that the girls had found difficult to spot even though they were pointed to the exact location of the camp. After travelling for another ten minutes the Vanars slowed down, looked around a little and then took the girls to a small shallow cave. Uncle Dhondiba was carefully placed on the floor of the cave ensuring that he was comfortable. The Vanars also placed his rucksack beside him. Thoroughly satisfied by their work, they turned to the girls.

"We will leave now, dear ones," said a Vanar named Vibhushan. *"Your uncle will be safe in this cave. It will take you less than twenty minutes to reach flat ground. Your camp is another ten minutes away. Go safely, for the mountains are very treacherous in these parts. Watch out for crevices. There are many, hidden below the ice. One false step can send one plunging a hundred feet below to one's death. Use that rope there to secure yourselves to each other. We would've gladly taken you right to your camp, but unfortunately, it will be dawn in a short time and we cannot risk being seen by the others. We will have to rush back. We all will pray for you to succeed in your mission. Please do not forget that our lives too are in your tender hands."*

The Vanar-escorts bid the girls farewell and began ascending the mountain. The girls were astounded by their agility and firm grip, for within a span of five minutes, they had disappeared.

"I'll lead the way," said Tina.

"Fine with me," said Varshika. "But let us secure ourselves with this nylon rope."

After they had secured the nylon rope to their waists, they began their slow descent. Tina led the way, followed by Varshika. Their descent was very slow and Varshika couldn't help but wonder how Tina had managed to climb the high cliff with such agility, just twenty four hours ago. She had climbed as if possessed - possessed by the devil. That was what Varshika had thought till they had met the noble Vanars.

Suddenly Tina slipped and landed with a thud.

"Watch it," said Varshika. "Is the Astra safe?"

"I have it safe," assured Tina.

Varshika reached her and helped her to her feet. When they looked up, both screamed simultaneously for right in front of them, some ten feet away, were three evil looking men dressed in white. They had mean-looking guns in their hands.

"Get them," commanded one, to the others.

"Run for your life," yelled Varshika as she began to run.

With a surge of adrenaline in their veins, the girls began running, Varshika in the lead, followed by Tina. They had not run for more than two minutes pursued by the men, when Tina let out a blood curdling yell. The ground under her just gave way and she plunged into a crevice hidden under the snow.

When Varshka heard Tina scream, she instinctively dropped to the ground and tried to dig in, until she felt the tug on her stomach. Slowly she began to slip towards the crevice, for she was tied securely to Tina.

"Tina, are you okay?"

"I'm dangling here. There is no place where I can grip the walls."

"Stop struggling," said Varshika. "With every tug, the nylon rope is cutting deeper into me. Is the Astra safe?"

"The Astra is safe."

Varshika kept tugging into the ice and felt something solid. It was a rock buried in the snow. Pleased with the discovery, she gripped on to it tightly. However in a few minutes, she no longer felt pleased, for right in front of her were the thugs whom they had encountered moments ago. The hoodlums must've worked their way around the crevice and were right in front of her. They had mean-looking faces. One of them removed his dark snow goggles.

"This is the other girl," he said with a cruel smile. "The one with the relic is in the crevice."

"Just kill them," said the one with a deep scar on his face, who was obviously the leader. "Do not touch any of them. Let boss figure what to do with that thing."

The man closest to Varshika drew out a pistol and pointed it to her forehead. She looked at him wide eyed. There was nothing that she could do at that moment. Immediately scarface rushed to the man and knocked out the gun from his hands.

"You dumb idiot! Do you want to get us all killed. The noise of the gun will trigger an avalanche. Use your machete."

The man looked irritated, but obeyed. He carefully drew out a huge machete. The blade gleamed in the snow. Varshika looked at the raised blade. It was surely curtains for them. She considered letting go, but then both of them would plunge to their deaths. As these thoughts raced through her mind, she saw someone huge come behind the killers. He swiftly knocked out two of them and reached the man with the machete. With a powerful blow to the jaw, he knocked him out too and immediately grabbed Varshika.

Varshika looked up at the man who had grabbed her. He was huge – very huge. Must've been close to six and a half feet and powerfully built, but had a kind face. He seemed like an educated man – no, not a man, probably a young man.

"Don't worry Varshika, I've got you," he said to an astounded Varshika. "Is Tina safe?"

"Yes, but dangling below," muttered Varshika.

He held on to the nylon rope and began to heave up Tina. Varshika felt much better, as the pressure of the rope on her reduced considerably. She managed to sit up and then screamed once again. One of the thugs had woken up and machete in hand reached the big man, who was busy hauling Tina. The thug began ruthlessly kicking the big man, who was helpless at that moment. If he let go, Tina would plunge into the crevice, taking Varshika with her. Hence he bore the blows silently. Varshika kicked the thug but he hit her hard and knocked her to the ground. By then the other two regained their consciousness and got to their feet.

After kicking the huge man, maybe fifteen times, the thug drew his pistol and pointed it at the big man.

"You have meddled with the wrong people and will die for it, you oaf. You shouldn't have left university..."

Varshika heard two distinct pings as the thug dropped his gun yelling in agony. The man clutched his right hand as blood dripped to the snow, making it red. She strained to see who was approaching them and heaved a sigh of relief as she saw two familiar figures in the distance. Ram and Rahim had come to their rescue. They had sophisticated silenced guns pointed at the trio. One of the other thugs raised his machete, but he too was shot in the hand and dropped it. The three thugs looked at each other and began running away. They were pursued by Ram and Rahim.

The commotion gave enough time for the huge man to safely pull out Tina. He carefully avoided touching Tina who clutched on to the relic. Varshika felt sorry for him. The thug had kicked him so savagely that he was bleeding profusely.

"Thanks for saving us," said the girls earnestly. "Who are you?"

"I am the apprentice of the Abbot of the African temple," he said. "The relic from the African temple has been stolen. We are in hot pursuit of the scoundrel who committed the shameful act. Our Abbot has instructed you to reach your temple as soon as possible and place the relic on the altar. He believes that would create some sort of force field around the temple and protect you against those creatures, at least temporarily."

"But how could someone steal the Astra from the African temple?" asked Tina. "Aren't they protected?"

"Yes they are," he said. "In fact, you must ensure that nobody touches it or they will surely perish. In our case..."

Suddenly they heard shots fire in the distance. With a look of concern in his eyes, Simba began running in the general direction of the shots. He paused a moment and turned back.

"The Abbot may be in trouble. I have to rush. Remember what I told you."

"What is your name?" asked Varshika.

"Simba," he said as he ran away.

The girls looked at each other. They heard more shots

170

in the distance and were a bit confused. Then Tina saw it.

"Varshika, look above you."

In the distance they saw a huge white wall descending towards them.

"It's an avalanche," yelled Varshika. "We have to reach a safe place, else we are doomed."

"Can we reach Uncle Dhondiba's cave?" asked Tina.

"Good idea, run for it."

They reached the cave in time, just before a blanket of snow covered the cave entrance. The avalanche had buried everything in its path, but fortunately they were safe in the cave. Varshika sat squeezed next to Uncle Dhondiba, while Tina sat some distance away, clutching the Relic. Everything around them went silent.

After sitting perfectly silent for about ten minutes, Varshika began fidgeting with Uncle Dhondiba's rucksack.

"What are you doing?"

"Looking for something to dig our way out of here," said Varshika.

She probed the sack, fished out something and let out a low whistle.

"What is it?"

"It is a walkie talkie," said Varshika. "Now let me see if it still works."

She began turning the knobs on the device and was disappointed to hear static. After persistant efforts, the set came to life and she heard someone frantically yelling instructions. It was Gopal from camp.

171

"Help!" yelled Varshika.

"O my God! Who's this?" asked Gopal.

When they revealed who they were, they heard a cry of jubilation from the other end. The girls tried their best to describe where they were. They even got a chance to speak to Tina's father who was relieved to know that the girls were safe and was double pleased that Dhondiba was with them.

The rescue team from 'Astro-Dreams' found the girls an hour later. It took them another hour to transport Uncle Dhondiba and the girls back to the base camp. Tina's father hugged both the girls tightly.

"I thought something bad had happened to you," he said. "You girls have been gone for more than twenty four hours. How did you survive? And, how did you manage to find Dhondiba?"

"Long story," said Tina. "We will fill in all the details on the way back. But we need to get back home urgently – I mean immediately."

The look in her eyes conveyed the urgency to her father. Hence he started making preparations for their immediate departure. The others were curious to know where the girls had been and how had they managed to survive, but Dr. Madhusudan was firm about them leaving urgently. After a lot of discussions, the course of action was planned. Three teams were to be formed. It would be the responsibility of the first team to ensure that Uncle Dhondiba was moved to the nearest hospital. Gopal headed the team. He assured the girls that Dhondiba would be transported swiftly to the nearest hospital for preliminary help and once his condition stabilized, he would be shifted to Shri Haripur. There they had excellent medical facilities and Dhondiba would recover soon. Dr.

Madhusudan reluctantly accepted the proposal, for he would've preferred Dhondiba being shifted to Batatawadai Puram.

The second team, the smallest team, was entrusted the task of taking Dr. Madhusudan and the girls safely to the airstrip. Since communications had been restored, it was possible for them to communicate with the others. They tried contacting Mr. Ishwar, but couldn't get through. However they managed to contact Nath and updated him. Hearing that the Asourbouts had been located raised their spirits a bit but the news that the condition of Xixorro was getting worse by the minute and the fact that there was absolutely no news from the boys, dampened their spirits considerably. Nath promised to convey the message of the rescue of Uncle Dhondiba to their families and everyone at the temple. Dr. Madhusudan requested him to contact Mr. Ishwar so that the aircraft in which they came would be there at the airstrip where they had been dropped the previous day.

Finally a third team was to stay behind, in their bid to rescue Ram and Rahim. Though the girls did not mention anything about the Vanars and had cooked up a fine story about their escapade, they did mention the attempt on their lives by the thugs and how Ram and Rahim had saved them. Everyone found it strange that Ram and Rahim too had disappeared as soon as the girls had disappeared and had not been seen since, but on the girls' insistence a team decided to remain behind. Tina and Varshika particularly asked Tina's father to thank Mr. Ishwar for sending such fine men to protect them. He promised to mention the fact as soon they contacted Mr. Ishwar.

Nothing more was said. Each team got busy with the task assigned to them. Gopal contacted the authorities at Astro Dreams. Glad that Dhondiba had been found alive, they immediately swung into action and made arrangements for him to be admitted to a hospital in a big city nearby. Once his condition was stable enough, he would be airlifted to Shri Haripur. Luckily the weather had cleared a bit and it was possible to fly in an air ambulance to the camp. The girls were by the side of Uncle Dhondiba as he was lifted up into the helicopter. So Uncle Dhondiba was the first to be rescued. They received news from Gopal an hour later that Uncle Dhondiba had been admitted to a very large hospital and was beginning to show signs of improvement. He conveyed the doctor's prognosis that Uncle Dhondiba was lucky to be alive and would probably take months to fully recover.

The third team set out to rescue Ram and Rahim, but had to return as the weather turned bad. Since the weather took a turn for the worse, Dr. Madhusudan and the girls, accompanied by two mountaineers immediately set out towards the airstrip. They absolutely couldn't risk getting stranded there at the base camp. Dr. Madhusudan tried to contact Mr. Ishwar one last time before they left, but gave up as they couldn't get through. The third team promised to keep trying to contact him and would relay it to the second team once they succeeded. Varshika and Tina were finally on their way to the airstrip.

It took them more than eight hours to reach the airstrip and the girls were terribly exhausted. However the plane was waiting for them at the airstrip. The very same pilot who had dropped them there a couple of days ago was there to welcome them with a big, broad smile on his face.

"Thank you for coming for us," said Varshika. "Did we keep you waiting?"

"I reached an hour ago. I left as soon as I received the message from Mr. Ishwar."

"We are sorry for the inconvenience that we have caused," said Tina. "But it is imperative that we reach as soon as possible."

"Please, please don't speak like that. I am indebted to Mr. Ishwar, and anyway the plane belongs to him. I am merely his pilot. I will try to get you to the big city in less than three hours. As soon as we are airborne, I will have a talk with Mr. Ishwar and make the helicopter available at the airport. So once all the formalities are completed, you can board the helicopter and reach your village."

It was then that they saw two grumpy looking men standing close to the plane. They stood with hands folded across their chests and were probably waiting for the party to board the plane, before they boarded it themselves.

"Are these men the replacements of Ram and Rahim?" asked Varshika, looking directly at the pilot.

"No," said the pilot with a serious expression on his face. "These are the original men."

"Original men?" asked Varshika puzzled.

"Yeah!" said the pilot. "These two men had been sent by Mr. Ishwar to protect you guys. However, on their way to the airport, when they halted for a cup of coffee, those other two guys took their place by spiking their coffee with sedatives."

"If what you say is true," said Varshika, "and these are the men originally sent by Mr. Ishwar, then who are Ram and Rahim and who sent them?"

"Haven't the faintest clue," said the pilot. "Anyway, hurry up and board the plane."

They were airborne in fifteen minutes. The girls and Tina's father sat together at the rear end of the plane while the grumpy looking men sat at the front. Though they had been trekking for the past eight hours, the girls had not gotten the opportunity to speak to Tina's father as they did not want to speak in front of the guides and whenever they found a hint of a signal on their cell phones, they had phoned Nath and updated him about whatever had happened in the past two days. They had always taken the precaution of being as far away from the guides as possible. As Tina and Varshika updated Dr. Madhusudan, his eyes became rounder by the moment until they resembled saucers. Finally when they had finished their tale some two hours later, he shook his head in disbelief.

"I can't believe it," he said. "So after all, our mythology is not pure myth. There is some reality in it. I feel blessed that I am one of the few to know about all those events and particularly feel blessed to have children like you. I only hope that the boys are safe wherever they are and soon we are united. And the big guy who rescued you…"

"His name is Simba," Varshika interrupted. "And he is the apprentice to the Abbot of the African temple."

"Yes," said Tina's father. "And he told you that the relic would protect us from those devil robots?"

"Not exactly," said Tina. "It will merely stall them - buy us some time till we can figure out how to destroy them."

Their gaze shifted to the two grumpy men sitting at the front of the aircraft.

"Those guys seem pretty bugged," said Varshika discretely pointing at the two.

"They sure are," said Tina's father. "Imagine being conned by those two men. I wonder who those two men are, but whoever they are, I bless them for saving your lives."

"They are good people and I hope they are safe," said Tina.

"Should we go home briefly once we return?" asked Tina's father. "The ladies must be really worried."

"No way," said the girls firmly. "The lesser the number of people involved the better. And it is imperative that we reach the temple and place the Astra on the altar."

"Ok then it is final," said Varshika. "As soon as we reach Batatawadai Puram, we rush to the temple."

"We should be landing in some time. Hope the helicopter is there as requested."

As there was nothing else to do, they decided to take a short nap before they reached their destination.

October 17ᵗʰ, 10 am (earth time)
Desert in Xixipoo

Guru trudged along, oblivious of the surroundings. He didn't even feel her weight. Of course, he had checked on her a number of times, even tried to revive her, felt for a pulse and tried to hear her heart beat. He knew that she was alive, but for how much longer, he could not tell. The hope that a rescue team would arrive and rescue them slowly dwindled and then died out completely. They were all alone and it was entirely up to him to ensure their survival.

However with every passing minute, he felt drawn more and more in the direction he had been travelling for the past few hours. He couldn't understand why he was feeling such a strong urge to travel in that particular direction.

He paused a moment and looked around. All he could see was the sprawling desert, dotted with giant sand dunes. These dunes were larger than any, seen on earth. Guru estimated that some of these could easily hold fifty storey buildings in them, may be a small city. He even imagined a city hidden away in one of these dunes, no not a city, but a village, a neat village with cottages, shrubs, lush green grass and water. He could literally see such a village in this big dune.

Stupid of me to hallucinate now! But is that really a mirage? It seems so real. I can even see the huge and magnificent doors. No, it can't be real. Is this it, am I dying..? What a way to go, and poor girl, she will die too... just because I wasn't strong enough to save her.

He tried to gather his wits. The giant dune reappeared. So, he was hallucinating after all, but it seemed so real. She lay limp on his shoulder. Suddenly, instinctively he gripped her

178

tighter and charged towards the dune, towards the door, towards the neat village that he imagined he had seen, a few moments ago. With that kind of momentum, he knew that he would probably bury both of them a couple of feet in the side of the dune. Then what? Would he lay there and wait for the inevitable? But he couldn't understand why he charged towards the dune in the first place. Had the heat made him crazy? These and numerous other thoughts flashed through his mind as he hit the dune. To his surprise, he went clean through the dune, tumbled a couple of times and lay sprawled on the floor besides her limp body.

Guru looked around, eyes blinking, for his vision was blurred. He was awestruck by what he saw. He was lying on the centre of a meandering path in a neat village. The atmosphere was much cooler here in contrast to the conditions outside. Lush green grass grew on both the side of the path. The landscape was dotted with a number of cottages. He could see farms on either side of the path bordered by trees. A number of people began to appear, but there was something wrong with them. They seemed so tiny, not more than three feet tall... like elves... magical creatures.

They are not real... can't be. I must be hallucinating, maybe dying. How can there be a village... and that too in this godforsaken desert? It can't be so cool in here... maybe my last moments... poor girl... but I feel sort of rejuvenated.

"It is a girl and a young man. She is injured... pierced by a sharp object. Get our Vaidyousse immediately. You young people carry them to my cottage."

Guru had been going on for so many hours on shear will power, but was rapidly losing consciousness and strength. Every inch of his body ached. He finally let go and collapsed. The world turned dark around him.

About six dwarfs carried Guru along the path, followed by others carrying Amy. A very old dwarf, who probably wielded a lot of authority, led the way. He was clean shaven except for a tuft of hair at the back of his head that hung down. He had instructed them to carry Amy without touching her, after the first one who touched her had collapsed. They reached a cottage that was visibly bigger than the surrounding ones and entered it, carefully, so as to not accidentally drop the two. The two were laid on two wooly mats on the floor. The mats however, were not long enough to hold the entire bodies of the two, so their legs rested on the floor. Another tiny man, followed by two young assistants, rushed to the injured teens. His garments were saffron in colour and resembled a loose version of a Kurta and Pyjama - attire commonly worn in India. His attire and hair resembled the old man's. His male assistant was a couple of paces behind him, carrying a bag. The female assistant has some sort of a contraption in her hands. He immediately knelt down beside Amy and scanned her with a rod like device. The device had two tubes, one attached to his ear and one in his mouth. He gently blew into the tube in his mouth and it emitted a sound. After examining the two of them, he gave quick instructions to his assistants who immediately began attending to Guru and Amy with strange looking instruments.

"How are they?" asked the old dwarf who had brought them there.

"They are not in good shape, O learned one. I'm surprised they made it this far."

"How long will it take for them to fully recover?"

"The boy will recover in a couple of hours, but it will take a few days for the girl to recover. She has lost a lot of blood. We are flushing her system right now. Both will live - lucky ones, I would say."

By then huge crowd had gathered outside his cottage. They peered at the two young people with awe and suspicion and whispered amongst themselves. It seemed that they wanted to talk to their leader but did not have the courage. The old man looked at them sternly.

"Speak out if you have to. Why is there such a lot of suspicion amongst you folks?"

A young man came out of the crowd. He was dressed exactly like the old man.

"Sir, may I ask who these people are and why are you so concerned about them?"

"Don't you people remember our code of conduct? Speak out young man."

"Our code of conduct is - to live and let live and not harm any living being"

"Then am I doing wrong in saving them?"

"Not at all, O learned one. We do not doubt your intentions but aren't we inviting harm to everyone, by harbouring these Asourousse?"

He laughed aloud. The tension in the air seemed to dissipate a bit.

"Now young man, I believe that you are learned enough. Please recite and explain to all these folks the meaning of our hymn 'Raukshouk Stoutrouse'."

The entire crowd looked at the young man with great anticipation, for he was regarded as one of the top seven learned people in the land. He first recited a hymn and then began to explain its meaning to the assembled crowd.

"The hymn is one of our most holy hymns, O learned one. It states that the Vamanousse have been blessed by the great one himself. No living being shall be able to breach the walls of our holy city. Only our hymns shall open and close the doors to this land and... and finally it says that if anyone ever breaches our holy land, then within him dwells the great one."

The crowd began to murmur once again. Suddenly there erupted cries of joy from within the crowd. Many of them started dancing and chanting hymns.

"You surely don't mean to say he is..." said the astonished young man.

"That is exactly what I mean to say young man," said the old man with joy in his voice. "This boy could just walk through our doors as if they didn't exist. I believe he could see us even though we are cleverly camouflaged. Even the Asourbouts with their modern technology have failed to locate us, but this boy could see us."

"But what about the girl?" he asked concerned.

The old man now addressed the very huge crowd that had gathered.

"Rejoice O Vamanousse – we have fulfilled our destiny. We came here fourteen years ago following the kidnapped princess. We have tried our best to locate her on this vast and hostile planet, but did not succeed. However, by the blessings of the almighty she has come to us. The girl lying here is none other than princess Amindita."

The chants grew even louder. Now the old man raised his hands in authority. The entire crowd felt silent.

"They need to rest now. You will resume you duties immediately."

The old man commanded such respect, that the scenario changed within a couple of minutes. Where there was utter chaos a few minutes ago, the scenario now depicted a normal day with the Vamanousse going about, performing their daily chores. He now turned to the young man.

"Look after them and call for me when the boy awakens. I leave them in your care. I need to pray. I see a storm coming – the mother of all storms."

He silently left as the young man watched him with awe. The young man wondered how this frail old man could command such respect just by raising an eyebrow. The old man had mentioned a storm, but not literally. Something big was about to happen in the next few hours.

"How are they now?" he asked the chief Vaidyousse.

"We have successfully flushed out the system of the princess. She has resilience, as never seen before. She will be fit in a few hours. We will subject her to the holy chants for the next few hours. The boy on the other hand..."

"Is something wrong with him?"

"On the contrary, he will awaken in a few minutes from now. He has been absorbing energy like I've never seen before. His body and soul are rejuvenating fast. This is not normal at all."

"Then I need to send for 'the learned one' immediately."

Fifteen minutes later the learned one and the young man were intently peering at Guru who had begun to stir. The old man was astonished at being summoned so soon. He had gone into deep prayer and was initially angry when he had been disturbed. In his years of experience he had never seen anything like that happen. He wondered how anyone could heal that fast.

Guru sat up five minutes later and looked around him. The world slowly came into focus. He saw two small men looking at him with undivided attention, studying his every move. They looked like midgets, yes midgets because they had a well proportioned body, only small in size. The older one must've been some three feet tall and the younger one a couple of inches taller. Both wore similar kind of loose clothes, of a material that Guru had never seen before. But that didn't surprise him for in the past few hours, he had seen things never seen by any human on earth. He was on Xixipoo, wasn't he? The old man seemed to literally radiate wisdom. Guru could not understand why he felt so, but knew that the old man was wiser than anyone he had ever met before. The young man beside him seemed to have a great deal of knowledge but exhibited a sort of impatience like all young men usually do. Again Guru failed to understand how he could read these two people standing in front of him. The old man approached him with folded hands and spoke. Guru could not understand a word of what he said.

"I am sorry, but I don't quite understand what you mean. Where am I and how is the Amy? Is she okay?"

The old man looked at him with astonishment in his eyes.

"Welcome to the abode of the Vamanousse. How do you speak the ancient language?"

"This is the language I normally speak," said Guru. "I am not from this planet. I am from a planet called earth."

"Incredible!" said the old man. "We all know that the Devousse left earth a long time ago and the Manousse inhabit the planet now. They are very ordinary beings, then how do you exhibit so many of the characteristics of the Devousse?"

Does everyone here, except for the Xixipians, use "ousse' after every word? This really irritates me. So what he probably means is, the 'devas' had left earth a long time ago and the 'manavs' that is humankind were left behind on earth. He wonders, how I, a common human, exhibits the characteristics of the 'devas'? Now, how the hell, am I to know that?

"Young man," said the old man calmly, "your soul is in deep turmoil. Can I try to open up your mind?"

So now, he too wants to read my mind. What's with these guys and reading minds? Don't they know it is rude to read others minds? My mind is my own and no one is reading it anymore.

He suddenly felt a sense of deep peace and felt as if he were floating in a bubble from where he could see the world but no one could see him.

"You blocked me out of your mind," said the old man, his voice trembling a bit, "no one has ever done that before."

"Well," said Guru, "I don't exactly know how, but yes, I have blocked you out... I can feel it."

"I will not read your mind without your permission. But eventually I will have to read your mind. Take your time, rest a bit, then we will meet when you are ready. 'Vamanousse Gopalousse' will show you around"

He pointed to the young man standing beside him.

"May I know your name, Sir?" asked Guru.

"You already know it, don't you?"

"Somehow I do," said Guru, "it is 'Vamanousse Hariousse'."

The old man left with a smile on his lips. Vamanousse Gopalousse kept shifting his gaze from his leader to Guru. He couldn't make out what was happening. Finally he turned his gaze to Guru. He had a look, half of fear and half of astonishment.

"Relax," said Guru laughing, "I'm cool."

He looked with greater fear, for he did not understand what Guru meant by 'cool'. He wondered how the old man understood the young man while he did not understand him one bit.

"Pease treat me as a friend. You can relax. I'm an ordinary 'Manousse' from earth."

"But you aren't ordinary. The 'learned one' says so."

"Ok," said Guru giving up, "then I request you not to treat me any differently than you would treat a friend."

Those words seemed to relax him a bit. His expression too changed, only a bit though.

"Would you like to eat now Sir?"

"Call me 'Guru'."

He merely smiled. Then he rapidly gave instructions in a language that Guru did not understand. Immediately a few men and women arrived with large platters filled with delicious looking food. They placed one in front of him and the other in front of Vamanousse Gopalousse, then silently moved away, but not before stealing a glimpse. They were obedient but curiosity got the better of them. The aroma made Guru's mouth water. He looked hungrily at the food in the platter in front of him. There were three varieties of vegetables, rice cooked in saffron, two bowls with lentils cooked in different ways. The platter also contained pickle, a piece of lemon and some salt. Finally he noticed a small bowl with a yellow substance. It was probably a sweet dish. He almost felt that he was in a restaurant in his very own village, but then reality dawned upon him. He was far away from home, in a strange planet, in a distant part of the galaxy facing conditions that threatened to destroy both planets.

"It will be an honour if you say grace before we begin," said Vamanousse Gopalousse.

Guru noticed that the tiny men and women who had served him food and who were now a few feet away were straining their ears to hear what he prayed. Now, Guru had this incorrigible habit of gobbling up food placed in front of him and asking questions later. Many a times he had gobbled up food specially made for Tina and although she had fought with him for it, he knew she loved him. Leave aside thanking God he never even thanked his mother for the delicious food that she painstakingly prepared. He felt a pang in his stomach. He really missed them. But here, were people looking up to him. How could he disappoint them? He vaguely remembered a prayer that he had learnt in school as a kid and recited whatever he remembered, with folded hands.

> *'Thank you God, for the world so sweet,*
>
> *Thank you God for this food we eat,*
>
> *Thank you God for the birds that sing,*
>
> *Thank you God for everything.'*

Guru looked around, to find everyone smiling. It was as if happiness had erupted from within everyone around. He was sure that no a soul, except maybe Vamanousse Gopalousse had even understood a word he said, but the mere fact that he said a prayer elated everyone's soul. He could wait no longer and ate with a lot of gusto. The meal disappeared within minutes. There were cries of joy from within – perhaps the cooks were celebrating. Guru felt nice to know that the cooks were rejoicing merely because he appreciated the food prepared by them.

Only after eating his fill did Guru notice the plate and bowls. They were perfectly shaped, only made from leaves.

"Are these made of leaves?" he said pointing to the empty plates. "Then how are they so durable?"

Vamanousse Gopalousse beckoned someone standing on the far side of the room. He had some sort of flute in his hand and meekly approached them.

"Please turn the plates to their original form for our guest here."

The man knelt before Guru's plate, which of course was empty and began to play a lilting tune. With every passing second, the durable material of the plate began resembling straw, woven in the shape of a plate.

"I can't believe my eyes," said Guru. "What just happened?"

"This plate has taken its original form – a plate woven from straw. The tune played by Vamanousse Kisnousse here, returned the molecules of the straw to their original form."

"You got to be kidding me. Can sound do that?"

"Yes, sound is far more powerful that earlier perceived. It can create as well as destroy. The plates woven from straw we subjected to sound of a particular frequency and volume. It rearranged the straw molecules and made the plate tough and impermeable. Now it has returned to its original form and can be converted to its basic elements."

"You mean that, you will recycle it, right?" said Guru with some admiration.

"I do not fully understand what you say, but if you are strong enough to accompany me, I can take you around our village and you can see for yourself."

"Anytime buddy," said an enthused Guru, "I'll be more than glad."

Vamanousse Gopalousse looked at him with a blank expression. Perhaps he had not fully understood Guru, but was sure that Guru was willing to take a tour of his village. He gave quick instructions and a couple of tiny people rushed in a pair of shoes and placed them in front of Guru. Again, Guru couldn't help but notice, the texture and material of the shoes. These too seemed to be made of leaves or woven straw and treated by sound. He slid his feet into each shoe, expecting them to be rather uncomfortable, but to his surprise they fit well and felt cozy.

"Thank you!" said Guru with genuine feelings, "but where are my shoes, I mean those I was wearing?"

"Sorry, O great one! They were made from the skin of the holy animal and had to be discarded. The Vamanousse do not use any product obtained by harming plants or animals. Can we leave?"

Guru followed him without a word. His admiration for these people kept on increasing. Once outside, they took the path in front of them and walked briskly. The path meandered and Guru had the distinct feeling that it was spiraling outwards.

"Is this path spiraling outwards?" asked Guru.

"Yes," said Vamanousse Gopalousse. "We are in the centre of the village. This is where the administrators of the village reside. The cottage of the learned one marks the exact centre of the village. He is our leader. Then we have the houses of the seven scholars. I am one of the seven."

"So you are judged according to your skills?" asked Guru.

Vamanousse Gopalousse merely nodded.

"Then as we spiral outwards, we have the houses of the various craftsmen and finally the houses of the farmers. Then

189

the fields begin. So it is convenient for the farmers to have houses on the outer edge of the village just before the fields begin. This region also has the largest number of water bodies and a lot of water is used for farming."

"What if one has to reach the edge of the village in a hurry?" asked Guru. "Will he have to travel all along the spiral path?"

"No, there are small paths radiating outwards from the centre of the village. These are not as wide as the main path, but are very useful if one wants to travel from the centre of the village to the outermost edges or back. In fact, you were brought to the centre of the village through one of those paths."

As they walked along, they saw people busy doing something or the other. However whenever they came near any such person, he or she stopped work for a moment and bowed low to Guru. Guru found the unwarranted attention rather irksome, but gave each one a broad smile lest he hurt their feelings. There were brightly coloured houses on either side of the path, made of mud walls and having intricate patterns on them. Guru felt a gentle and cool breeze on his face. It made him feel fresh. For the first time he carefully looked all around and even above. He felt as if he was in a dome. Clear light filtered in from all sides of the dome. It was probably natural light, only less intense.

"Where exactly are we?" asked Guru.

"Don't you already know? You saw us didn't you? You saw us even though we are well camouflaged by the sand dune."

"So, I really did see this village in the sand dune," said Guru affirmatively. "But how is it so bright in here? It is as if, the dune is made of glass."

"The dune rests on a dome made of a material only known to the Vamanousse. This material is harder than any known material. It is neither metal nor non-metal, neither conductor nor insulator, not in any of the known states of matter and can withstand large amounts of heat and pressure and is almost indestructible."

"Then how did you guys mould it in the shape of the dune, and how is light passing through the dune?" asked Guru. "I distinctly remember seeing an opaque dune."

"I attribute this to our in depth knowledge of sound and music. While this material, known as Vamandhatousse is made, it is subjected to certain sounds. This makes it soft and pliable like putty. It is then given the desired shape and form. Then it is subjected to a powerful hymn which makes it indestructible. That is how we constructed this dome. This material also has other remarkable properties. When subjected to certain specific frequencies of sound, it can convert heat to light. So what is happening is the sand above the dome is getting tremendously heated up due to the planet's sun, which we call Suryousse. Once this heat reaches the dome, it absorbs the heat and converts it into light similar to the light emitted by the Sourousse. We have reduced the intensity of the light to make it practical to use but not unpleasant."

"It is amazing that you have such advanced technology, yet you live such primitive lives," said Guru.

"The Vamanousse have taken the holy oath to never intentionally harm any other living being."

By then they had left the residential area of the village and had reached an area where there were huge fields. Guru was surprised by how lush green the grass was. The fruits on the trees planted on the borders of the fields looked luscious. Guru felt like plucking a few mouth watering fruits and sinking his teeth into them.

"But then, how do you carry out your farming and animal husbandry? Plants too have life, don't they?" asked Guru.

"They definitely have life and are considered sacred by us. We only use that part of the plant, which can be obtained without harming the plant. For instance, the function of the fruit is to ensure continuation of the species. We have developed plants that live very long and bear many fruits. These fruits are plucked without harming the plant. We gently shake the plant, which causes the fruit to fall. Similarly we have developed rice, corn and other plants that live for many years. When the seeds mature, the grain clusters just fall off. We merely collect these. The plants are tended till they live and once they die, they are plucked out of the ground with due respect to enable new plants to grow."

"Then what about your animals and insects?"

"As you can see, we have limited species of animals. We do not kill and eat animals like the Asourousse. The only animal product used by us is milk. Our cows and goats are bred to yield much more milk than required by their young ones. Once the young ones have had their fill, we extract the rest of the milk, which is plenty. This is used to make cottage cheese, butter and ghee. Wool yielded from our goats is modified to make garments that protect us from both heat and extreme cold."

"What about your insects – bees and butterflies," asked Guru.

"They have a section in our village with limited number of plants. We do not venture there and they cannot come here unless we let them come and..."

"Let me guess," said Guru. "You use music to summon them to pollinate your fields when farmers are not present and when they've had their fill, you send them back to their section."

"Absolutely right," said Vamanousse Gopalousse beaming.

They moved further ahead and saw a huge cottage. It was probably a school where various vocations were taught. It had a huge compound with a lot of shrubs interspersed by open spaces. In each of these spaces were groups of pupils, learning an art from a teacher. Guru could not help, but notice that music was present in every sphere of their life, right from agriculture to tool making.

"How do you guys put music to use in every sphere of your lives?" asked Guru.

"We are the founders of music. Rhythm exits in every aspect of life."

"You mean that, my body functions due to music?" questioned Guru.

"No, your life force or energy flow controls your body, but rhythm keeps it going perfectly. If this rhythm is disturbed, your life functions would also be disturbed. The same is true, for other plants and animals. We use the same on non living objects, whose molecular structure can be altered by subjecting them to different types of music. Thus, a material that is hard and indestructible can be made soft and pliable."

"Do you have any other materials like the Vamandhatousse?"

"Yes," said Vamanousse Gopalousse, "we have a sacred material called Paramdhatousse. This material is of two types, Pravritti Paramdhatousse and Nivritti Paramdhatousse. They are in the true sense the opposites of each other and if they come in contact, there will be complete annihilation."

193

"What happens?"

"If these two dhatousse come in contact, they will draw such a lot of energy from the surrounding, that the surrounding region will experience Param Shunyousse."

"Wow," said Guru, "you mean 'absolute zero' temperature will be attained."

"If that is what your people call it... Once the combination of the two dhatousse have obtained enough energy from the surrounding, during which, they may attain temperatures equivalent to that present inside the Suryousse, they will suddenly release this energy and then there will be nothing."

"I get it," said Guru, "you possess matter and anti-matter and when they come in contact, matter itself gets nullified and releases tremendous energy."

Vamanousse Gopalousse looked at him with a blank expression on his face.

"I didn't quite understand what you mean."

"Never mind," said Guru, "Do you possess this material?"

"Not abundantly, but we have supplies of these materials. We store them in the form of tiny grains locked away safely, for energy liberated from a single grain could destroy the dome."

Guru's mind was working faster than time itself. Maybe he finally had the solution.

"Tell me,' said Guru, "how good are you people as craftsmen?"

"The very best," said he, "however only seven of us have mastered the hymns and are respected by all."

"You mean only you can bring about all these changes?"

"Yes, we are the seven Bhramousse or high priests. 'Vamanousse Hariousse' is the most learned one and is considered the Paroum Bhramousse or chief. The other seven of us, including me are his inferiors."

"Why do you people do even the menial tasks when you possess such technology," asked Guru. "For instance, why do those boys and girls have to keep playing music in the fields or why are those others fetching water from that pond? Can't you device machines to do that work for you?"

"If the so called machines do all our work for us, then what would we all do? Probably idle away somewhere and get into evil habits. We have been given this fertile mind to learn and learn we do. Similarly we have been given this body to work and we definitely work. But that does not mean we do not enjoy. Once all the work is done, each one of us has time to enjoy activities of our choice. We dance, sing and play our instruments. We even express ourselves by painting our houses. We have great festivals and competitions. We work hard, enjoy and help one another. We never fight like the Asourousse or the other inhabitants of this planet."

"Your houses do not have doors. Aren't you scared of intruders?" asked Guru.

"We are scared of intruders, but not from within our village. Our dome is impenetrable. However our houses do not have doors, as anyone is welcome to our houses. The only places where we have doors are for privacy. We have a deep respect for each other and do not need doors to guard our houses."

He paused for a moment. Then he pointed to a structure at the far end of the village.

"Do you know what that is?"

"Nope," said Guru.

"That, my friend, is where we dispose all matter that has ended its existence. There are powerful beings that break down all matter to its simplest form and return it to the surroundings. From this simple matter, the cycle of life begins anew."

Their walk was interrupted by a person who came running to them. He spoke briefly to Vamanousse Gopalousse and left.

"Princess Amindita is awake and asking for you."

They rushed through one of the radial roads and reached the house of Vamanousse Hariousse in fifteen minutes and found Amy sitting on her bed. Guru couldn't take his eyes off her for she looked stunning even though her face was swollen and eyes looked terribly tired. Seeing him, she smiled and Guru felt as if his heart would leap out of his chest.

"Hi there sleeping beauty," he said as he held both her hands. "I thought we were goners."

"But... but how can you touch me?" she asked astonished.

"I told you before, didn't I? It is very easy to touch you, since you are gorgeous, stunning and bewitchingly beautiful."

"Don't be silly," she said blushing. "I am cursed. No one can touch me or the very life force will be drained out of them."

"What rubbish."

"She is not lying," said Vamanousse Gopalousse. "She has the ability to draw out the life energy of anything she touches. She is unique. We had to transport her without

196

touching her."

"I am touching her right now, but am not fainting."

"Only our learned one, Vamanousse Hariousse, would be able to answer your question. He will meet you soon."

"I will leave now. The sevoukousse of this abode will help you if you need anything."

"Who are the sevoukousse?"

"They serve this household. They will attend to all your needs."

He bid them goodbye and left.

"So, no one has touched you, hugged you or kissed you, because you are the 'holy one'?"

"No," she said.

"Can I give you a hug?" he said with outstretched hands.

"Maybe you are pushing your luck too far," she said, punching him playfully.

"Ouch! Ok, ok," said he, "but it was worth a try. Can we be friends?"

He extended a hand to her that she accepted. Her touch sent waves through his body, but these weren't waves of energy – they were something else.

"Where are we and who are these people?" she asked, "How did we get here?"

Guru spent the next hour explaining how he had defeated the Rakshousse, located water and Xiboras, dressed her wound, found the village in the dune and ultimately about all the experiences he had had in the village.

"Try the food," he said, "it's delicious and I wouldn't

mind having one more meal with you."

After a sumptuous meal, the two of them spent some time talking. She listened with awe as Guru told her about planet earth, Batatawadai Puram, his school and all his friends. He could see in her eyes how impressed she was. Then he asked her about herself.

"I have been a virtual prisoner in the palace. My only companions were the four ladies who took care of me. They taught me everything I know. We were confined in a huge section of the palace. No one visited that section and we had it all to ourselves."

"But where did you come from and who are you?"

"My caretakers never told me much, only that I was their princess and that my parents were far away. I have spent fourteen years of my life wondering who I am and where my home is, for I am sure that I am not from this planet. Whenever I insisted on knowing about my origins, my caretakers only answered that I would be told everything when the time was right. Probably they were terrified of Mooisausooura, since like me, they too were captives."

"I can't understand," said Guru, "Why did this Mooisausooura character keep you guys alive? Why take the trouble of keeping you in captivity when he could've easily bumped you off?"

"Initially he kept me alive to use me as a hostage if my people attacked. However later he kept me alive because he discovered the full extent of my powers – all along he knew that I had some powers. One day when I was about four, I threw a fit because I wanted to go out. Mooisausooura arrived as I was throwing tantrums and tried to hit me, but the moment he touched me, he collapsed and almost died. He never interfered with me ever again but ensured that security was doubled and we had no chance of escape. He visited me regularly and tried to find the source of my power. Then he subjected my caretakers to various forms of torture in order to learn more about my powers, but couldn't get anything out of them."

"When did your caretakers tell you about yourself?"

"About two years ago, I saw you guys..."

"You saw us on earth..?"

"No, I somehow connected to queen Xixandra's mind. She must've been in a zone that amplified her thoughts..."

"Does something like that even exist?"

"Hey," yelled Amy, "how do you expect me to complete if you keep interrupting? Yes there are spots like that, not only on this planet but also on earth."

"Sorry."

"Where was I..? Ah yes, I could read her thoughts clearly. I saw you both and immediately knew that you held the key to defeating Mooisausooura. From then, I kept on reading the mind of Xixandra, whenever I could and relayed it to my caretakers. Unfortunately the news spread to Mooisausooura via his spies and he subjected them to severe torture until they cracked and told him about earth. This happened a few months ago and since then Mooisausooura began all his preparations to invade earth..."

They were interrupted by a sevoukousse, who told them that the Paroum Bhramousse wanted to meet them urgently. He led then to a chamber where the old man was seated on a mat. He beamed as soon as he saw Amy.

"Come to me, my little one," he said beckoning her to

approach.

Amy took a few reluctant steps towards him.

"You cannot hurt me, my precious one," said he, "you were a few months old when I first took you in my lap. Do you know it was I, who named you?"

Her eyes brightened up as she rushed to him, got down on her knees and bowed before him. He fondly ran his hand over her head.

"I am the chief priest of your father, Emperor Ramabhadrousse. It is believed that you are the direct descendent of the great Lord."

"How did we come to this planet and where are my parents?"

He looked at Guru, who was standing a few steps behind her and beckoned him to sit.

"Do sit down both of you. This planet is in peril and it is time you two know the story of the Great Lord and how some of us ended up on this planet fourteen years ago."

They both sat in front of him.

"How do you know that the planet is in peril?" asked Guru a bit worried.

"...because I managed to project my consciousness and have seen a huge army of non living beings getting ready to annihilate the planet."

"Didn't you try to project your consciousness before, in order to locate Amy... er I mean Amindita."

He laughed out loud and his eyes sparkled.

"You can call her Amy. Don't take this old man to be

naïve. I know exactly how you feel about her."

Guru blushed and his cheeks turned pink as Amy turned and looked straight into his eyes.

"Yes young man, I have tried many times to locate the princess. Projecting oneself is not an easy task and drains all the energy out of your body. It may even kill you. I have tried a number of times, but failed each time. Mooisausooura hid her in such a place where even powerful minds could not pry."

"Then how did you do it now?" asked Guru as Amy pinched him.

"Something has happened in the past six hours. Somebody has deployed a device that has virtually blocked all communication between all those Asourbouts... sorry, but I got the name from the princess' mind."

"Great!" said Guru, "It is definitely the work of Queen Xixandra and her people. They must've deployed some device. It means Sri is okay. Amy, can you read the queen's mind?"

"Sorry Guru, but I have temporarily lost that ability. I am sorry...really sorry."

"But first listen to me," said Vamanousse Hariousse, "You must know the story of the Lord and our people and the princess. Only then can you take right action against Mooisausooura and his army of Asourbouts."

Vamanousse Hariousse began narrating the story of the Great War on earth, the lord and the consequences of the war – the same one narrated by the Vanars to Tina and Varshika.

"So you were the descendents of the Devas who left earth through the portal opened by the Lord?" said Guru.

"Yes," said Vamanousse Hariousse. "Our ancestors rounded up all the Asourousse, Rakshousse and Pischasousse,

201

and transported them on huge ships, built by the Asourousse, to this part of the universe. They managed to locate a planet much similar to earth and decided to settle down. The Great Lord had strictly instructed us not to destroy the evil ones as a lot of blood had already been spilt. The Devousse too were ashamed of the devastation of earth caused by the war. But the King of the Devousse was well aware that given a slight chance, the evil ones would try to rise to prominence. Therefore as a punishment, he ordered the powers of all the beings to be locked away. Our ancestors were the ones who made all the special beings forget their powers. We achieved this by use of certain Mantrousse. The evil ones were reduced to mere Manousse."

"What about the good beings? Were their powers too taken away?" asked Guru.

"Yes, many other special beings accompanied us, but their powers too were taken away by the King. He then made our ancestors forget the Mantrousse, lest we accidentally reverse what we had done."

"What a waste," said Guru. "What if the good beings needed their powers later?"

"The wise king was aware that a situation may arise when we needed to unlock the powers of the good beings. We retained one Mantrousse that would unlock certain powers of the good beings. We were forbidden to ever use that Mantrousse and it was passed on from one generation to the next. Only the high priests of the Vamanousse know the Mantrousse and how exactly to use it."

"That Mantrousse would've come handy now," said Guru, "but unfortunately we have no special beings here, on this planet."

"You are mistaken, young man," said Vamanousse Hariousse, "for there are about a thousand such beings on this planet. I saw them with my mind."

"Then we need to locate them and ..."

"They are too far away and we will not reach them on time..."

"Oh..."

"... but your friends could reach them, your alien friend..."

"You mean Xixandra and Sri?" asked Guru, "How do you know where they are?"

"I sensed their presence near the Gandharvousse, but cannot contact them, for I cannot latch on to their minds – they are too far away. If I knew where they were, then I could have contacted them, but you have a chance and for that I need permission to read your mind."

Guru readily agreed and the old man asked him to lie down. Then he gently stroked Guru's forehead as he recited some verses. Guru felt a lot of pain. It was as if someone was drilling his head, probing into that part of his life, hidden deep in a secret place. He got up with a start. Amy was wiping blood of his nose. The high priest was lying on the floor, blood oozing out of his nose and ears. He was being attended to by the Vaidyousse. They were back to business in five minutes.

"You have a very powerful mind, young man," said Vamanousse Hariousse, "and now I can help you contact your friends. You are very close to Sri and have shared a lot of significant moments of your life with him. It won't be very difficult for you to reach out to him, but first let me continue the story..."

"Yes," said Guru, "I need to know how you got here and why is Mooisausooura trying to destroy all humans?"

"Once the powers of the special beings were curtailed, peace reigned on our new planet named Prithvousse. Many millennia passed and we continued living peacefully. The population of the Devousse and Vamanousse greatly dwindled while the population of the other beings gradually increased. Knowing the powers that remained locked away in the evil ones, the Devousse continued ruling our new planet for millennia. This was resented by the Asourousse, who by now had grown in numbers. There began agitations on our planet for equal rights for all. Since the Devousse and Vamanousse retained their powers, it was not difficult to control such agitations and we always managed to maintain peace. Then fifteen years ago, something happened that changed everything."

"The Asourousse got back their powers?" asked Guru.

"Not exactly," said Vamanousse Hariousse, "but it has something to do with our first king – a secret that he did not share with the others."

"What kind of secret?" asked Amy.

"Just before the Evil Asourousse King went to fight his last battle with the Lord, he copied all his memories onto a master computer..."

"Is that even possible?" asked Guru.

"The Asourousse were very smart and had a great knowledge in the field of cloning. The Evil Asourousse King was aware of the fact that the Great Lord would destroy him and so took the precaution. He believed that his memories could be transferred into a new cloned body, in case he perished. This master computer which already had intelligence of its own and all the memories of the Evil Asourousse King was placed in a

204

small sphere. The sphere was so special that no rays could penetrate it. The Evil king ensured that his memories would remain safe in the sphere. This sphere, he handed to his wife with instructions how to open it. He told her to have his body cloned if he perished and open the sphere. The master computer would do the rest."

"So he was really smart!" exclaimed Guru.

"Yes he was, but fate had something else written for him. When the Great Lord killed the Asourousse King, his body vapourized. There was not a trace left and so no chance of obtaining his DNA or cloning him. Being proud, he had not allowed his DNA to be extracted when he was alive. Moreover the war devastated earth. When the evil ones were rounded up and banished, the Asourousse Queen approached the commander of the Devousse army and handed the sphere to him in exchange of freedom for herself and her children. She promised never to use her powers again and that she and her children would live like an ordinary Manousse. The Army commander, who was to later become the first king of our new planet, felt pity on her. He let her slip away and did not inform the Great Lord about the sphere. He carried this sphere to the new planet Prithvousse. However he ensured that the sphere would be lost forever and had it buried deep inside our planet in some sort of secret chamber. There it remained buried for millennia.

Then a smart Asourousse boy named Mooisausooura was born in an affluent Asourousse family some forty years ago. Right from a young age he exhibited extreme powers, not known to any Asourousse. When the news reached our King Raghupungavousse, father of our present king Ramabhadrousse, he was alarmed and had the boy brought to the royal palace. When the king realized the extent of the boy's powers, he decided to keep him under his direct observation, in order to curtail his powers. The king spoke to Mooisausooura's family and mentioned that he had special talents. He requested permission to keep the boy with him so that his talents could be properly honed. The family gladly agreed and Mooisausooura went to live in the palace. There he befriended the prince Ramabhadrousse and everything went on well for some time. All that while the king, with the help of the Vamanousse managed to keep the powers of Mooisausooura well under control. Mooisausooura grew up to become a fine young man under the guidance of the Devousse.

Then King Raghupungavousse unexpextedly passed away and his son, Ramabhadrousse had to ascend the throne at quite a young age. He was shocked to learn about the powers of Mooisausooura from us and resented our methods of keeping his powers under control. However we managed to convince him to let us continue with our methods. King Ramabhadrousse married Lakshaki, a very beautiful Devousse princess. Mooisausooura was the King's best man in the wedding – such was the love between the two friends. The couple was blessed with a daughter, Amindita and she too began to exhibit special powers. The Vamanousse advised the king to isolate her from the others and not let anyone know about her powers. Four ladies, one of whom was not affected by the special powers of the Princess were chosen to be her caretakers. Amindita was kept isolated and only her parents and the caretakers were allowed to touch her.

This made Mooisausooura suspicious and he began his research. I tried to warn the king, but he did not take me seriously, for he was too worried about his daughter. So Mooisausooura continued his research as he had access to all the information of the Devas. The more he learnt, the angrier he got.

Due to his intense research, he managed to locate the

sphere in the underground chamber and disappeared for many months. We tried our best to locate him, but he was well hidden. We still have no clue as to what exactly he did during that period but know that he somehow managed to open the sphere and gained access to the Master Computer. He learned the history of the Great War and got even angrier as he felt cheated by the Devousse. He also realized that the Devousse had somehow locked the power of the Asourousse.

He decided to assemble a secret army of his own and managed to convince a hundred Asourousse to join him. He was unanimously declared the king of the Asourousse. They began exploring ways to unlock the powers of the Asourousse but miserably failed each time. It was then that Mooisausooura decided to find a way back to earth, since he believed that the answer to unlocking the powers of the Asourousse lay on earth. However the Great Lord had ensured that earth remained hidden away from prying eyes so earth was not visible. The Master Computer began scanning space systematically, trying to locate earth, but needed more power. So Mooisausooura made arrangements to supply a large amount of power to the Master Computer. That was a grave mistake on his part, for we could easily locate him by tracing the spot where such enormous amount of energy was being diverted.

King Ramabhadrousse immediately launched an attack on Mooisausooura who was aware that if the king's army reached him, the Master Computer would be destroyed. Since he had lived in the palace for most of his life, and knew every nook and corner, he hatched a plot to kidnap Princess Amindita from the palace and use her as a hostage. His band of Asourousse launched a sudden attack on the palace and managed to capture the four caretakers along with the princess.

The king's army surrounded the place where the Master Computer was located, but couldn't destroy it because of the hostages. They decided to cut power to the Master Computer to curb its activities, but by then it had become very powerful. It managed to open a small portal that directly took them to Xixipoo. Mooisausooura could literally walk into Xixipoo using the portal.

Normally portals are opened in space, but the Master Computer opened this one directly from the surface of one planet to the other. It was a very unstable portal, but Mooisausooura and a few of his Asourousse followers with the Master Computer reached Xixipoo. A few were left behind to defend the portal while others launched an attack on the king's army.

After a fierce fight, the Asourousse left behind to defend the portal were defeated. The king had no other alternative but to close the portal permanently. That would mean losing the princess forever, but the fate of Prithvousse was more important and so he ordered the portal to be closed so that Mooisausooura and the Master Computer could do no further damage. They decided to find another way to the planet. It was at this juncture that we Vamanousse requested the King to let us follow Mooisausooura, because we were the only ones with the knowledge to control his powers. He was reluctant to let us through, firstly because it was too dangerous and secondly because there were no soldiers to accompany us. All the soldiers were busy fighting the other followers of Mooisausooura who had launched a fierce attack on them. They had developed dangerous weapons and the soldiers were trying their best to prevent them from deploying the weapons.

As the portal was getting more and more unstable, I defied the orders of the King and along with a hundred

Vamanousse entered the portal. In a short time we reached this planet, but reached an altogether different location. Any normal being would've perished, but we had carried along with us sufficient quantities of whatever material we needed to set up a small village. We had taken that precaution, in case we got stranded on the planet for a long time, and that's exactly what happened. Then the portal closed completely and we were alone on the planet with two tasks – surviving the harsh climate and locating the princess..."

"But you said just now that there are other beings..." said Guru.

"You are right. I thought that we were the only ones who got through before the portal closed. That was because the Master Computer had somehow managed to curb our powers of projection for so long. We have been trying for fourteen years but couldn't project our consciousness, but a few hours ago I could and located some more beings that may be able to help us."

"So some Devousse managed to get through," asked Guru.

"No, but I located a group of about a thousand Gandharvousse..."

"Who are they?" asked Guru.

"They are beings whose ancestors could fly. They were very talented beings, but lost most of their talent when their powers were curbed, millennia ago. At one time, they had magnificent wings and were the best archers in the world, but now they live as grotesque and deformed creatures with protruding backs. That was where their wings were..."

"But just now you told us that you can revive a part of their power..."

"I indeed can, but they should have the will to change and right now they are very angry."

"Why?" asked Guru.

"That, your friend will have to find out and you will have to project your consciousness in order to connect to him. Since you two are so close, you may be able to connect to his mind, but there are risks involved. Are you willing to take the risk?"

"Why not?" asked Guru. "I am ready whenever you are. Just show me how..."

"We will need the help of the seven high priests and ..."

"Sorry for interrupting you," said Guru, "But tell me about the Pravritti Paramdhatousse and Nivritti Paramdhatousse."

"What do you have in mind, young lad?"

"Read my mind and see for yourself what I am visualizing."

"You are a genius," said Vamanousse Hariousse, "I will immediately summon all our craftsmen. It may take five or six hours, but we will make them."

"Make what..?" asked Amy, "...for she couldn't understand what was going on."

"Special arrow heads – thousands of them," said Guru.

"How do you propose to stop and army of thousands of Asourousse using mere bows and arrows?"

"Just wait and watch..."

Guru now turned to Vamanousse Hariousse and looked at him intently.

"I am ready to try to project my consciousness and

contact Sri. My body is ready and my soul is more than ready."

"Then let us start," said Vamanousse Hariousse, "but let me warn you of the consequences. You would face tremendous pressure, you could go crazy..."

"Not a problem," said Guru. "I'm already crazy. What more could happen..?"

The tiny priest gave him a look that was hard to define. Then he sent for the other high priests. They arrived shortly and sat down in a circle, holding hands. Guru and Vamanousse Hariousse completed the circle. Amy stood a few paces behind Guru. The tiny priest asked Guru to close his eyes and concentrate on his friend Sri, to think of all the good things they shared. Then the high priests began chanting some sort of a verse, in a chorus.

Amy did not understand what they were chanting, but she presumed that it was something very powerful because in a minute or so she saw Guru's body go into spasms. The spasms started increasing in frequency and intensity and Guru began shaking violently. A scream escaped Amy's lips as he collapsed. She ran to him and felt for a pulse and was relieved to find a weak one. She tenderly wiped his nose that had begun bleeding once again.

"Don't worry he will be up in a couple of minutes. The strain was perhaps a bit too much." said Vamanousse Hariousse with an expression of amusement.

Guru was up in a couple of minutes. He blinked his eyes a few times and looked around. Then he sat up with a start.

"What just happened? For how long was I out?"

"Just a couple of minutes," said Vamanousse Hariousse. "Could you connect with your friend?"

"It's difficult to say. It was like a dream... I thought I was speaking to Sri, but don't know. I feel terribly tired..."

Just then a Sevakousse rushed in and asked for forgiveness for interrupting. He spoke something into the ear of Vamanousse Gopalousse before rushing out of the chamber.

"Is something the matter?" asked Vamanousse Hariousse.

"The Sevakousse reports of a strange chariot flying around our dune and making a buzzing sound. It is unlike anything we have seen before."

He then went on to explain what the Sevakousse had reported. Guru listened intently then stood up.

"According to your description, it seems to be a World War I plane," said Guru, "but how can that be possible? Let's go out and explore... er and is there any way we can signal the craft, say a smoke signal or something."

He described what he wanted and then rushed out of the chamber. He was followed by Amy and Vamanousse Gopalousse. It took them ten minutes to reach the gate of the city. They exited and were out in the open. Guru scanned the skies, but not a thing was in sight. Then he heard a buzz in the distance the buzz seemed to be getting louder and a very tiny shape became visible.

"Is the smoke signaling device ready?"

A tiny man came carrying some sort of pot in his hand that was spewing out thick smoke. He placed it on the ground, sat down, took out a pipe and began playing. The smoke immediately got thicker and began spiraling upwards. In a few minutes the craft was very close and it was apparent that they had seen the smoke signal, for the craft went ahead, circled and began descending. Guru couldn't believe his eyes. The descending aircraft looked exactly like a Viker's Vimy aircraft of the World War I era. The aircraft approached them and landed some forty feet away. Two Xixipians, one male and one female got out of the aircraft and approached Guru, Amy and the Vamanouse who had accompanied him out of the dome. One of the aliens was dressed weirdly. He had a tomahawk haircut, earrings in both ears, golden chain around his neck and was dressed in jeans and a sleeveless jacket. Strangely, he had goggles on and approached them confidently.

"Yo Guru!" said the Xixipian, "Your rescue team had just arrived."

"Xixalstats!!!" exclaimed Guru, "How on earth did you find me? And look at you..!"

"Hey buddy," said the Xixipian, sounding very cool, "It was difficult, but me n the wife decided not to go back unless we found you."

The female Xixipian had by then reached them. Xixalstats pointed to her and spoke.

"Meet m' wife, Xixillia," said Xixalstats, "remember her?"

"Hi Xixi!" said Guru. "You were Xixandra's wing-woman."

"Yes," she said, "But now I assist Xixalstats in our scientific lab. Our situation has not changed much. Initially we were trying to kill each other, now we are merely trying to survive."

"Don't worry," said Guru, "Everything will soon change for the better. But how did Xixalstats change so much? I remember him as the nerd following KingXixorro."

"C'mon," said Xixalstats, "Am chief scientific advisor to the king now."

"I didn't mean that," said Guru. "What's with the punk look?"

"Now I'm a cool dude man."

"Is that a Viker's Vimy from World War I?"

"Cool, isn't it? I built it here. The principle's the same but it can fly long distances – really long. And it has no electronic parts, so is unaffected by the waves. I left behind a smaller two-seater aircraft in our city."

"Guess, you were instrumental in whatever is going on – I mean blocking communication."

"Yeah man," said Xixalstats, "We managed to fry all the electronic equipment on the planet, but sadly many Asourbouts survive and so does the Master Computer."

"You mean that all your modern equipment is finished?"

"Do you think I am so foolish? We have stashed away a few spaceships where they will be safe, but we cannot use them unless we stop transmitting the waves."

Guru was so busy talking to the alien couple that he almost completely forgot Amy and the others. Amy cleared her throat, to draw his attention. The alien looked at her and went close to Guru. He nudged Guru with his elbow and whispered-

"Introduce me to your girlfriend before she gets angry."

"Ah... this is Amy, My gir... eh the princess and this here is Vamanousse Gopalousse, one of the chief priests of the 'Vamanousse'."

Both the aliens bowed before the priest and politely greeted Amy. By then Vamanousse Hariousse came to where they were standing, followed by some Sevakousse. He looked enquiringly at the aliens.

"They are friends," said Guru. "They came here in search of us."

He then went on to introduce the Param Bhramousse to the duo. They bowed low.

"But how on earth did you manage to build these aircrafts?" asked Guru.

"I got the design from the books you had given me when we were at Batatawadai Puram for a week. Once I got the basic design, modifying it was easy. Moreover one has to have some privileges being the King's first cousin."

"Wicked..!" exclaimed Guru. "I didn't know you were the first cousin of Xixorro."

"I am," said Xixalstats, "My father and his mother, are siblings. My father was the chief scientific advisor of the king, until the day he disappeared. We initially thought that Xixandra and her people had something to do with the disappearance, that was when we were enemies and so after we became friends I asked her, but..."

"We had nothing to do with the disappearance of his father Xixeinstein," interjected Xixillia. "He was a very noble man and even we respected him a lot though he was our enemy then."

"Can you take me to the Gandharvousse in that flying device of yours?" asked Vamanousse Hariousse.

"Pardon me? Where..?"

"If I show you the place in your mind, would you be able to recognize it?"

"Yes sir," said Xixalstats, "I will surely recognize it if

you show me and it will be an honour to take you there. But why do you want to go there?"

"Only I can restore the lost power of the Gandharvousse and will have to go there personally to do so. We need the skill of the Gandharvousse, if we have to win this war."

"Sir," spoke Guru, "Can we also send the special arrow heads along?"

"Yes, we can. As we speak, the Vamanousse are busy manufacturing the arrow heads under the guidance of the Bhramousse. But that will take another four to five hours."

"I guess, we can wait for five hours," said Guru. "And it is turning dark. Won't the temperature go way below freezing, as soon as it turns dark?"

"You are absolutely right," said Vamanousse Hariousse, "Neverthless, I want you and the Princess to leave in the flying contraption right now. You will travel to a palace, made of crystals. These crystals are impenetrable to our thoughts and it is likely that Mooisausooura has hidden the Master Computer in there. Locate that evil device of Mooisausooura and destroy it."

"Pardon me," said Xixalstats, "But do you mean we have to go to 'The Royal Palace of Xixibamba'?"

"Yes, they will have to go there. Will you take them?"

"No problem!" said Xixalstats, "If that is where the so called Master Computer is located, we can go there and attempt to destroy it."

"No," shouted Vamanousse Hariousse, "They both have to go. It is their destiny."

"Ok, ok, chill out. I know a place where I can leave

them. It will take about a klaak and a half to reach..."

"What..?"

"He means, 'three hours'," interjected Guru.

"Yes," said Xixalstats, "But then they will have to walk for a long time - many hours to reach the Palace. That spot is as far as we can go, unnoticed."

"So, if you leave now, you can return in six hours?"

"Definitely..!"

"Then will you take me to the Gandharvouse?"

"Your wish is my command sir."

"Then get ready to leave. But first please come into our city and enjoy our hospitality. I have some important business with the boy. Vamanousse Gopalousse and the princess will accompany you two. Bless you!"

Guru and Amy looked at each other for a moment. Then Guru silently followed Vamanousse Hariousse, while Amy followed Vamanousse Gopalousse.

October 17th, 8 am (earth time) Xixibamba

Mooisausooura paced about angrily. Every living cell in his seven foot frame seemed to be emitting fire. He couldn't understand how everything was going terribly wrong. He had meticulously planned for the past fourteen years and now in a span of a couple of days things were going seriously wrong. First the Princess and her caretakers had managed to escape. He had kept her alive so that he may use her powers when the right time arrived, but now wondered why had he kept her alive in the first place? He should have wrung her neck when he had the chance. Then those jinxed boys had landed on the planet and things got worse. The only Rakshousse on the planet had been slain by one of the boys. And suddenly an hour ago, when they were about to invade the underground city of those nosy little aliens and gain access to all their technology, all his electronic equipment ceased to function.

He had to hurriedly shift the Master Computer to the most secure location inside the crystal palace – so secure that the enemy waves could not penetrate. But now he was left without any support. He was happy that the Master Computer had at the very last moment transferred all control of the Asourbouts to him, but was not sure of their efficiency. He had to protect the master computer at all cost, for it was close to unlocking his hidden powers. Then he would go to planet earth and find the way of unlocking the hidden powers of all the Asourousse clan.

A wave of anger surged through him when he thought of his friend King Ramabhadrousse. He felt betrayed by his friend. Who had given the Devousse the right to control all the beings on their home Prithvousse? He was aware that the

218

master computer had the memories of the Great Asourousse King stored, but it had never offered to share them with him. He also knew about the Great War and how the Lord of the Devousse had destroyed the Asourousse King. He held no grudge against the Great Lord, for he had fought in a fair manner and had even spared the Asourousse from total annihilation, but why had the Devousse king snatched all their powers. They could've used those powers to enrich their new planet Prithvousse. Moreover they were so much better than the Manousse. Why had the common Manousse been given the right to rule planet earth? They were slowly poisoning and ruining the planet. They had to be eliminated.

He then wondered about the six Asourbouts sent to earth. Had they succeeded in their mission? He had hatched a perfect plan to mislead the Alien King into attacking them and getting infected by the virus. He had even spent hundreds of hours with the Master Computer, perfecting the virus that would wipe out all humans from earth, but not damage any other species. The information that they had successfully landed on earth had elated him and then someone had blocked communications. It was sheer bad luck – those confounded boys were bad news.

He thought about all the hardships they had had to face when they were transported to Xixipoo fourteen years ago. The planet was cold and dead and they had almost starved to death. The master computer too couldn't do much as it had been rendered weak by the King's final assault, just after it had opened the portal. It had taken them ten years to partially restore the master computer and that too because they had found equipment abandoned by the Xixipians which they could use to strengthen the master computer.

Then a couple of years ago they had noticed activity on the planet. Those darned aliens had returned to their planet.

Imagine the shamelessness of those aliens – first wipe out an entire planet and then return as if nothing had ever happened. By then the Master Computer had become strong enough and began manufacturing the Asourbouts. His own cells had been used to create the bodies of the Asourbouts. In a way they were his children, although a hundred times more powerful than him. However one good thing about the aliens was that they had led him to earth. It was because of them that the Master Computer had located earth and it was possible to plan the invasion of earth. But they had become increasingly nosy and so he had decided to eliminate them. Anyway only a handful of them were left and they had no business returning back to a planet that they had destroyed. However he had underestimated their power and technology and was amazed by how they had managed to evade the sophisticated Asourbouts.

Finally he had located their hidden city, but they always seemed two steps ahead. Now they had gone and deployed a device that destroyed all electronic equipment. But what was the point worrying? He had to launch an attack on the Xixipians and would do so, even if the Asourbouts had to run all the way to the underground city. It would take some more time, but their sheer numbers were enough to destroy the handful of Xixipians. He decided to visit his army of Asourbouts, judge their present abilities and give them fresh orders.

Mooisausooura, accompanied by the handful of Asourousse (who had managed to escape along with him through the portal), marched out to where the Asourbout Army was stationed, ready to attack. When he reached, he was dismayed at what he saw. No doubt they looked terrifying in their armour and all but something was amiss. The army was still, as if made of stone. Normally they would have been tinkering with the crafts, perfecting them, checking their weapons – lively. But here they were standing like a bunch of idiots, mouths agape.

"Attention!" barked Mooisausooura. "What are you doing, you morons? Why aren't you trying to repair the crafts?"

Five commanders marched towards him, while the others remained stationery.

"Sir," shouted an Asourbout, "At your service."

"Listen, you idiots, why are you not trying to repair those confounded crafts?"

"They are beyond repair Sir." said one of the Asourbout commanders.

"What do you mean, beyond repair?"

"Fried Sir," said the commander, "They are completely destroyed."

"Then what about my army?"

"Limited abilities Sir..."

"Explain..."

"When those waves struck, half of the army was lost. Those of us, who remained functional, did so by blocking an emergency circuit in our bodies from those deadly waves. So we have lost eighty percent of our abilities. That is why the army is still, conserving power..."

"I am not interested," said Mooisausooura, "Just tell me how strong you are."

"Maybe, twice as strong as you," said the Commander. "But we have lost our connectivity. We are no longer connected to each other and to the Master. Nevertheless there are ten thousand of us functional."

"I want you to attack the city of those confounded aliens. I don't care how you do it. Destroy that device and wipe out every one of those aliens. For all I care, run from here to there."

"It will take us twelve klaaks to reach..."

"How many hours...tell me how many hours?"

"Twenty four hours Sir," said the commander, "But..."

"But what?" roared Mooisausooura, "Scared of dying?"

"You are well aware that we have no emotions. We are programmed to obey and will gladly perish, but right now we have limited energy and will lose most of it, reaching there..."

"Not my concern," said Mooisausooura with disgust. "Obey my order or perish trying. Do not return to show me your dark faces if you fail. Now get going and take all those buffoons with you..."

"Your wish is our command."

The Asourbout Commander, followed by the four other commanders ran to the assembled soldiers. Then he gave some orders. Immediately the army came alive, picked up sticks, rocks and sharp objects and began running. They raised such a cloud of dust that Mooisausooura was caked in dust. He walked away in a huff, closely followed by a handful of Asourousse.

"See what those idiots are reduced to! Till now they had the most sophisticated weapons and now they are going into battle with sticks, stones and spears. Savages! If only the Aosurousse had their powers! We could have squashed those tiny aliens like insects."

He hurried towards the palace, still followed by the Asourousse, and then stopped so abruptly, that a couple of them bumped into him.

"Why are you nincompoops following me? Don't you have anything better to do?"

"We are guarding you Sir," said the very fat Asourousse closest to him.

"Do I look like I need guarding? Have those waves affected your brains too?"

They stood with their heads bowed.

"Go guard the palace. The princess may return. Break her neck."

"What weapons do we use?"

Mooisausooura couldn't control his temper anymore. He bent and picked up a brick and rushed towards them. The Asourousse fled.

"Guard the palace and don't show your faces again."

He walked briskly into the palace. Normally he would've travelled by hover-chariot but presently nothing was working, so he had to walk. The safe chamber was fifteen levels below, but he had to go, had to talk to the Master Computer. The deeper he went, the eerier it got but he did not stop, even to catch his breath. He finally reached a huge wall and knocked in a rhythmic manner. Immediately crevices appeared in the wall and a door opened. He went in and the door shut behind him. The walls of the chamber were made of some sort of crystal – probably a type of diamond and glowed in the light. At the centre was a sphere and as he approached it, the sphere opened up into two hemispheres and an image was projected out.

"What news do you have, my emperor?"

"Stop calling me that," snapped Mooisausooura. "I am not an emperor and probably won't be one ever."

"Why do you say so?"

"Because, you have not shared all that you know, with me. I activated you. You were dormant for millennia and it was I who got you out of the dormancy, but you continue to keep things from me. Some friend you are..."

"What do you want to know?"

"Everything!" said Mooisausooura, "I want access to the thoughts of the great Asourousse King. I want to know about his powers. Transfer his thoughts into my mind."

"Are you ready to pay the price?"

"What price?"

"If I transfer his thoughts into you, a part of him will live inside you. You will no longer be yourself."

"I don't care. Just do it."

"Then go and relax your mind, for you have to be very calm and in total control when I transfer the information into you. Come back to me in twenty four hours. But I still ask you to consider the consequences."

"You are a computer. How do you speak as if you have emotions?"

"I am a Master Computer. I am intelligent and definitely have evolved... I do have emotions."

"Whatever..." said Mooisausooura, "I'll be back tomorrow."

October 17ᵗʰ, 6 am (earth time)
Batatawadai Puram Temple

They were all seated around the makeshift table in the huge room of the lower level of the temple. Nath idly gazed around the room. He saw Ghasitaram's vegetables neatly stacked in one corner, but he was not to be seen. Perhaps he was out in the open, cooking something sumptuous. Sleeping bags lay on the floor. The hum of the table fan was distinct.

"May I have everyone's attention please?"

Nath stiffened a bit and turned to the Principal who was seated at one end of the table. Seated to his right were Sri's father, Keshava and Dr. Naik while Gendamal was seated to his left. Nath was at the other end of the table. Everybody looked terribly tired. Nath noticed that Dr. Naik seemed to the person affected the most. He had hardly slept in the last couple of days and had spent almost every waking hour trying to help the alien king. He had black sacs under his bloodshot eyes and looked very weak. The principal too looked very tired as he had been using all the resources at his disposal, to try and locate the abducted boys. His worst fear was facing the mothers of the missing boys. How would he explain their disappearance? Moreover if the Asourbouts succeeded in reaching the ailing king, humankind faced potential extinction. Gendamal and Keshava had been running about, but seemed much better than the others since they were getting some sleep.

"It is now more than forty eight hours since this crisis began and I thought we should meet and strategize further," said the principal in a tired voice. "Now each one of you, narrate your findings to the group and let us together plan the further course of action."

Dr. Naik was the first to speak. He informed the others that despite trying his best, the condition of King Xixorro was steadily getting worse. At that rate, he would not last for more than forty eight hours. He had been delirious in the past twenty four hours and time and again was affected by some sort of muscular spasms. The scientists had been working round the clock, but had made very little progress. The virus present in the king's body seemed to be bioengineered and was waiting for some sort of trigger. The doctor believed that some sort of biological trigger would fully activate the now dormant virus and if that happened, mankind was doomed.

Then Keshava and Gendamal narrated their experiences in the past two days. They had been visiting the camping site owned by Maya under some pretext or the other and been keeping an eye on the Asourbouts. They confirmed Nath's observations and also the fact that the six Asourbouts looked exactly alike. Though they outwardly resembled humans, their behaviour and the way in which they moved proved beyond doubt that they were engineered beings. On one occasion Gendamal had seen one of them move so fast, that confirmed the fact of their being cyborgs. They had stopped visiting the site as their frequent visits had begun to raise suspicions among people. However, Gendamal had sent Riya a couple of hours ago to go and spy on the campsite and he mentioned that she was expected shortly.

Finally Principal Sandipani spoke solemnly.

"You all have gone way beyond your call of duty and I thank you for it. I am indebted to Nath for his contributions. He has behaved so maturely despite being so young. Had it not been for him and his fast thinking, we would probably be yet searching for the Asourbouts and let us not forget that he has devoted a lot of time at the communication centre. Though we had a communication blackout with the Himalayas, it was he who was persistent and finally managed to establish some contact with the team at the Himalayas. We have not failed in every endeavour, as Dhondiba has been rescued and I am told that the girls Tina and Varshika have some sort of device with them that may protect us from the Asourbouts. I have spoken to Ishwar and he will arrange for a plane to be sent to the airstrip at the foot of the Himalayas. Hopefully they will be back in about ten hours.

"Sir," interrupted Nath. "Do you think our village will be in any sort of danger, if those robots attack?"

"If I am right, they will not venture near the village. In fact when the time comes, they will launch a full scale attack on the temple. So we need to worry more about ourselves at the moment. I have discussed this with Ishwar and both of us agreed that considering the present circumstances, we can wait for not more than forty eight hours. Then we will have to contact the authorities.

"But why?" complained Nath.

"Why..? - Because things are already getting out of hand. We are not equipped to deal with such a major crisis."

"But the authorities will come and take away King Xixorro and perform all sorts of experiments on him," said a worried Nath. "The military will come snooping around our temple and its sanctity will be lost. We have to find a way out. Moreover, what if the aliens decide not to return Guru and Sri? If they realize that the king is in the hands of the authorities, they may sever all ties with earth."

"I share your concern, but I cannot go beyond a limit.

So pray that the crisis gets resolved in the next forty eight hours."

"You have to give us more time sir," said Nath. "We all are trying our best. I even brought Mr. Bose's equipment from my house."

"Mr. Bose's equipment?" said the principal raising an eyebrow.

"Yes sir. He had left a bag full of equipment before he disappeared. I have not entirely gone through his stuff, but there are a lot of gizmos in the bag and believe it or not, he is a genius. I just need some time to figure out his stuff."

"I am sorry kid," said the Principal, "but time is something that we don't have, at the moment."

Their conversation was interrupted when Riya came bursting in. She was panting heavily and sweat dripped from her forehead.

"I have news," said Riya, "and it isn't good."

"What happened?" asked a concerned Gendamal.

"The Asourbouts have disappeared from the campsite.

"Disappeared?" asked the Principal.

"I kept an eye on the campsite for three quarters of an hour. When nothing stirred, I went nearer."

"That was a dangerous thing to do," said Gendamal. "What if they had attacked you?"

"C'mon dad, I took precautions," said Riya, "and then, when I was convinced that the site was deserted, I visited it. The tents were empty and the Asourbouts were nowhere in sight, so I looked around and found this."

She handed a piece of equipment to the Principal.

"That looks similar to King Xixorro's communicator," said Nath. "Looks like, communication with Xixipoo has not been established yet. The Asourbouts have been trying hard and have failed."

"But didn't King Xixorro mention that they are linked to the Master Computer on Xixipoo?"

"Yes," said Nath. "But when their internal communication failed, they must've tried other options."

"Then why have they disappeared from there?" asked the Principal.

"Because they must've sensed that the condition of King Xixorro is taking a turn for the worse. And they must be getting ready to attack us."

"Wait a minute," said the Principal. "We are jumping to conclusions. Let us first try to confirm that they have indeed deserted the camp and will not return. Keshava and Gendamal will keep an eye on the campsite for the rest of the day. Also they will make discrete enquiries about the Asourbouts. Someone would've surely seen something. In the meanwhile we will be extra cautious here. We can also start patrolling the forest around the temple cautiously. We are bound to notice something. Let's wait till the girls and Dr. Madhusudan return before deciding our further course of action."

They dispersed – all except Riya and Nath.

"I've decided to camp here tonight," said Riya.

"But, it may be dangerous," said Nath. "What if they attack tonight?"

"That is exactly why I want to be here," asserted Riya. "If those devils attack tonight, then I want to be here. Will

229

you accompany me home? I need to pack some equipment."

"What sort of equipment?"

"My bows and arrows..."

"Really?" asked Nath. "Do you think mere arrows will stop them?"

"Maybe not," said Riya. "But we can't fight with them bare handed. Moreover I am a good shot."

"Give me fifteen minutes. Let me check the communication equipment once again and then we can leave."

They left for the village half an hour later. Nath accompanied Riya to her farm where she packed her archery equipment and some clothes for the night. Then they visited Guru's house. Nath had expected to find his mother there, but was disappointed to know that she was in Dr. Madhusudan's dispensary. The dispensary had been shut for the past two days due to his absence, so she had opened it to complete pending paperwork and also take the delivery of dentures meant for some patients. However Guru's and Sri's mothers were there. They seemed extremely happy and were having breakfast together. Ever since Nath had conveyed the good news of Uncle Dhondiba's rescue, there was great jubilation in the three houses. Sadly, the ladies had no clue of the imminent danger and also that their dear sons had disappeared in a spacecraft.

"Why are you two so glum?" asked Guru's mother. "I bet you are missing your friends and would've liked to be with them, but can't you see how big a role you have played in locating my brother? Principal Sandipani told us everything – how you have hardly slept for the past two days and have been constantly monitoring the communication equipment."

"He did?" asked Nath.

"But what about the other two rascals?" asked Sri's Mother. "You told us nothing about them. Did they get into any sort of trouble there?"

"Not at all," lied Nath. "On the contrary they behaved in a very mature way. In fact though it was decided that Tina's father would accompany Uncle Dhondiba to the hospital, they insisted on accompanying him and asked Tina's father to proceed to the village with the girls."

"You mean, they are not coming tonight," asked Guru's mother dismayed.

"No," lied Nath again. "Right now they are in the hospital with Uncle Dhondiba. I spoke to them an hour ago. They will leave, once Uncle Dhondiba is declared stable by the doctors."

"But why haven't they spoken to us in these two days?" asked Sri's mother. "They could've easily phoned us from the hospital. They left without saying goodbye, haven't spoken to us. I fail to understand what is going on with those boys. I'm really worried for them."

"Don't worry," said Nath. "They can take care of themselves. Have done so on many previous occasions."

"You are not hiding anything from us, are you?" asked Guru's mother.

"Why would I do so?" asked Nath keeping a straight face. He could not bear the pang of guilt that he felt in his stomach. At that moment his cell phone rang and he had to answer it, as the call was from Gopal, who had accompanied Uncle Dhondiba to the hospital.

"Hello Mr. Gopal. How is Uncle Dhondiba?"

Nath glanced around nervously as the ladies watched

him with hawk eyes.

"He's fine. The doctors say that he had a close call. It will take many months for him to fully recover."

"What about Guru and Sri?"

"How am I to know? They are with you, aren't they?"

Nath pretended as if he had not heard that part of the conversation.

"Tell them that their mothers are really cross with them for not phoning home."

"What in God's name are you talking about? You very well know that they are not here."

Nath once again ignored the last comment and spoke assertively.

"If they are around, then their mothers would like to speak..."

He did not have time to complete his sentence because Guru's mother snatched the phone from his hand.

"Hello Mr. Gopal. This is Radhika, Dhondiba's sister. How is my brother? And is my boy around? I would like to give him an earful. Imagine running off without telling his mother and what about that friend of his? Hope they are not causing you a lot of trouble?"

He spoke to her for the next five minutes and she listened wide eyed. Nath was sweating profusely. He was worried what the man would say. Would he spill the beans? However after about five minutes Guru's mother handed him the phone. He placed it to his ear.

"I don't know what exactly is going on, but I played along. I told her that Guru and his friend have gone to the pharmacist to get some medicines for Dhondiba. Also I promised that they would phone once they got back. You better explain what is going on."

Nath once again kept a straight face and spoke.

"Thank you so much sir. I appreciate all that you have done for me – for us. I will surely call you once I am out of here."

There was a beep from the other side. Gopal had hung up. Nath heaved a sigh of relief. He looked at Riya. She had been there beside him all the while – frozen like a statue.

"Why are you so pale Riya?" asked Guru's mother in a very jovial tone.

"Has your mother returned? And why do you have all that equipment?"

"My mother will return in four days," stammered Riya. "I have this equipment because I have a big competition coming up."

"Hope you win."

"So do I," said Riya, "for it is the most important competition of my life."

"O, how silly of us," said Guru's mother. "We are enjoying our breakfast and haven't offered you any. Please do join us."

"Thank you, but we just had breakfast. I will be in touch as soon as I hear from Tina and Varshika."

"You better do that boy," said Sri's mother. "Is there anything that you want to convey to your mother?"

"Just tell her to take care," said Nath.

"Radhika, our boys are growing up fast," said Sri's mother. "Now they are asking their mothers to take care."

Nath and Riya did not utter another word and left. They had a long day ahead.

October 17th, 7 am (earth Time)
Foot of the Himalayas

The high priest was pacing up and down the tent. Simba had never seen him so angry, ever before. He briefly looked at Simba and then at the others seated in the tent.

"What a bunch of murderers that scoundrel has gathered around him," he said as if he were spitting fire. "Look what they have done to my poor Simba."

"More than half of them perished in the avalanche, O noble one," said one of the men seated beside Simba. "The others barely escaped."

"We were lucky that the noble Vanars came to our rescue, else we too would've perished," said the priest. "How are our injured warriors?"

"They are being taken care of," said Simba. "I've arranged to send them back to Africa."

"I want you to personally take them home," said the Abbot.

"With all due respect Sir," said Simba. "That is one order that I cannot obey. You know very well that a wild elephant would not be able to pry me away from you. Moreover, I have promised my grandfather, the king, to always be by your side. So I beg of you not to give me orders that I won't be able to obey."

"Don't be obstinate boy," said the Abbot. "You are hurt and need to rest. I absolutely cannot permit you to continue on this mission."

"Sir," said Simba. "The medicines administered to us by the noble Vanars have worked wonders on all of us. I am much better now."

"He speaks the truth," asserted the others.

"Ok," said the Abbot. "Have it your way. But we must leave soon."

"Are you sure that they are going to that village?"

"Yes," said the Abbot. "Somehow that scoundrel is always one step ahead of us. This time I want to be two steps ahead of him. I ensured that he heard about the girls taking the relic to their village. He has our relic and will be eager to obtain theirs. So right now he is on his way to their village with his bunch of murderers."

"You mean, whoever survived," said Simba.

"You're right. But don't for a second underestimate that bunch. They are highly trained killers."

"So are we, O Abbot..." said the others. "We are the best warriors of our clan."

"To Batatawadai Puram we go," said the Abbot. "But remember, don't touch the relic whatsoever, for if you touch it, you shall perish. We shall leave in an hour."

October 17ᵗʰ, 2 pm (earth time) Fringe area of the Xixidorra Desert

Xixandra and Sri had been flying for about eight hours scanning the terrain below. Sri was pretty tired. The craft vibrated a lot and had probably been made in a hurry, but it travelled fast. Ever since he had landed on the planet, he had been running around and was tired - so tired that he dozed off. The rhythmic hum of the aircraft sounding like a lullaby acted as a catalyst so Sri drifted off to a deep slumber.

He dreamed of his village... dreamed of the pranks that Guru and he played... they had planned an elaborate prank on the Chemistry teacher... a stink bomb... Guru was beside him, tugging him...

Sri, Sri, where are you? Can you sense me? Amy and I are safe with the Vamanousse. The chief priest wants you to find the Gandharvousse. They are located below a mountain, whose peak is shaped like a crescent moon. Go there and convince them to join our cause. Tell them that the princess needs them...remind them of their vow...

Sri woke up with a start.

"Guru spoke to me just now," said Sri in an excited tone. "He wants us to meet these people called the Gandharvousse and enlist their support..."

"Impossible!" said Xixandra. "You are tired and must've been dreaming."

"Exactly!" said Sri. "I was dreaming and he spoke to me in my dream, but it sounded so real. Didn't you yourself say a few hours ago that the princess can read minds? What if

237

Guru...?"

"The princess can read the minds of people in her close vicinity. We are very far away from Guru and so high up in the sky..."

"But he described the place in detail. It is at the base of a mountain with a tip shaped like a crescent moon..."

"What..?"

"He did!"

"You have never ever been on this planet and you couldn't have known about that peak. Yes, I believe you."

"Then let's go there and find these Gandharvousse. How far is that place from here?"

"It will take three of your hours to reach there but then it will start getting dark and temperatures will plummet. Once we land we have very less time to locate the beings."

She looked at the sun, probably to get her bearings and then turned her craft in a particular direction. Sri realized that with no sophisticated instruments, she must be navigating using the planet's sun. Sri, once again drifted to sleep. Three hours passed, yet Sri did not show the slightest indication of waking though Xixandra had been repeatedly calling him.

"Wake up," yelled Xixandra loudly and Sri woke up with a start.

"Huh? Have we reached?"

She merely pointed a long finger. Sri saw a very tall peak ahead. Its tip distinctly looked like a crescent moon. The queen began to descend and they landed at the foot of the peak in five minutes. As soon as they alighted from the craft, Sri felt the biting cold breeze on his skin. Though he had a protective jacket on, it felt as if he was being jabbed with thousands of knives.

"Hope we find the Gandharvousse soon," said Sri, "It's freezing out here."

The queen handed him a shawl that he gratefully accepted and wrapped around himself.

"It is made of a special material and should keep you comfortable."

They explored the region for fifteen minutes, but everything around seemed cold and dead.

"Are you sure Guru mentioned this very place?" asked the queen. "It seems so cold and dead."

But Sri was not paying attention to her. He was looking at the tall boulders around them. Something was moving. Then in a jiffy, they were surrounded by beings brandishing swords and spears. The beings were fifty yards away and encircled them. Sri concluded that they were indeed the Gandharvousse, but they seemed hostile.

He once again hurriedly looked around. More and more heads were becoming visible by the moment and then one of them boldly approached the duo. Sri studied the approaching being, that was close to six feet tall and extremely thin – pencil thin. His back had a visible hunch and so he was bent. He carried a huge spear with a diamond tip.

"What are you doing in our territory?"

"Are you the Gandharvousse?"

"Who wants to know?"

"I am Xixandra, the queen of Xixipoo."

He looked around and laughed aloud.

"This little pipsqueak is the queen of the aliens," he yelled as the others made hooting sounds. "We have ourselves a nice hostage..."

"Listen Idiot," yelled Sri, "She is the queen of this planet and you will respect her."

"Or else what?" asked the being putting his spear to Sri's chest, pricking him a bit.

"Do that one more time, and I will stick that spear..."

Sri had no time to complete his statement. The being was upon him and hit him on the face. Blood oozed from the left side of his lip. Sri was up fast and faced the being with clenched fists. However before he had time to react, the being somersaulted over him and hit him on the head. Sri fell down feeling dizzy but got up in a jiffy. The queen had her sword drawn but Sri motioned her to stop. The being once again somersaulted over Sri – a mistake, for Sri was ready and landed a well aimed blow on him sending him sprawling. Immediately a couple more of the beings joined the fray and were upon Sri. He was outnumbered.

"Stop, you cowards," shouted someone.

Everyone turned to the voice. Then there was absolute silence. It was as if every one of those beings was facing a dilemma. Then the being that had attacked Guru spoke-

"The old fool who led us to this wretched planet is back."

The old man ignored the remarks and looked straight at the crowd that had gathered.

"Do not forget that you are the Gandharvousse. You are bound by vow to protect the Devousse or lay down your lives doing so. Have you lot forgotten the holy oath you took, before initiation? Do not listen to Vishvavasu, for he is blinded by hatred."

They looked at him with heads slightly bowed.

"Bretheren," shouted the being that had first attacked Sri, "Remember the hardships that we have faced on this planet for the past fourteen years. Remember how this very man, fourteen years ago led us into that portal, because he wanted to be a hero and rescue the kidnapped princess and the Vamanousse leaders?"

"I had to," said the old man. "It is the duty of every soldier to protect the Devousse..."

"But we were ten years old – trainee soldiers..."

"I had no other alternative. At that time we were closest to the portal and there was no time to wait for the soldiers to arrive. The portal would've closed..."

"We've met the princess," said the queen. "She is very much alive and needs your help at the moment."

"That won't happen," said Vishvavasu, "I am their leader and I alone decide who to ally with?"

"Then I, Paravasu, former leader of the Gandharvousse, challenge you to a duel, in order to challenge your leadership."

"You think you stand a chance, old man? Did you forget how I defeated you seven years ago and threw you out of the tribe?"

"I have grown feeble and don't have it in me, but she does," said Paravasu pointing to a young girl, who quietly walked to him and took a place next to him. She is of royal blood, for she is your sister. We have been in exile for seven years and now she has come to claim her position in the tribe."

"Mrugakshi my sister," said Vishvavasu, "Why are you listening to the old fool? Didn't he bring you here as a two year old baby? Didn't he separate you from our mother?"

"That is no way to speak of your father," said Mrugakshi. "I am aware that he brought us to this planet, separated us from our mother, but he had no other alternative. As a Gandharvousse, he was bound to help the Princess. At that time you were the only soldiers with him. I was in his care and he had to bring me along because a fierce battle was raging. He couldn't have left me amidst the fighting. I am not defending what he did, but am asserting that whatever he did, he did with pure intentions."

"No," said Vishvavasu, "He did it because he wanted to be a big hero."

"This planet is in peril and I am requesting you to obey him, else I shall be forced to fight you."

"Then we fight," said Vishvavasu. "I hope he has trained you well."

The circle widened as the others moved back. She had some sort of stick in her hand whereas he had a spear. Sri couldn't help noticing how beautiful she was. Her eyes were big and looked like a doe's eyes. She was very thin, but extremely beautiful - enchantingly beautiful, but had a protruding back and a bend, just like her brother and the other Gandharvousse.

They sized up each other for a moment then suddenly began fighting. Sri was astonished by the speed at which they fought. It all seemed like a blur and lasted for a minute and then was over. She had landed two powerful blows on his head and he sat on the floor, blood oozing from his head. She had her stick to his throat. He sat there motionless for many minutes, with the crowd looking on in silence. Then she turned

242

to the crowd-

"I am your new leader and order you to obey my father," she said in a commanding voice.

Everyone got on their knees and bowed to her. Then there were cries of jubilation.

"Banish him," said the crowd in a chorus. "Throw him out the way he threw you out."

However Sri stepped in and raised his hand. The crowd fell silent.

"Friends, we need Vishvavasu. He is a brave warrior and powerful leader. This planet is in peril and we need every warrior."

He gave his hand to Vishvavasu, who accepted it and pulled him to his feet. He was surprisingly light. A couple of Gandharvousse approached Vishvavasu and gently wiped the blood of his forehead.

"Even if what you say is true, there is little we can do," said Vishvavasu. "I have seen those creatures. They are not living beings and we don't stand a chance."

"I am sorry to interrupt," said Xixandra, "but you are mistaken. We have destroyed half of them and considerably slowed down the rest."

"There are about a thousand of us and ten thousand of them, if what you say is true. What chance do we stand?"

"The odds are not favourable, but if we do nothing at this juncture, then they will eventually destroy all of us, one by one."

"How far away is your kingdom?"

"Very far away," said the queen.

"Then how do you suppose we reach there in time?"

"Just prepare for battle and leave the rest to us," implored Sri. "I am sure we will find a way."

"Get you bows and arrows ready," shouted Vishvavasu. "Get ready for battle and pray well tonight. It just might be your last prayer."

The weather had turned bitter and unbearable by then, so the Gandharvousse welcomed Sri, Xixandra, Mrugakshi and Paravasu to their dwellings amongst the rocks. The dark clouds of war loomed ahead.

October 17ᵗʰ, 9 pm (earth time)
Batatawadai Puram Temple

It was just after nine. Nath and Riya were in the communications room, hungrily eating the food served to them by Ghasitaram. They had been there, ever since both of them had returned from Guru's house that morning and discussed the events of the past hours as they ate.

The first thing that Nath had done on coming there was phoning Gopal. He apologized for whatever had happened in Guru's house and explained that the disappearance of the boys was connected to the Himalayan incident. He assured Gopal that both Sir and Guru's father were aware and had purposely kept the women in dark to avoid panic. Gopal did not wish to know any more and assured Nath that if the ladies phoned him, he would handle the situation. He also offered to help them. Nath thanked him and assured him that he had already done more than his share in helping find Uncle Dhondiba. Nath promised to keep him posted and hung up.

Then Nath had spent the next hour on his laptop editing recordings of Guru and Sri's voice. He added a lot of static in the background so that their voices would be barely audible but ensured that their voices would be recognizable. Once done, he called Guru's mother and played the recording. When he was sure that they were satisfied, he disconnected the call and hoped that they would not call him or try to contact him for the rest of the day.

In the meanwhile Riya had got her Archery equipment ready. She had assembled her bows and mended damaged arrows, then had packed her quiver full of arrows and kept all

245

her equipment handy.

Then both of them had spent the rest of their afternoon carefully going through Mr. Bose's equipment that Nath had brought the previous day. Riya wanted to know why Nath was so obsessed with Mr. Bose and Nath had answered that according to him, the man had one of the best scientific minds on the planet. Nath agreed that the man was a bit – not a bit, but terribly queer, but that did not change the fact that he was a genius. They had found a number of gadgets, but couldn't figure out any of them. There were a couple of glove like gadgets and Nath was sure that they were more than mere gloves, but even those, they couldn't figure out. Finally after tinkering with the equipment for three hours, they had given up and carefully packed all the equipment in a huge travel bag with the name 'Bose' written boldly on the side.

They realized that they were terribly hungry because they had skipped lunch and were about to go to Ghasitaram to get something to eat when the phone rang. It was Varshika. So they had spent the next few hours talking to the girls because the call dropped a number of times. Nath and Riya couldn't believe their eyes when the girls had narrated the story of Vanars and that Tina had in her possession an Astra that could protect them and potentially close the portal. However Nath was terribly worried when the girls mentioned that they would come straight to the temple and not go home. He really did not know for how much longer they could keep on lying to the ladies. He had requested the girls to convince Tina's father to go straight home and cook up some story. He had also assured them that Riya's father would be at the farm to receive them when the helicopter arrived and would bring them straight to the temple.

They had been interrupted on two occasions by Riya's father who told them that the campsite was indeed empty.

Gendamal and Keshava had searched the periphery of the forest but their search had been futile. Then Nath had requested them to pick up the girls from Gendamal's farm and bring them straight to the temple and convince Guru's father to go home. So it had been agreed that the duo would bring the girls to the temple while Nath, Riya and the others would stay put at the temple. Thus the two men had left.

Then at about half past seven, there had been another emergency. Dr. Naik had come shouting that one of the alien king's hearts had stopped beating. He had two hearts and one had stopped. They had all rushed into the room where the king had been quarantined, only to be promptly driven out by the scientists. Finally half an hour later, the two scientists along with Dr. Naik had managed to get the alien king's heart started. They had used a pump to resuscitate him and injected Adrenalin into him. But the dose had probably been high because the king got up and tried to run out. He begged of them to let him go home to his wife and children. It had been almost impossible to manage him and so the scientists had pumped him with sedatives and laid him on the bed. Seeing the condition of the king, Principal Sandipani had almost thrown a fit.

At around nine, Ghasitaram had served dinner to everyone present in the temple. That included Dr. Naik and the two scientists, Principal Sandipani, Nath and Riya. Seeing the steaming food, the teens had realized how hungry they were.

So now they ate the food with great gusto as they summed up the events of the past hours.

With food in their tummy, both felt much better. After food, Nath went to the communications room briefly and noticed Varshika's tarantula pacing up and down the tank. He realized that in all the confusion, he had forgotten to feed the spider and it was probably very hungry so rushed to the glass tank, carefully opened the lid and emptied the dead insects that he had collected the previous night into the glass tank. He was about to put the lid on when he heard a blood curdling scream from Ghasitaram. Nath immediately rushed to the upper temple followed by Riya who had a bow fitted with an arrow ready in her hands. They saw Gahsitaram on the floor at the entrance of the temple, being pacified by the Principal.

"It was the devil," he said crying and hitting his head. "It will kill me."

"Now relax," said the Principal, "and describe exactly what you saw."

Riya cautiously moved to the entrance of the temple, bow in hand followed by Nath. It took a lot of guts to peep out, but they did. There was no one outside. However Nath noticed some blades of grass spring up. Someone had been there recently. As there was no one in sight, the duo made their way back into the temple and found Gahsitaram on his feet, drinking water from a glass that he held in his shivering hands. He was obviously petrified. When everyone had just begun to calm down, they heard a loud crash from within the subterranean temple.

Nath rushed below with Riya close to his heels, followed by Sandipani and Ghasitaram, who probably did not want to be left alone. He rushed into the communications room, just in time to see the mamba sink its fangs into King Xixorro. Apparently the sedatives had been insufficient. The king had wandered into the communications room and had come face to face with the tarantula that had escaped from the glass tank because Nath had forgotten to put on the lid when Ghasitaram had screamed. The startled king had lost his balance and landed on the other glass tank, knocking it over and releasing the mamba. The irritated mamba had done what it does best – and that was, repeatedly sinking its fangs into the alien king.

"Oh God!" lamented the Principal with both hands on his head. "What has happened now?"

Riya rushed to help the king, but Nath grabbed her before she could touch him. She did not have any protective gear on and risked being infected by the virus. For that matter, there was no saying whether any of them were safe because of their close proximity to the alien king. One of the scientists appeared with protective gear on, lifted the king and took him to his quarantine quarters. They tied a tourniquet around his arm just above the bite. Remembering that the critters were free, Nath rushed back to the communications room, only to find the principal with a stout stick in his hands.

"I'll kill the damn snake," he said, "or it will kill us all."

"Leave the snake alone," said a loud voice.

Varshika had returned, followed by Tina, Keshava and Gendamal. She immediately rushed into the communications room and grabbed the snake by its head. Nath lifted the fallen tank and placed it on the table. The glass had a crack, but the tank was in one piece. Varshika carefully placed the snake in the tank and covered it with a makeshift lid as the original lid lay shattered on the ground. Then she swiftly grabbed the spider and placed it in the other tank and covered that too.

"What exactly is going on?" asked a baffled Tina.

Nath did his best to explain whatever was going on in a few words. Then they all rushed to see the king. The scientists and Dr. Naik were trying to revive him. His body went into convulsions and he began to sweat profusely.

"We need to place the Astra on the altar immediately," said Tina.

She rushed into the main sanctum of the temple closely followed by Nath, Varshika and Riya. The torches made by Nath were burning brightly. They assembled in front of the statue. Some kind of glow seemed to be emanating from it. The glow began to increase as Tina opened the purse that contained the Astra. Once the Astra was out, the statue seemed to be emitting light of its own. Tina stood in front of the statue enraptured. She had held the Astra in both hands. Everyone, except Varshika, had to cover their eyes as the glow was too powerful for them to see.

"Where do we place the Astra?" asked Varshika almost in a whisper.

"I know," said Tina.

She carefully removed the stone from the hands of the statue and placed it near its feet. Then she placed the Astra in the depression where the stone stood. The result was spontaneous and magnanimous. Both of them could literally see ripples of energy radiate out in all directions exactly like ripples formed on the surface of a pond when a stone is thrown in it. The others could not enjoy the spectacular sight because the burst of energy was too much for them to bear. The temple seemed to tremble as if struck by an earthquake. Then, as if nothing had happened, everything returned back to normal.

"What just happened?" asked Nath.

"I believe that an energy field had been created around the temple," said Varshika. "We are probably safe from attack – at least for the moment. Now let's go and see if we can help the king."

She rushed out, followed by the others and bumped into someone. He was a small person, for the collision knocked him to the floor. He had a large head, unkempt hair and a beard. His tiny spectacles lay on the floor.

"And who exactly are you?" asked Varshika.

"Mr. Bose, you came!" exclaimed Nath simultaneously. "I was praying that you would. We are in serious trouble."

"Where is Xixorro?" asked the small man.

"And how do you know him?" asked Varshika, with arms folded in defiance.

He looked at her with a hint of a frown on is brow as Nath helped him up. They rushed to the alien king.

"Explain exactly what happened to him, in all details and fast," he said looking at Nath in the eye.

He rushed to the king and began examining him as Nath meticulously explained the events of the past three days. The scientists tried to intervene, but he waved them off with some authority. This Mr. Bose seemed to be an altogether different man from the meek and shy Mr. Bose that Nath had known. Here was a man, confident and authoritative, a man who knew exactly what he was doing.

"I will need my bag – the one I gave you," said Mr. Bose. "But unfortunately there is no way we can leave this place."

"Why is that so?" asked the Principal.

"Because those cyborgs have surrounded us," said Mr. Bose. "I do not know how you created such a powerful energy field around this place, but it is keeping them out. However, the very same energy field has activated some sort of failsafe in them. They seemed determined to reach here and will destroy anyone coming in their path or be destroyed trying to reach here. Nothing goes out of here or comes in."

"Who exactly are you?" asked the Principal.

"Never mind who I am. Our first priority is saving the king and for that I need my bag."

"I have it right here," said Nath as he handed the heavy bag to the small man.

"Good boy," said the small man. "You have learned well and I am proud of you. Now everybody leave me alone and let me do my work. I shall not tolerate any disturbance."

He spoke with such authority that everyone including the Principal left the quarantine quarters. Mr. Bose went to the king and began performing some tests on him.

The others gathered in the big hall. Since the makeshift table did not have enough seating arrangement, they sat wherever they could find place and spent the next two hours exchanging information and sharing their personal experiences. After two hours, a tired but relieved Mr. Bose came in and sat down. Everyone looked at him in anticipation as he wiped his brow and began to speak.

"The king is out of all danger. I collected a few samples of the dead virus from his body."

"Dead virus?" asked Nath.

"Yes," said the small man. "It was the poison from the snake that killed the virus. However the dose of poison in king Xixorro's body was so high that had I reached five minutes later, he would have perished. I have neutralized the poison. But he will take a few hours to recover. I need more poison from the snake to create a vaccine. I will inject each of you with the vaccine so that you are safe, in case you have been infected."

"Who exactly are you?" asked the Principal once again, "For you have performed a feat that no human can perform."

"That is because I am not a human," said Mr. Bose as everyone looked at him, mouths agape. "My name is Xixeinstein, chief scientific advisor to king Xixorro. I also happen to be his maternal uncle."

"Then why are you living on earth?" asked the Principal.

"Because I was fed up of the war, that's why. I am a man of science and was against the war right from the beginning. I tired convincing the erstwhile king, Xixorro's father, to put an end to the nine hundred year long conflict and make peace with the other clan, but he did not listen to me. Xixorro and I were close and I knew that he was kind hearted, but it was too late by the time he ascended the throne. We had spent many centuries outside our planet fighting against our own. I longed for a home but alas our planet was dead. I discovered the portal, quite by accident and decided to come to earth. Here I designed a bio-suit and began living amongst you guys. My respect for you increased manifold when you managed to end our nine-hundred year long war in a few days, by your good sense and deeds. This boy, Nath, has been very kind to me and I love him as much as I love my nephew Xixorro. When you guys helped Xixorro and Xixandra end the war, I was pleased and wanted to go back to Xixipoo right then, but refrained from doing so, because I wanted the younger generation to try living their lives peacefully without the interference from our generation. But since my people had arrived on earth, I was scared of my cover being blown, so I decided to get myself incarcerated in a mental asylum. I had planted certain spy devices in the many gifts that I had given to Nath and kept tabs on him. Finally when I got the news of Xixorro, I came to help you guys."

"Can you help us destroy the Asourbouts?" asked Varshika. "Do you have any weapons that can destroy them?"

"I do have a couple of weapons, but no energy source to run them, at least not here."

"Then where?" asked Nath.

"At your place," said the small man. "Remember the crystal ball that I gave you? It can recharge my weapons."

"It is on my study table at home," muttered Nath.

"But as I told you before, no one goes in or comes out. Those Asourbouts will kill us. We will have to use whatever we have here, to protect ourselves."

"But isn't the king cured and the virus neutralized?" asked Tina. "Then why will they attack us now?"

"That is because their failsafe is activated. Now those robots have only one mission – kill us all and try to extract the virus from the king or perish trying to do so. They will eventually reach us. It may take them some hours, but they will find a way to penetrate the energy field."

Just then Tina's phone rang. It was her father.

"Dad, am I glad to hear your voice?"

"What's going on? Why haven't you guys returned?"

She hurriedly explained the current situation to him.

"No, don't try to come. They will kill you."

"But don't you need the energy source that is on Nath's study table."

"We do, but no human can get past the Asourbouts and we are surrounded."

"I'll figure out..."

The line abruptly went blank.

254

"They have jammed our signals," said Mr. Bose. "Now it's us and them."

"Then let's fortify ourselves," said Keshava. "That way, we will at least stand a chance."

"You are right," said Sandipani. "But there are other tasks to perform. Let us split up into groups. One group can concentrate on fortifying the temple and let the other group concentrate on the Astra. Didn't the Abbot tell you that you will have to figure out yourselves, how to use it."

"But three Astras are required to shut the portal and we have only one," said Tina.

"At least try to figure out how the Astras work," said their Principal.

"I have been working on that," said Nath as he drew out a small diary from his pocket. The inscriptions on the walls of the temple hold the clue to closing the portal."

"Then figure out how the Astra works, while we figure how to hold out against those devil Asourbouts when they attack."

So Varshika, Tina and Nath tried to figure out how the Astra worked not only because they bonded well but also because Tina was the only one who could touch the Astra. The others began helping Xixeinstein in fortifying the temple – all except Dr. Naik, who continued closely monitoring the alien king.

It promised to be a busy night...

October 17th, 11 pm (earth time)
Fringe area of the Xixidorra Desert

Mrugakshi looked at Sri and smiled. She had never been so happy before. They had used the rocks around them as reclining chairs and were gazing at the stars. The bitter cold made it very uncomfortable to be there, but they didn't care because they wanted some privacy. They had wrapped themselves in thick blankets – blankets manufactured by the Gandharvousse.

She recollected the events of the past few hours. Guided by her father and brother, the Gandharvousse had made themselves battle ready. The warriors had checked and rechecked their bows and repaired arrows. Soon there were quivers full of arrows. Swords and spears had been sharpened. The elders had discussed a few war strategies, but that was it. There would be no further planning unless some mode of transport was made available in order to transport the thousand odd Gandharvousse to Xixarappa and hope seemed to be dwindling by the minute. Finally Vishvavasu had ordered the fighters to have their dinner and rest awhile.

Queen Xixandra had been very anxious because her city was in extreme danger. She had decided to wait for a few hours for new developments else she would fly back to Xixarappa. It was better to die amongst her people rather than wait for help from an army that could not reach her city on time. Sri had promised to accompany her back to the city and fight alongside.

After a meager meal (for the Gandharvousse ate less and anyway were starving) they had some free time. It was

256

then that Sri had approached Mrugakshi. Initially she had given him the cold shoulder, but after interacting with him for ten minutes found him irresistible. They had spent the next two hours out in the open, talking to and knowing each other better. The temperatures beyond the rocks had plummeted to thirty degrees below freezing point however the rocks of that area had some sort of minerals in them that trapped the extreme heat of the day. This made the rocks considerably warmer than the surroundings and the temperature amidst the rocks was a couple of degrees above freezing point.

A distinct hum drew them out of their thoughts. The silence of the night was disturbed by the sound that seemed to be getting louder every minute. Sri was up in an instant.

"Looks like the aircraft sent to rescue Guru has found us," said Sri turning to Mrugakshi. "Get the queen here while I draw their attention to us."

But there was no need to draw attention towards themselves, for the many fires of the Gandharvousse could be seen from a great distance. The aircraft got louder and maintained its course towards them. It was descending rapidly and touched the ground on a relatively clear patch of ground, fifty feet away from where Sri was standing.

Two Xixipians, followed by a midget alighted from the craft. Sri peered into the darkness to get a better look at the approaching beings.

"Yo Dude Sri!" shouted one of the Xixipians approaching Sri.

Sri blinked his eyes for a minute and once again stared at the approaching Xixipian. It couldn't be him, for the last time they had met, he was a perfect geek.

"Xixalstats, is that really you???"

257

"Hey man, you gone and hurt my feelings bro..."

"What in the world happened to you? And why are you dressed like a punk?"

The Xixipian couldn't wait any longer and ran towards Sri. They hugged each other.

"Thanks for changing me man," said Xixalstats. "I have followed your path and am now enjoying every moment of my life."

"Unbelievable!"

"Meet the wife," he said pointing to Xixillia, "And hope our queen is fine?"

"She is ok. Is that really a Viker's Vimy from World War I?"

"Yeah dude and your friend Guru went crazy seeing it."

Sri stiffened a bit as his gaze fell on the approaching midget. He looked at Xixalstats enquiringly.

"Show a lot of respect to the small dude," said Xixalstats in a whisper. "He is somebody very important and even kings and queens bow to him."

Sri greeted Vamanousse Hariousse with folded hands as he approached them. Then before a word was spoken, someone shouted loudly –

"It's the Param Bhramousse. He has personally come to us."

Paravasu ran and fell flat at the feet of Vamanousse Hariousse. The Param Bhramousse blessed him and looked around at the gathering crowd.

"What have you done Paravasu? These youth seem so

miserable."

"Forgive me Sire," said Paravasu, "I only performed my duties. We were bound by oath to protect you. When you went through the portal, I followed you..."

"With these children...?" said Vamanousse Hariousse sternly. "What were you thinking?"

"I was only thinking about your safety and the safety of the princess, Sire."

"If king Ramabhadrousse encouraged you, then I resent his behaviour. The Vamanousse have special powers and we easily adapted to the harsh conditions on this planet, but these youth have been living a miserable life."

He then turned to the Gandharvousse, who were curiously watching whatever was going on.

"Listen, O lost children of our planet," said Vamanousse Hariousse, "I know you have been wronged and I have no right to ask for help from you, but it would be wrong on my part not to enlighten you about the true facts. This planet is about to be overrun by creatures that don't live. They will destroy all of us unless we put up a front."

"We are ready to fight till our last breath," said Vishvavasu, "but are outnumbered. Moreover the enemy has far advanced technology."

"You are no ordinary beings but are divine. You ancestors have fought alongside the Great Lord himself."

"With due respect sire," said Vishvavasu, "We are deformed beings who have evolved to be warriors."

"I am the Param Bhramousse and have the ability to restore you to your original form. However the mantra that will supposedly transform you has not been tried for millennia and I am not sure of the consequences. Is anyone willing to try?"

Everyone looked at each other with uncertainty in their eyes. Then before Sri could stop her, Mrugakshi walked to the Param Bhramousse and bowed.

"I am ready to try."

"Then kneel down in front of me."

She knelt down and he began chanting some sort of verse. His chants must've really been powerful, for everyone could feel the vibrations and power of the chant. Mrugakshi was writhing in pain and Sri couldn't control himself when he saw a patch of blood on her back. He rushed towards her but was caught by Vishvavasu.

"She has chosen the path by her own free will and has to face the consequences."

Suddenly Mrugakshi stood up straight, the bend in her back disappearing. The back of the attire she had worn tore off and she sprouted a pair of magnificent wings. Then she ran, wildly flapping her wings and was airborne in a few paces. She kept flapping her wings and reached very high altitude in a short time, zoomed around for a couple of minutes before abruptly descending and landing a couple of feet in front of Sri.

"How was I?"

"You are enchantingly, ravishingly and breathtakingly beautiful," said Sri.

"I asked, how my flight was," she said nudging him in embarrassment.

"Oh that," said Sri, "It was excellent, just superb!"

Cries of joy pierced the night sky. There was a lot of excitement in the air. Then the Param Bhramousse raised his hands. Everyone felt silent.

"You are the Gandharvousse or the Gandharvas, the ancient beings that can fly. You do not know the extent of your powers yet, but will learn gradually. Now who else wants to transform?"

The air was once again filled with cries of joy. Amidst all the chaos, Queen Xixandra ran to the Param Bhramouse and bowed down before him. Tears flowed freely from her eyes. The old man gently blessed her.

"Do not worry, little queen," said the tiny man, "When the Almighty has given your species a second chance, he will also ensure that you are protected."

"Thank you," said the queen in a choked voice.

Mrugakshi ran to Xixandra and took both her hands in her own.

"We will fly to Xixarappa and defend the city."

Sri looked on with amazement. It was going to be an interesting night...

October 18ᵗʰ, 7 am (earth time)
Crystal Palace, Xixibamba

"Wake up," yelled Amy, shaking Guru. "I've been trying to wake you up for so long now."

Guru opened his eyes partially. The planet's sun was way above the horizon. He realized that he must've been fast asleep. Amy, seated beside him, looked heavenly. A cool breeze blowing in their direction carried her fragrance to him and he longed to keep looking at her.

"Wakey, sleeping beauty," said Amy sweetly, "We have to leave, so freshen up."

Guru stretched himself and yawned loudy. He got up with some reluctance and looked around and recollected that they were at the base of a hill, amongst Xibora shrubs. The view above was simply spectacular with the Crystal Palace of King Xixorro twinkling in the bright sunlight. Guru was sure that they would not be spotted from above as they were well hidden amongst the Xibora and other desert shrubs.

"If you walk a couple of minutes in that direction you will find a small stream," said Amy, "You can freshen up there. I will be right here waiting for you. Then we can plan our further course of action."

Guru walked in the direction pointed out by Amy. It had begun to get unpleasant as the sun was well above the horizon. He had to move carefully amongst the shrubs to avoid the sharp thorns that could easily blind one. After walking for about three minutes, he came to a stream. It was much bigger than the one he had seen before when they were lost in the desert and there were many more shrubs on the banks. He got down on his knees, scooped some water in his joined palms and splashed it liberally on his face. The cold water made him feel fresh and alert.

After doing whatever had to be done, Guru was on his way back to Amy and was about to enter a patch of shrubs when he saw a movement from the corner of his eye, so turned to his left to explore. A fox like creature swooped down from the air and gazed at him. It was tinier than the foxes found on earth but very fluffy and cute. The creature approached him, tail wagging gently. Guru felt like cuddling it, but had more urgent tasks at hand, so shooed it away. But the creature had no intention of leaving and held its ground, then another came out of the bushes and another and another. In a span of a minute, Guru was surrounded by fifty odd creatures showing their teeth – razor sharp teeth. He realized that though the creatures looked cute and cuddly, they were far from that and had probably come for a mid-morning snack. He was surrounded with absolutely no weapon to defend himself.

Suddenly, the creatures began sniffing the air and bolted. Guru heaved a sigh of relief on seeing Amy approach.

"What did you do to scare them away?"

"Nothing," said Amy. "They must've sensed my abilities and fled."

"Great, let's go. How long do you think will it take for us to reach the palace?"

"About half an hour," said Amy. "Then we scout the area and find a way in."

"How many of them will be guarding the palace?"

"Haven't the faintest clue," said Amy. "There are only a handful of Asourousse. It is the Asourbouts that worry me."

They returned to their camp, packed whatever little they had and set out towards the Crystal Palace. Guru let Amy take the lead, because he believed she knew more about the terrain than him and it would be prudent to let her lead. He followed her closely as they ascended the rocky hill.

While ascending the hill, Guru's mind drifted back to the events of the past few hours. He literally began reliving the events of the past few hours and felt a sense of déjà vu.

Before they left the village of the Vamanousse, he had followed the Param Bhramousse to his special prayer chamber. On the way he had seen all the Vamanousse engaged in activity, fervently instructed by the seven Bhramousse.

The prayer chamber was tiny and on entering it, Guru felt strange. It felt as if he had entered an altogether different dimension, so much so that Guru couldn't make out top from bottom. It was if he was suspended in space and he may well, have been in space.

"You have to concentrate now," said the Param Bhramousse, "... concentrate as you have never concentrated before, for I am going to transfer some knowledge of music to you. You need to have that knowledge before I hand over the Astrousse to you. This Astruosse will destroy the Master Computer."

He placed his fingers on Guru's temples. For a moment, Guru felt as if someone was drilling his head with a pneumatic drill. But the pain passed and he felt a sort of calmness fill his entire being. He began having visions. Once they were done, the Param Bhramousse handed him an object. It looked like a conch, only the material was different from the ordinary conches that Guru had handled a number of times.

"I have no knowledge on the use of this device."

264

"That," said the Parambhramousse, "...is up to you to figure out. And when you are enlightened, you will have to lock the knowledge in your mind and block anyone that tries to read it."

"Does the Master Computer have the ability to read our thoughts?"

"It does not have a soul, so cannot read our thoughts, but its ability to read your body language will surely surpass the ability of any living being. It may be able to judge your thoughts by judging your body language, so be careful."

"Why aren't you passing on this knowledge to Amy?"

"You know the answer to that question," said the little man. "The Master Computer will try to break you, remain strong, don't buckle under pressure."

"What are our chances of making it out of there alive?"

"Very slim," said the Param Bhramousse sadly.

Guru bowed low in front of the Param Bhramousse and got up to leave.

"You will be in my prayers."

"Don't pray for my safety or success," said Guru. "Instead pray that I do not falter and perform the task given to me, to the best of my abilities."

Guru left a bit depressed. When he reached Amy, he had a strong urge to embrace her, but refrained from doing that. He very well knew that her ability of reading minds was returning, (for she had temporarily lost that ability when she was injured) and he had to block his mind from her.

The two Xixipians were waiting for them. Once ready, they bid good bye to the Vamanousse and were on their way out of the village towards the airplane. Vamanousse Gopalousse accompanied them, to see them off.

"You have been gone for quite some time. What took you so long?" asked Amy. "Xixalstats has been telling all sorts of stories of your escapades. You guys are devils!"

Guru smiled feebly but did not comment. He took her hand in his as they walked towards the plane. She looked at him enquiringly, but he did not meet her gaze. However his mood drastically changed, once they were on their way because Xixalstats nonstop chatter took his mind off the more serious thoughts.

Xixilia piloted the plane because in the words of Xixalstats she was the better pilot and moreover he had a lot of catching up to do. It was clear that the duo had put in a lot of efforts to make the interior of the airplane plush and cozy. It had space to seat ten, but the luxuries in the craft allowed only six seats to be fitted. Guru and Amy sat side by side while Xixalstats sat in a seat facing them.

"Let me show you some of the cool gadgets that I have invented," said the little Xixipian. "You may borrow a couple of them."

They were so engrossed in their talks that three hours seemed to fly by. Only when Xixilia called them, did they realize that they had arrived at their destination. They alighted from the craft and looked around.

"You will have to go on foot from here," said Xixalstats. "It will take you eight hours to reach the base of the palace. However be careful, for it has turned dark and is freezing. These clothes that you are wearing will protect you from the extreme cold. Just touch your burning torches to them every ten to fifteen of your earth minutes. The fabric is special. It will absorb the heat and keep the heat within it. The fire will protect you from all wildlife. Good luck my friends and for all our sakes, hope you suceed."

The duo left almost immediately as they had to take the Param Bhramousse to Sri and Xixandra. Guru and Amy looked around for a few moments then began their journey to the Crystal Palace.

"What did the Param Bhramousse tell you back there?" asked Amy.

"Nothing much," said Guru. "Just showed me the Master Computer in my mind and the possibly ways to destroy it."

"It there anything that you are not telling me?" asked Amy.

"Read my mind."

"Somehow, I can't," said Amy.

"Then don't worry. We'll figure out a way when we confront it. I am counting on your ability to draw out energy from anything you touch."

"Oh."

So they had walked, hand in hand for many hours, taking short breaks. Amy wanted to know more about Batatawadai Puram and kept pestering Guru for information. When they reached the base of the hill on which the palace stood, the weather had become almost unbearable and so they had decided to sleep for a few hours.

"We've reached," said Amy, drawing out Guru from the past to the present.

October 18ᵗʰ, 8 am (earth time) Xixarappa

Almost a thousand Gandharvousse had assembled at the top of the flat mountain, above Xixarappa. They were armed to the teeth and were waiting for the Asourbouts to attack. There was a lot of excitement in the air. Some of them were flapping their wings, probably exercising them. Sri found their enthusiasm hard to believe, for they had flown hundreds of miles to reach Xixarappa.

Since Xixilia had flown off to a secret location in one of the airplanes, Xixandra, Sri and Xixalstats had flown alongside the flying Gandharvousse, in the other airplane. Time and again a couple of Gandharvousse would land on one of the wings of the airplane to catch their breath. The most frequent among those was Mrugakshi, who had been landing on the airplane not just to catch her breath but to get a glimpse of Sri and speak to him.

The Param Bhramousse had transformed all the Gandharvousse into their ancient forms and enthusiasm levels were very high. He had instructed them how to use the special arrow heads manufactured by the Vamanousse. After seeking his blessings they had undertaken their journey, to prove their worth.

Sri and Mrugakshi stood, hand in hand, at the centre of the flat mountain close to the hatch that led to Xixarappa. The hatch was presently open but would be sealed tight once the battle began. Queen Xixandra and Xixalstats were beside them.

"Be careful," said Sri to Mrugakshi.

"You too, for you are far more valuable to me than

anything else. The Asourbouts will target you because you are guarding the device."

"Ah, don't worry," interrupted Xixalstats, "We're going to have a ball of a time. You guys be careful and precise."

Then they heard the sound of the conch. The Asourbouts had been spotted. The battle had begun.

"Attention!" shouted Vishvavasu.

The Gandharvousse stood in attention.

"Now listen very carefully because the success of this mission depends on how precise our timings are. Each one of you has twelve special arrows. You will discharge these arrows only on my command so be alert. Make every arrow count and once you've started discharging the special arrows, do not stop under any circumstances. You have two minutes to discharge the twelve special arrows and then fly straight up to this mountain top. No Asourbout should reach the top of this mountain with those arrows embedded in him, for it may cause great damage to the city below. May the mighty Lord be with you and protect you."

He blew the conch once again. Simultaneously all the Gandharvousse took to flight. It was a spectacular scene. In the distance the Asourbout army was visible. Just like army ants, closing in on their prey, they approached the mountain from all directions. Mrugakshi took an extra minute to wish Sri 'luck' and then was airborne, bow and arrow in hand.

Sri looked around and wielded his sword.

"That's so un-cool of you dude," said Xixalstats.

Sri turned to him and almost rolled over laughing. He had changed his attite and was now dressed like a commando with a cartridge belt across his torso and wielded what looked like a Tommy-gun.

"Where did you get that?" asked Sri.

"Made it myself, and the bullets are special. A direct hit with my bullets will vapourize those scumbags. Got an extra gun, wanna use it?"

"Sure buddy," said Sri, "But I am not dressing up like a joker."

"You insult me chum. My uniform is flawless."

He handed a gun and cartridge belt to Sri.

"Let me teach you how to use it."

Just when Sri had learnt the technique to use of the gun, Xixandra approached them, sword in hand namely because the waves had rendered their other weapons useless.

"What in the name of the devil are you two up to? And why did you throw down your sword Sri?"

"Swapped it for better equipment," said Sri.

Giving a look of disbelief, she ran to the edge, to get a better view of whatever was happening below. The Asourbouts were running towards the mountain at astounding speed. The Gandharvousse descended upon them and began firing their arrows, but they could hardly stop any Asourbout. Then the queen saw Vishvavasu rise high up into the sky. He was accessing the situation from high above. When he was satisfied that a large number of Asourbouts had assembled close to each other, he gave the signal to his people.

With renewed vigour, the Gandharvousse descended on the Asourbouts and began shooting them with their special arrows. They were really good and most of the arrows found their mark.

270

"What's with those arrows?" asked Xixalstats.

"It was Guru's idea," said Sri. "The Vamanousse have a special element that is of two types like matter and anti matter. These elements on their own are harmless but if combined can turn deadly. The arrow heads contain both the elements separated by a small gap. Once they pierce their victim, the matter and anti matter will combine."

"Wicked..!" said Xixalstats, "Then what will happen?"

"The substance will draw out tremendous energy from the surroundings and then there will be a monster explosion..."

However Sri could not complete his sentence, for he saw a number of Asourbouts reach the top of the mountain. Sri's estimated that a hundred of them must've breached the Gandharvouse line of defence. That was not bad, considering the fact that about ten thousand of them had attacked. They charged to where Sri and Xixalstats stood, for their prime target was the device that had fried all the electronics.

Sri lifted his gun and fired a volley of shots, but the Asourbouts were fast and easily dodged the bullets. The situation was grim because there were only a dozen of Xixipians along with Sri, stationed on top of the mountain to defend the device. At that juncture, the queen and a few of her subjects join the fray. The queen was fast with her sword and cut down five Asourbouts in a minute. Her guards too were fast and the Asourbouts found them really tough to handle. When they realized that the odds were turning against them, the Asourbouts changed tactics. While the others engaged the queen and her handful of soldiers, ten of them, started making their way towards where Sri and Xixalstats stood. Sri fired one more volley and managed to vapourise two Asourbouts. But the others kept coming. He turned to Xixalstats to plan their strategy.

"Let's stand back to back and fire. That way we will get more of these scumbags and won't end up shooting each other."

"Sane idea," said Sri.

They stood back to back and began firing wildly, managing to destroy six more Asourbouts. The remaining two were upon them in a jiffy. Xixalstats managed to get one as they jumped high into the air targeting the device. The other almost managed to reach the device – almost, because before he could reach it, Mrugakshi, who had been keeping a close eye on Sri, swooped down upon the Asourbout and grabbed him. She flew with him and tossed him down. Taking cue from her, hundreds of Gandharvousse swooped down upon the Asourbouts, and threw them down the mountain.

By then it had started getting very cold and Sri guessed that the arrows had started working. The sky turned dark as all the Gandharvousse descended upon the top of the mountain and crouched low. Within a couple of minutes, the surroundings turned orange as the explosions happened, Temperatures soared and it was almost unbearable. For a minute, Sri felt as if he was burning in hell and then the surroundings turned silent, eerily silent.

One by one the Gandharvousse got up and looked around. They were all safe, but the terrain below was ravished. The explosions had wiped out the Asourbouts. Only traces of them were visible in the form of tiny specks in the flat terrain below.

A cry of joy went into the air and everyone began dancing and strangely enough, it began to rain. Xixidorra had never experienced such heavy rain before, but that was not any ordinary day, it was the day the mighty Asourbouts had been vanquished.

272

In the middle of their dance, Mrugakshi suddenly hugged Sri and planted a kiss on his cheek.

"What was that for?"

"For being you... I love you Sri!!!"

Sri promptly returned the kiss and began dancing in a wild frenzy.

October 18th, 8 am (earth time)
Crystal Palace, Xixibamba

Guru and Amy crouched behind a clump of shrubs some four hundred meters away from a side entrance to the palace. The huge and exquisite Crystal Palace glittered in the bright sunlight. Guru had never seen so many diamonds ever before. An open ground separated them from the palace. Bodies lay strewn all around them - bodies of Asourbouts that had probably been hit by the first waves and had been caught unaware.

"So you spent fourteen years of your life here?"

"As a prisoner," said Amy.

"If I were you, I would've flicked a couple of those stones for myself."

"Are you crazy?"

"Just joking," said Guru. "Now how do we reach the gate without being noticed by that buffalo, Mooisausooura?"

"We wait and observe the movements of the patrolling guards and keep moving ahead when the window of opportunity presents itself. The palace is very huge and there can't be more than a handful of guards, guarding this gate. The only danger is the Asourbouts. What if, some of them are alive?"

"No chance," said Guru. "They are cyborgs, not living beings. If they had even a bit of energy in them, they would've been up and guarding the palace. The waves sent by Xixalstats must've been very powerful."

"What if Mooisausooura is not in there?" said Amy. "What if he is leading the attack on Xixarappa?"

"He won't do that," said Guru. "The Master Computer is far too valuable to be left alone in the care of the Asourousse, who have probably gone soft. He is very much in there."

"It is quite a large distance from here to the main gate of the palace. How do we reach the gate without being noticed?"

"It's not all that difficult," said Guru. "Tune into the minds of the nearest guards and see the path that they are following. Then we can keep moving towards the gates when they are not around. If one happens to be near, we simply lie down amongst the dead Asourbouts."

"Won't they spot us?"

"That's why I asked you to read their minds," said Guru. "In that way we will get to know who amongst them is the least alert and we move when that one is in the vicinity."

So they waited patiently. Guru keep a sharp eye on the palace to judge the activities going on, while Amy did her best trying to latch on to the minds of the guards that were closest to them. She realized that there were only three guards posted at the side entrance while all the others were at the main entrance or elsewhere at strategic locations. Maybe they were confident that no one would attack them or perhaps they would not have imagined in their wildest dream that a couple of kids would attack them, and that too almost unarmed. Whatever be the case, there were only three of them at that particular entrance. However they knew their job well and ensured that the entrance was not left unguarded at any time. She realized that the stupidest amongst the three was a very fat Asourousse called Bakasourousse.

The palace had a protective wall around it and a passage separated the main building from the wall. The three guards patrolled that passage and had so timed their patrolling, that one of them was always within reachable distance from the entrance. Each one of them carried a club and some sort of sharp weapon.

Amy and Guru moved ahead foot by foot, crawling and lying still beside the Asourbouts, whenever Bakasourousse was closest to the entrance. Slowly but surely they reached the outer wall of the palace. Guru learnt from Amy that an Asourousse named Ivalousse was closest to the entrance at that moment. Guru crouched just outside the entrance, with a club that he had picked up from the ground. He asked Amy to tune into the Asourousse' mind and signal him when the being reached the entrance. On her signal, he rushed into the entrance and jabbed the surprised Asurousse in the stomach. The blow was enough to knock the wind out of Ivalousse who fell down coughing. Before he got up or raised any alarm, Amy rushed in and grabbed his neck knocking him out with her power. The commotion attracted the second Asourousse named Vatapousse who came rushing at them. He was powerful and swung his club at Guru with such ferocity that he knocked out a couple of diamond bricks from the wall. Guru managed to duck fast and missed being pulverized by a couple of inches. However before Vatapousse had the opportunity to lift his huge club again, Amy was on him and knocked the daylights out of him by a mere touch.

"We need the third one conscious," warned Guru. "We need to extract information from him."

"How..?"

"Touch him briefly."

After dragging the bodies of the unconscious Asurousse outside the entrance, Guru boldly entered the compound of the palace. Bakasourousse had just turned the corner and on seeing Guru, rushed to him, club raised. He was extremely fat and the ground shook as he ran towards them.

"Bakasourousse, you moron, what are you doing?" said Guru in a commanding tone.

"How do you know my name?" asked a baffled Bakasourousse. "Are you one of those confounded boys?"

"Do I look like a boy, you idiot. I am an Asourousse Prince and have been sent from Prithvousse to get you back."

"How..?"

"We have opened a portal," said Guru, "similar to the one through which you came here."

"Where..? Where..?"

"Right here," said Guru pointing just outside the entrance.

As Bakasourousse peeped out, Amy who was standing just outside the entrance grabbed his hand briefly and left it. He fell down, stunned. Guru went near him.

"Now listen carefully you big fat oaf," said Guru to Bakasourousse who was looking at him with wide and terrified eyes, "... one more touch from the princess and you die a horrible death. Do you want that?"

Bakasourousse shook his head.

"Then answer my questions, and fast," said Guru. "Where has Mooisausooura hidden the Master Computer?"

"I don't know what you mean," said a terrified Bakasourousse.

"Then you are of no use to us," said Guru.

"No, no, I promise I am not lying."

"Ok, then tell me where is that buffalo Mooisausooura at the moment?"

"He is deep down inside the palace. No one is allowed to go there. Maybe he has some secret hidden down there."

"Tell me exactly how to go there and how many guards we may encounter on the way."

He told them exactly how they could reach the lower chamber. He also mentioned that they would not encounter any guards on their way down as no one was allowed there.

"Thank you and sweet dreams," said Guru as Amy grabbed the neck of Bakasourousse.

They boldly ran into the palace, following the instructions of Bakasouousse. Guru couldn't believe his eyes. Though the walls of the palace were made of diamond bricks, the main palace itself was carved from one single piece of diamond. Guru couldn't believe that a diamond of that size even existed and wondered what would be the value of one, that size, on earth.

They reached the steps that lead to the secret chamber and began descending carefully. When they had descended a few levels, Amy wanted to know why Guru was carrying a club. Guru just shrugged. By the time they reached the lowest level, they were out of breath.

The chamber was a ten by ten foot room. It was a perfect cube and seemed seamless. It led to nowhere.

"Is this it?" asked Amy. "Have we been had?"

"No," said Guru. "We have reached the right place."

He sat down, took out a flute and began playing a lilting tune.

"What are you doing?"

"Announcing our presence to the Master Computer..."

"Are you mental? Have you gone nuts?"

Amy couldn't utter another word, for she stood, mouth agape looking at the chamber. A neat door appeared and opened slightly. Guru got up and approached the door.

"It's a trap," said Amy.

"I know," said Guru. "But we will go in all the same ... and fulfill our destiny."

Amy gave one long look at Guru as tears welled up in her eyes and began streaming down her cheeks.

"I know what you mean," she said. "I know exactly what I have to do. I will go in and grab the master computer and when I draw out enough energy from it, you will strike. We die, but destroy the Master Compuer."

Guru did not speak, but merely entered the door with Amy close to his heels. Once they entered the chamber, the door automatically closed behind them. It was a huge chamber made of some sort of crystal that was not translucent but completely opaque. The walls were perfectly white and twinkled. The chamber was empty except for a piece of furniture that resembled a reclining chair with Mooisausooura on it, in a deep trance. There stood a sphere, about one foot in diameter, on a pedestal beside him that was discharging something like lightning onto his head. When the two of them approached, the discharge momentarily stopped.

"Welcome to my abode," said a sweet voice.

Guru kept looking at the sphere. Then light beams, similar to that of a laser show, shot out of the sphere creating a petite lady.

"My name is Param Sanganakam, better known as the Master Computer."

"Why are you trying to destroy earth?"

"You are mistaken young man. I am not at all destroying your planet. I am merely repopulating it."

"What do you mean?" asked Guru.

"Answer me boy," said the sweet voice. "What do you do when pests invade your precious fields or homes?"

"Pest control," said Guru.

"Exactly," said the voice. "That's exactly what I am doing on earth. I am destroying all humans. I call that 'pest control', got it?"

"Who gave you the right to decide?"

"You humans have been plundering this planet for eons and you talk about my rights? You are like a cancer on the planet and if not eliminated, you will consume the entire planet."

"How far away is my planet Prithvousse from here?" said Amy.

"I would say, a hundred light years away and so is earth. The three planets Earth, Prithvousse and Xixipoo are located on the three vertices of a triangle. It will take a lifetime to travel directly from one planet to the other. The only way is through a portal. Unfortunately your father closed the portal from Prithvousse to here, so we will have to occupy earth."

"I won't let you do that," said Amy rushing towards the sphere.

A powerful light shot out of the sphere hitting Amy and throwing her across the room. She landed on the floor writhing in pain.

"You think I do not sense your intentions," said the voice.

The commotion woke up Mooisausooura. He got up and looked around. Then he moved towards Amy.

"I shouldn't have kept you alive. But now, I shall correct my folly. I will break your neck. I have the memories of The Great Asura himself. Your powers can't harm me anymore."

Guru, in the meanwhile, took out a conch from his pocket and blew it with all his might. The sound began reverberating. In turn the Master Computer also produced sound that seemed to cancel out the sound of the conch. So intense were the sounds that the conch began to crumble.

"You are a common Manav," said the voice. "You underestimate my powers. The sound waves produced by the conch should've caused serious damage to me, but I produced an exact mirror image of the waves sent by you and canceled your waves. Now your conch is destroyed. You humans never learn, do you?"

"Actually we do," said Guru as he crushed and tossed a small object the size of a lemon into the open hemisphere. "The conch was a mere distraction. You destroyed it, exposing the Param Dhatu that was concealed in it. Now get out of this one, genius..."

"Mooisausooura, leave the girl alone and help me. Get this device out of me. It is sucking energy out of me at alarming proportions."

Mooisausooura now turned towards the Master Computer, but Guru occupied a position between him and the Master Computer. He brandished a small knife.

"Listen pipsqueak," said Mooisausooura in a thundering voice. "You really think you can stop me with that."

Guru merely pointed the blade to him and pressed a lever. The blade shot out of the knife with tremendous speed and pierced Mooisausooura's thigh, just above his kneecap. He fell on the floor hollering.

"Surprise!" said Guru. "That's a Russian Ballastic Knife, however it has been made right here by my genius friend Xixalstats."

Then he turned to the Master Computer.

"I know we have less than five minutes and will all die, but at least I die with the satisfaction that earth is safe."

A very powerful beam now shot out of the Master Computer and a glowing vertical eye like sructure structure began forming. There was a lot of turmoil inside this structure.

"Mooisausooura," said a faint sweet voice, "I have opened a portal for you with the last of my energy. Get out of here. You have most of my memory and also the memory of the Great Asura. Nothing can stop you now."

Without a second thought, Mooisausooura got up, limping and walked into the glowing eye. As he left, he turned to Guru and spoke-

"We will surely meet again..."

Then he was gone and the portal disappeared. The room started getting cold as Guru rushed to Amy.

"Are you okay," he said as he helped her to her feet.

"I love you Guru, always have..."

"What???"

"I said I love you... I fell in love with you, the moment I saw you."

"This is unfair," said Guru. "You are telling this to me now that we are going to die in less than five minutes."

"Give me a kiss," said Amy.

However they had no time for a kiss. There was a loud explosion and a hole, the size of a small cupboard appeared in the wall. Xixilia came in through the opening.

"Xixilia!" said Guru. "What have you gone and done? Why did you come? We are all doomed here. This place explodes in less than four minutes and we cannot get out in that much time. Even if we could, we can't escape the explosion."

"Shut up and wear this fast," she said handing them jumpsuits.

They quickly got into them. Then she asked them to follow her outside. There she threw an object, the size of a huge bag, on the floor. It immediately inflated into what looked like a jet scooter.

"Hop on," she said, "and grab each other tightly. We are going to have the ride of our life."

"They jumped on, Xixilia in front, Guru behind her and Amy behind him. A flame shot out of the rear of the device and they ascended almost vertically.

"What in the world is this contraption?" yelled Guru as they ascended.

"One of my inventions," she yelled back. "Do you think, you friend Xixalstats is the only genius around here? This portable jet-scooter has five minutes worth of fuel. We can fly very high in that time, away from the blast. But first we have to maneuver my scooter out of this confounded castle."

"But what happens when the fuel gets over?" yelled Guru.

"Wait and watch," said Xixilia.

They held on tightly to each other as they shot out of the Crystal Palace and rose into the air at incredible speed. The palace got smaller by the minute and then was a mere dot. Suddenly an orange glow engulfed the crystal palace and the colour of the sky changed. They felt a sudden burst of heat and then there was silence – absolute silence."

"Eeeeeho!" yelled Guru. "Xixilia, you genius, I could kiss you right now, but on second thoughts, no, cause I have to kiss her first."

Amy punched him from behind and embraced him tightly. Then suddenly the fuel got over and the jet stopped. The scooted began descending fast."

"What now," asked Guru.

"Just pull the chords by you side, simultaneously."

Guru did just that and two huge balloons inflated. They began floating.

"No electronics whatsoever!" said Xxixlia.

It began to rain.

"Amy! Xixi!" yelled Guru, "Is that what I think it is?" Is it raining diamonds?"

They could see small twinkling specks in the rain. It was literally raining diamonds!

October 18th, 10 am (earth time)
Batatawadai Puram

It was close to ten in the morning. The teens had been racking their brains trying to figure out how the Astras worked but came across a dead end on every occasion. They had hardly left the altar of the temple the whole night and had relentlessly tried to figure out the carvings on the walls but every answer figured by them pointed them to a statue of the Lord that did not exist in the temple.

It was a statue that depicted the Lord in dance pose. One of his hands was raised as if he was holding something while the other hand was curled and close to his lips. He seemed very graceful in that pose.

"This statue holds the answer to closing the portal," said Nath. "I've been trying to interpret the writings for the past couple of days. They all point to this figure."

"What message does the statue convey?" asked Varshika.

"I know," said Tina in a trance. "The statue represents the highest form of energy and purity. The Lord is dancing – meaning that he is trying to bring back the lost rhythm of the universe. In his right hand, he is holding a damru (pellet drum) and shaking it vigorously – meaning that he is driving out the evil from the universe. In his left hand he is holding a conch. After the evil has been driven out, he will fill the earth with the auspicious sounds of the conch. His heart is a lotus radiating out consciousness into the surroundings."

"How do you know all this?" asked a surprised Nath.

In response, Tina collapsed on the floor.

"She's has had one of her visions," said Varshika rolling her eyes. "I've got it now. It is this statue that will hold the three Astras."

"How do you know that for sure?" asked a dumbfounded Nath. "We don't even know what the other two Astras look like."

"I am certain," said Varshika. "The other two Astras are a Damru and a Lotus."

"Don't be silly," said Nath. "Didn't you guys yourself tell me that even the Vanars had no clue about the third Astra?"

Tina by now was on her feet.

"She is right," said Tina. "The statue itself holds the third Astra. In fact the heart of the statue is the third Astra. I saw it in a vision. It is right here in the temple above."

"What," said Nath. "There is nothing but the stone deity in the temple above and that too badly damaged."

"Follow me," said Tina as she rushed out of the lower temple, then rushed across the curved stone staircase to the upper temple. The others followed her anxiously. They reached the idol which seemed to have been affected by the burst of energy - the energy released when Tina had placed the Astra in the palms of the huge statue below, previous night. It seemed badly damaged and the stone had a number of cracks. Nath went to touch the idol but was stopped by Tina.

"Don't touch it," said Tina. "It may hold the Astra."

Tina carefully ran her hand over the rough cracked stone and felt a surge of energy. She was now sure that the second Astra was somewhere inside the idol. As she ran her hands, a piece of rock got dislodged from the damaged idol and fell to the ground. That seemed to set off some sort of a chain reaction and for a moment everyone felt that the idol was crumbling to pieces, but they were wrong. It was merely the crust that was falling away, revealing a beautiful core, for there was another statue inside the first one. Tina hurriedly cleared out the remaining pieces to see the idol behind the crust of rock. Meanwhile, Nath rushed below to get one of his torches and handed it over to Tina, who promptly fixed it in a notch in the wall close to the statue, so that everybody could get a closer look. It was the same idol depicted in many places on the walls of the subterranean temple. It was the very statue that they had been trying to locate for so long. The six foot statue was made of some kind of transparent crystal and was exactly as described by Tina. The light passing through the statue, made visible a lotus deep inside the bosom of the idol. However Tina had not mentioned one tiny detail. Fixed upright, next to the idol was a big bow and three arrows. What material they were made up of, was anybody's guess, for the material seemed not from this world. Then all hell broke loose.

The Principal, followed by Gendamal and Keshava came running in. They were panting and sweating profusely.

"We've got company," sang the principal. "There is a lot of activity in the forests around the temple and we just got a glimpse of the first Asourbout. It is about three hundred metres away from the main entrance and is armed and dangerous. It was shooting at something in the forest and we saw a couple of trees vapourize right before our eyes. Therefore I initiate our emergency protocol."

"And what's that?" asked a defiant Varshika, hands on her hips.

"All of you will occupy the big room underground and barricade yourselves from inside while Keshava, Gendamal and I defend the temple," said the principal. "Now hurry up and ..."

"Fat chance," said Varshika.

"Girl, are you disobeying your principal?"

"Maybe sir," said Varshika in a matter of fact tone, "but honestly none of you are in shape – I mean, shape to fight the Asourbouts."

"Rubbish," said the principal as he brandished a revolver. "My World War II gun..."

"Now really..?" said Varshika. "With due respect SIR, I don't think you ever fought in World War II – you were probably not even born then..."

"But I purchased it from a soldier who promised that he used it in the war."

"...And though in your eyes, we are mere kids," continued Varshika, "we've been through a lot and deserve some respect. So let's not waste time and face this challenge like a team. Moreover if those devils reach the temple, it will take more than a gun and a barricade to stop them."

"Ok," said the principal, giving them one long look, "what do you propose?"

"Well," said Varshika, "Let's barricade Xixorro and the scientists. Tina and Nath can stay here and try to figure out the Astras. An extra burst of energy can buy us some more time. You sir, can take up positions in the rear with your gun, while Mr. Kehava and Mr. Gendamal can guard the two sides and finally Riya and I can guard the entrance with our bows and arrows."

The principal was about to protest when the entire structure vibrated as if an earthquake had struck. Everybody was thrown off their feet.

"That was pretty close," said Varshika. "Let's take up our positions. Tina, now figuring out the Astra is left to you. Nath, help in barricading the others."

Principal Sandipani rushed to the rear of the temple, gun in hand. Gendamal ran to the right side of the temple armed with a stout stick while Keshava ran to the left side. Riya stayed at the main entrance of the temple a few feet within the temple, bow drawn. The temple shook as one more series of explosions rocked it.

"Varshika..." yelled Riya. "Better get here fast. They are attacking something, and that something seems to be approaching the temple."

Varshika rushed to the entrance. Both the girls peered into the thick foliage some two hundred metres away. Something was definitely running through the foliage. Then one more shot was fired at the foliage, followed by a huge explosion. It was then that Varshika heard a familiar yelp as something jumped out of the foliage, right into her arms as Varshika screamed. It was Cuddly. Varshika gave her a hug and she whimpered softly. Her tail was singed indicating that she probably had a close call. Varshika rushed in, still carrying her, cursing aloud.

"I'm going to kill something, I am," said Varshika. "Nath and Tina hurry up here and see if my baby is hurt."

Tina was the first to reach the upper temple. She had the Astra in her hand. She had probably gone below to fetch it. A few moments later Nath came huffing and puffing. Tina carefully placed the Astra at the foot of the idol and approached Cuddly.

"Come here darling," she called, as Cuddly went to her with a slight limp.

The three examined Cuddly who seemed alright. She had a small bag around her neck. Then before Tina could protest Varshika rushed to the altar and plucked out the bow and three arrows.

"You guys take good care of her and hide her. I have some business that I need to take care of," said Varshika as she stormed out. Both Nath and Tina stood dumbfounded.

Meanwhile Riya who was at the entrance of the temple, noticed some movement about seventy metres away. It was one of the Asourbouts and it was struggling to reach the temple. So far the energy field was making it impossible for the creature to reach, but it was only a matter of time...

Riya took good aim and let an arrow fly off her bow. The arrow found its mark and pierced the Asourbout's chest, but the cyborg merely snapped the arrow, letting a piece protrude from its chest. Then Riya shot two arrows in succession, one of which pierced the cyborg's forehead. It was a mistake for the cyborg looked straight at her and lifted its hand pointing it towards her. A glove like device began glowing on its hand. It was preparing to fire. At that moment, Riya heard two shots fired in succession. Principal Sandipani too seemed to be in some sort of trouble.

"Move," said a voice. "They've messed with the wrong person."

Surprised, Riya turned around to find Varshika standing a few paces behind her. She had a bow in her hand, almost as tall as herself. It was unlike any bow Riya had ever seen – and believe it or not, Riya had seen all types of bows. Without wasting any more time, Varshika boldly took a few steps outside the temple and let an arrow fly at the abomination. The arrow found its mark. Then a strange thing happened. The cyborg was engulfed in a bright glow and vapourized. Both the girls let out

291

a cry of ecstasy.

"How did you do that?" asked Riya

"It's the Lord's bow and it was bound to have powers," said an excited Varshika. "Let's get them."

Both of them rushed out of the temple and moved towards the rear. They passed Riya's father who was crouching behind a rock. His lip was trembling a bit. They gestured him to stay low, but he got up on seeing the teens.

"Why did you guys leave the ..."

Riya cut him off before he could complete the sentence.

"Don't worry dad, we've killed one of them. Keep an eye while we go and help Sandipani Sir."

He once again assumed his position behind the rock and looked at them with a bit of suspicion as they ran to the rear. He wondered if they were lying. And if they were telling the truth, he couldn't imagine how the little devils had managed the impossible.

On reaching the rear of the temple, the girls saw the principal with his gun drawn. He had taken cover behind a very huge rock. Seeing them, he placed a finger on his lip and pointed to the rock. The Asourbout was probably on the other side, very close. He then extended his hand and fired a shot through a gap. The creature on the other side retaliated with a shot. However the energy of the Astra protected them to some extent, for the shot did not reach them. But a few rocks got dislodged and one landed very close to the principal. The commotion gave the girls enough time to reach a cluster of smaller rocks that gave them a good view of the Asourbout. The cyborg was some sixty feet from the huge boulder at the rear of the temple and stood there in the open without any cover. Probably it considered itself invincible – a common mistake committed by both man and intelligent machine.

It is often said that the errors of machines are nothing but the manifestation of human errors, but the machine, that Varshika and Riya we facing, was supposed to be intelligent – far more intelligent than any human. However it had committed a grave error by not taking cover – its final error, for Varshika's second arrow found its mark and the cyborg vanished in a bright glow – never to rise again.

And then they saw something rise high, some distance away, following a trajectory, aimed at the top of the temple. It was an Asourbout that had managed to catapult itself high up in the sky and was rapidly descending towards the temple. The cyborg had probably figured out that the energy field was relatively weaker at the top of the temple and had adopted an unconventional approach. Wasting no time, Varshika fitted her last arrow in the huge bow, took careful aim and let the arrow fly. The cyborg was engulfed in a bright light, some twenty feet above the apex of the temple and disappeared. Then they heard a lot of commotion in the foliage at the right hand side of the temple.

"I have no more arrows left," said Varshika, "... and there are three more of those devils out there."

"What if the energy field is weak at the top? What if..."

Riya hadn't enough time to complete her statement. The fourth Asourbout had catapulted itself high up in the air and was descending towards the temple. Riya fixed an arrow in her bow. The two were startled by someone behind them. It was Nath and he had some kind of glove in his right hand. It was building up charge with a loud hum and then Nath carefully aimed his hand to the descending Asourbout and discharged his weapon. It must've been a very powerful discharge, for the cyborg vapourized some fifty feet above them.

"Cuddly brought us the power source," said Nath beaming, "and we could charge Mr. Bose's weapons."

"We managed to get three with the Lord's bow and arrows and you killed one, so there are two of them left."

"Piece of cake," said Nath pointing to the device in his right hand.

"Let's all move to the highest point on the rock," said Mr. Bose who had arrived beside them. He had a similar glove in his hand. "We'll have a better field of vision from there."

"Yes, let's finish the scum once and for all," yelled Nath as they moved towards the rear of the temple in order to scale the huge rock.

The principal was still behind the rock with his gun.

"Good work fellas!"

They were about to scale the huge rock when they heard Tina's scream.

"I'll go and see," said Varshika as she turned to run. "It's definitely not the Asourbouts."

"Be careful - take this," said the principal tossing his gun to Varshika.

Gun in hand, Varshika ran to the front of the temple and entered. In the dim light of the torch, Varshika saw Tina standing close to the altar, tightly clutching the Astra. Close to her was a man with an automatic weapon in his hand. He had pointed it to Tina.

"Now hand me the relic," he said in a menacing tone.

"Don't," said Varshika pointing her weapon to the man

who was partially visible in the dim light. His body was bruised as if he had been in a fight.

"You have an old revolver, while I have an automatic weapon," he said with a wicked gleam in his eyes, "I can pump her full of lead before you blink. Now put down your gun and move back."

Varshika knew it was futile arguing with the madman. So she carefully placed the gun on the floor and moved a couple of steps back.

"But you will die if you touch it," said Tina.

The man suddenly violently pushed Tina who fell on the floor and banged her head. He picked up the Astra that had rolled out of her hands.

"Stupid girl, do you think you are the only one in this world who can handle it?"

He carefully placed the Astra in a small sling bag and rushed out of the temple dropping his gun. Varshika ran towards Tina who lay on the floor.

"Are you okay" said Varshika. "Your head's bleeding."

"Don't worry about me. I'm fine. Go and get the thug. He has the Astra. We are doomed without it."

By then the scientists and Dr. Naik reached them. They had probably heard the commotion. Knowing that Tina was safe, Varshika picked up Sandipani's gun from the floor and rushed out of the temple in pursuit of the scoundrel who had stolen the Astra. He had taken the path that would lead them out of the forest and into their village and was running fast that it took Varshika some time to catch up with him. When she finally caught up with him, they were on the narrow path with a steep drop on either side. The drop must've been a good three hundred feet. The gap between them was about fifty feet.

"Stop," said Varshika. "You can't escape."

However he did not stop and continued running. She was very tired and knew that it would not be possible to catch up with him, so she fired a couple of shots at his feet. A bullet hit his right leg above his ankle and he dropped to the floor howling in pain. The gap between then was now about twenty feet. The man dragged himself some distance with his hands and sat upright leaning his back on a huge tree at the edge of the path. He had the sling bag in his right hand.

"It's over. Hand over the bag," she said. "The Astra needs to be returned to its rightful place."

He looked at her with loathing eyes, opened the sling bag and took out the conch shaped relic that he had stolen from Tina.

"You want it? Go get it," he said as he tossed over the edge.

Varshika couldn't believe her eyes. What kind of a mad man was she dealing with? She rushed to the edge and peeped below. To her amazement, the relic was lying at the edge of a ledge some six feet below.

"You lose," said an elated Varshika.

The man couldn't believe his eyes. He dragged himself to the edge and peeped below then a cruel smile formed on his lips.

"No, you lose. The relic is at the very edge of the ledge and will roll off any moment now. You will have to watch it fall."

Varshika once again looked at the Astra at the edge of the ledge. The thug was right. It was precariously balanced and was likely to fall at any moment."

"You lose," laughed the man. "Or perhaps you could be a hero, jump down and prevent it from falling, - but wait, won't you die if you touched the relic?"

Varshika felt a burst of anger surge through her body. She felt like punching the man repeatedly in the face.

"Then I die," she said calmly as she started climbing down onto the ledge.

Once on the ledge, Varshika looked below. The sheer drop made her feet go numb and cold. So she went on all fours and crawled towards the Astra. Her whole body trembled. She knew that touching the Astra would surely kill her, but if it fell into the ravine below, a lot of lives would be lost. But what if she touched the Astra and passed out before getting it to safety? No, she would have to ensure that her sacrifice was not in vain. So she decided to grab on to the Astra, simultaneously pushing it under her body and lay flat on top of it. In that way even if she died, her body on top of the Astra would prevent it from rolling away.

As planned, Varshika grabbed the Astra and pulled it under her as she lay on it with her eyes closed, waiting for the inevitable. A couple of moments passed and then a few more, but nothing happened. So she carefully opened her eyes and looked around. She was very much alive and so carefully got on all fours with the Astra held tightly in her hands. She couldn't believe her luck.

"How is that possible?" said a surprised voice from above. "I'll kill you."

Varshika, who had by then managed to stand up, was close to the wall of the ledge. She looked above. The injured thug had managed to stand and had a rock in his hand. He meant to throw it on her.

"No you don't," said a familiar voice.

Someone roughly pulled the thug away and she heard a distinct crack and a groan. That someone had probably broken one of his bones. She wondered who was above, when she saw a head appear. It was Simba. He had a broad smile although his clothes were torn and he was badly bruised.

"She's alive boss, she's fine," said Simba to someone behind him. "C'mon, give me your hand."

"Don't," warned the voice. "She has the Astra in her hand. Touch it and you will perish."

"But how in the name of the Almighty is she unharmed though she holds the Relic?"

"Probably inherited the powers from me," said the familiar voice as one more head appeared.

"O my God! Dad!" cried Varshika as he lay on the ground and gave her a hand.

"Darling, first hand over the Astra to me and then we will pull you up."

Once up, she gave him a tight hug.

"How did you reach here? And how can you touch the Astra?"

"That's because he's the Abbot of our temple in Africa," said Simba proudly.

"Impossible!" said Varshika. "You're too cool to be an Abbot."

"And who told you that Abbots can't be cool?" asked her father.

"Is that why I could hold the Astra?"

"Yes," said her father. "We are probably the descendents of those who swore to protect the temple in Africa, many millennia ago. My uncle was the Abbot of the temple in Africa. His son, the scoundrel lying there, was supposed to take his place in the temple, but somehow switched sides and began working for the evil ones. "

He turned to the man lying on the floor.

"Vicky, you scoundrel, you had everything – brains, power and respect, but you blew it because of your greed," he said with fiery eyes. "Moreover you tried to harm my daughter and for that, the tribal council will punish you."

He then put his hand in the sling bag recovered from Vicky and took out the second relic. As predicted by Varshika earlier, it was a pellet drum made of the same kind of crystal. He held it near his bosom and said a prayer. Then he turned to Simba.

"Have the other thugs been rounded up?"

"Yes sir."

"Then make arrangements to have them discretely transported back to Africa. They all will have to face the council."

"What about you sir?" asked Simba. "Won't you be joining us?"

"I will join you later. Still have some unfinished work here and after the work is done, the relics have to be returned to their respective temples."

"And er... will you be joining university again?"

"Yes, and so will you. You have a thesis to submit in order to get you PhD."

Varshika was listening to the conversation wide eyed.

"He is doing his PhD?"

"Yes," said her father, "one of my best students."

"But why did he join you?"

"...because he also happens to be the crown prince of the tribe that has been assisting our family for thousands of years. But that doesn't mean that he should give up his studies."

They heard whistling and saw two figures in the distance, approach them, from the direction of the village, guns casually slung over their shoulders. When they were clearly in view, Varshika let out a gasp.

"Ram and Rahim..!"

"Yup," said her father. "They are our men."

"But they accompanied us to the Himalayas."

"I sent them to protect you. Do you think I would have let you go alone?"

"Varshika, are you ok?"

She turned behind and saw an anxious Tina approach, followed by Principal Sandipani, Keshava, Gendamal and Riya. In the rear were Nath and the Alien scientist involved in discussions. They were probably catching up. Cuddly, barking loudly appeared from somewhere and ran straight to the man next to Varshika and began jumping on him and licking his face.

"I'm fine," said Varshika hugging Tina.

"What happened here?" demanded the principal, "... and who are these men?"

"I think introductions are due," said Varshika's father.

"I am Varshika's father, Dr. Kris, that is Krishant and this is Simba. Those two are Ram and Rahim, my close aides and finally the scoundrel tied up there is my first cousin Vikesh. He is the one who stole the Astra from our temple in Africa, also tried to steal the other Astras and probably has something to do with whatever has been happening in the past few days."

"Dr. Kris is the Abbot of our temple in Africa," interjected Simba.

The Principal extended his hand to Dr. Kris but he politely refused showing the Astras in his possession.

"Your greetings are humbly accepted sir, but guess we cannot shake hands at this juncture."

"But then how were you holding Varshika?" asked Tina.

"The Astras won't harm her."

"How?" asked everyone in a chorus.

"Long story," said her father. "She'll tell you later."

"Now please update me on what has been going on in the temple."

"I will," said Nath with a smile. "The Asourbouts have been destroyed and King Xixorro is well..."

"I'm not sure about the last one," said the very short man next to Nath.

"But I'm sure I got it," complained Nath.

At that moment Nath's cell phone rang. He received it and as the conversation progressed, the smile on his lips got wider.

"Communications with Xixipoo have been established. It seems that Guru and Sri were involved in some kind of World

War in Xixipoo..."

"O my God!" said Sandipani. "What have they gone and done now?"

"Defended our planet, Sir" said Nath proudly. "They will soon be on their way back."

"Then let's hurry back to the temple and speak to them," said the teens in excitement.

"We still have to figure out how to use the Astras to close the portal, but only after the boys have arrived," said Varshika's father.

October 18ᵗʰ, 10 am (earth time) Xixarappa

They were travelling at breathtaking speed in an egg shaped craft. Xixalstats and Xixilia side by side in the front and Guru and Amy behind.

"We should reach in half an hour," said Xixalstats. "You missed the action. We wiped out them Asourbouts."

"You mean, every one of them," asked Amy.

"Every last one of them, but Xixidorra's a wreck."

"So is Xixibamba," said Xixilia. "This guy blew up the Crystal Palace."

"You what?" said Xixalstats, "Wicked! But Xixorro's going to kill you. That was our palace for almost two millennia."

"So what?" said Guru, "We saved your planet, didn't we?"

"You got a solid point there."

They quickly descended into the hatch and came to Xixarappa. There was great jubilation in the city. On seeing them, the queen ran to them and gave each a tight hug.

"Communications with earth have been restored. Xixorro is safe and the Asourbouts have been destroyed."

"I don't believe it," said Guru. "You mean my guys there achieved the impossible?"

"Yes they did," said the queen, "...but with a little help. They were helped by none other than Xixeinstein. Yes Xixalstats, your father is alive and well."

Just then Sri appeared from somewhere. He ran to Guru and they hugged each other, simultaneously jumping up and down.

"Meet my girlfriend," said Guru to Sri as he took Amy's hand into his own.

"And this is Mrugakshi, my girlfriend," said Sri beaming as he proudly pulled an embarrassed Mrugakshi towards him.

"Gosh!" said Guru, "You have a girlfriend who can fly."

Everyone fell silent as the small person approached and instinctively bowed to the Param Bhramousse.

"Well done girls and boys," said Vamanousse Hariousse. "We have overcome the crisis, but you will have to leave in a couple of hours from now. The portal has become unstable."

"I don't want to go," said Guru. "Moreover the party's just begun."

"Sorry, but you will have to leave. Your planet needs you. We have won the battle, but the war is far from over. Mooisausooura has managed to escape and will be back for vengeance. His powers have grown beyond imagination and if he reaches the other Asuras, he will unlock their powers and will have a very powerful Asura army under his command."

Guru and Amy looked at each other sadly.

"And I forgot one thing," said the Param Bhramousse, "You will take Amindita with you to earth. She will be safer there."

Guru and Amy couldn't believe their ears. They got locked in a tight embrace.

"Can Mrugakshi come too?" asked Sri.

"That is up to her to decide."

Sri turned to Mrugakshi. She came to him and took both his hands in hers.

"Sri, the Almight alone knows how much I love you, but I cannot accompany you now. My people need me. But I promise you that we will be united soon. Are you willing to wait for me?"

"I'll wait my whole life for you," said Sri, "for you are the one for me and I can love no other."

They spent the next couple of hours partying. Queen Xixandra couldn't hold back her tears and cried her heart out. They were tears of joy. She invited the Gandharvousse to stay in Xixarappa and they gladly accepted the invitation, for they had suffered enough for the past fourteen years. The Param Bhramousse too asked them to come and spend time with them in the holy city, so that they could connect to their roots and learn the true extent of their powers. The hours had passed merrily and it was time for the boys and Amy to leave.

"Xixalstats and Xixilia will pilot the craft that will take you to earth," said the Queen. "Xixorro and Xixeinstein will return in the same craft."

Amy gave the queen and Mrugakshi a tight hug. She was happy to be going home, not her home, but Guru's home, in Batatawadai Puram, the home of the Great Lord. Sri bid farewell to Mrugakshi who promised to meet him soon. A very huge spaceship was neatly parked on the flat top of the mountain above Xixarappa. The five of them left for earth in the craft.

October 18th, 8 pm (earth time)

The party was in full swing in Guru's house. The ladies had left no stone unturned in their efforts. The dining table was loaded with different types of food and everyone was tucking away large portions of food. The atmosphere seemed carefree.

"Finally I could properly speak to my boy," said Guru's mother. "I am happy that he is safe, but seems changed. I am sure there's a girl involved. My boy has made a girlfriend."

"Don't be silly," said Tina. "I know Guru well and he won't fall for that stuff."

"And I know him better. I am his mother after all."

"Kris," said Sri's mother, "It is so nice of you to come. Varshika is really happy."

"We had an educational conference here, so I decided to pay a visit. I will be leaving in a couple of days. We have excellent exchange programs in our university and it will be great if all the children come to Africa for some months as exchange students. I could arrange it with your principal, if you agree. The gang will have a great time and it will be an enriching experience for them. Moreover we have a very large house and everyone can stay with me."

"We will surely give it a thought," said Nath's mother, a bit worried.

Guru's father, who was out, attending a call, joined them.

"I have some news for you folks. Dhondiba is being

306

shifted to Shriharipur by his friends. They are not happy with the present hospital and want him shifted there."

"But we have better facilities here in Batatawadai Puram," complained Guru's mother.

"That's what I told them, but they wouldn't listen. So Guru and Sri will be accompanying him and will return as soon as he is safe in Shriharipur."

"Can you excuse us," said Tina. "We are going to the Riya's house."

"It's late," said Sri's mother. "You must be pretty tired."

"Let them go," said Dr. Kris. "They are not kids anymore. They can take care of themselves."

The children left in a hurry. They had decided to go straight to the temple. They were eager to meet Xixorro and Xixeinstein who were at the temple and would also get a chance to speak to Sri and Guru.

Epilogue

They were all solemnly seated in Principal Sandipani's huge living room. Dr. Kris was the only one standing. A large sofa was occupied by Amy and Guru, who were sitting hand in hand. Nath and Riya sat beside them. Another huge sofa was occupied by Gendamal, Keshava and Madhusudan. Sri sat in between Tina and Varshika on the third sofa while the Principal occupied a huge recliner. Ghasitaram was busy in the kitchen.

"May I have your attention please," said Dr. Kris to everyone seated. "We are the only ones who know what exactly happened in the past few days. Our planet was in extreme peril and we managed to avert the crisis. This is not the first time that our planet has faced a crisis of such magnanimous proportions and probably won't be the last. Whether you like it or not, you have all become a part of a secret society that protects this planet whenever such a crisis presents itself. My family has been doing this for millennia.

The first question is regarding whether we should try to close the portal. I firmly believe that we should do nothing at present. From what I gather, the portal has become rather unstable, so we wait and watch what happens. The king and his entourage are on their way to Xixipoo and will contact us as soon as they reach. We will be in regular touch. Nath can handle the communications from this end and Simba will handle the communications from Africa.

The second question is regarding this girl Amy. I suggest she stays here with Varshika. You can introduce her as my niece from Africa. That will put awkward questions to rest and people will not find it odd that she knows very little about India. In the meanwhile, she can learn about life here and try to blend in. However may I caution you not to underestimate her power. She is as powerful as the Astras themselves. Anyone other than those who can handle the Astras touches her and it is curtains for that person.

The third question is about the Astras themselves. I take the responsibility of returning the Astras to their rightful temples. The conch will be returned to the noble Vanars and the damru will be returned to the temple in Africa. The third Astra will continue to remain in the temple here and it will be your responsibility to protect it.

The last and pertinent question is about your selves. You may be wondering if everything will ever return back to normal. Sadly, it won't. Such knowledge demands a price and since you have acquired this knowledge, you all will have to pay the price. Life will never be as it was before. You may continue leading apparently normal lives, but now you are not part of society, but way above it. You will have to keep your secrets buried deep in your hearts and watch your backs. Anything could happen anytime, so be prepared and train your selves. Some of you have special skills, hone them. You were lucky this time but may not be so lucky the next time, so train hard and acquire new skills.

I will arrange for all of you to visit Africa for a short period but will take the kids for a longer time. They will be trained there. With the Principal's cooperation, we can arrange for an exchange program. However it will be up to you to convince the ladies. I shall leave in the morning.

Remember, my dear ones, we have won the battle, but the war is far from over. This is the calm before the storm – the mother of all storms.

****

The three men stood idly beside the old ambulance. They were in the outskirts of Batatawadai Puram. The tall man was trying to pacify the very fat man and the old man.

"Calm down," he will return soon.

"But who will take care of us, Biswajeet?"

"I will," said Biswajeet, "at least until he returns."

"What is that you keep wearing in your hand?"

"It is a gift from him," said Biswajeet. "Just like the loads of money that he left for us. We don't need to ever work."

"Yiii, what is that," said the fat man pointing to something crawling towards them.

They peered at the creature that was crawling towards them. It looked like a human but was certainly not one. It had half a body and the other half, waist down, was missing. It kept pulling itself towards them.

310

"Help us Biswajeet, save us," shrieked the other two.

Biswajeet was petrified. He pointed a hand towards the hideous creature crawling towards them and then the strangest thing happened, a bolt of light shot out of his hand instantly, vapourizing the creature.

"How did you do that?" asked the astonished fat man.

"Didn't I tell you that I will protect you?"

They took turns to kiss his hands.

"From today, you are our protector – our God."

www.ingramcontent.com/pod-product-compliance
Lightning Source LLC
Chambersburg PA
CBHW021217260626
47172CB00002B/475